P9-CLG-600

# 666
## THE NUMBER OF THE BEAST

# 666

## THE NUMBER OF THE BEAST

POINT

ISBN-13: 978-0-545-02117-3
ISBN-10: 0-545-02117-0



Library of Congress Cataloging-in-Publication Data
is available on request.

12 11 10 9 8 7 6 5 4 3 2 1 7 8 9 10 11 12/0

Text type was set in Lino Letter Roman.
Text design by Steve Scott.

Printed in the U.S.A.
First printing, September 2007

# TABLE OF CONTENTS

## EVIL

## DARKNESS

# BEASTS

*Let him that hath understanding count the number of the beast: for it is the number of a man; and his number is six hundred threescore and six.*

REVELATIONS 13:18

EVIL

# CHANNEL 99

**Peter Abrahams**

"Are you all right?" Mom said. "You look a little pale."

"I'm fine," said Becky.

Mom laid her hand, soft and cool, on Becky's forehead. Her eyes, tired-looking, with red veins here and there, darkened slightly. Two minutes later, Mom was squinting at numbers on a thermometer.

"One-oh-one point five," Mom said. "Back in your jammies."

"Back in my jammies?"

"You don't go to school with one-oh-one point five."

"But—" Back in her jammies, a day off: how pleasant that would have sounded in the past. But ninth grade was turning out to be so much harder than eighth, and Becky, already struggling in math, could think only about falling further behind.

"No buts," Mom said. "I'll take a personal day."

"Don't do that, Mom." Mom only got two paid weeks off a year, plus Thanksgiving and Christmas, and five personal days, with no pay. So wasting one just because—

"Of course I'm doing it," Mom said. "You can't stay home alone."

"I'm fourteen."

But Mom, already dialing work, wasn't listening. She was wearing the nicest of her work outfits, in Becky's opinion—Mom had five, one for every day of the week, rotated on a complicated schedule only she understood—the blue suit with the gray pin-stripes. The skirt no longer fit right, a little too loose. Mom was still losing weight although she'd never needed to, had lost a lot since Dad died, blown up by a car bomb in a far-off roadside village with a name Becky had trouble pronouncing.

Mom had a habit for when she sensed things starting to go wrong. She'd take a lock of hair and twirl it behind her ear. She was doing it now. "But—" she said. And then, "I see. But what if—" Mom twirled faster. "No, that wouldn't . . . of course I'd never . . . yes." Mom hung up, turned to Becky, still twirling her hair.

"It's all right," Becky said. "I'm fourteen."

Becky got back in her jammies, cozy flannel ones with a floral pattern. Mom gave her two aspirins, set her up on the couch in the den, laid a tray within arm's reach—water, toast and jam, vitamins, a chocolate chip cookie, and a bottle of her favorite soda, Orangina—and handed her the remote.

"No going out or anything like that."

"Of course not."

"Call if you start to feel worse."

"I won't feel worse."

"Just relax."

"Okay."

"Watch TV."

"Mom. You're going to be late."

* * *

Becky drank some water, took a bite of toast, found she wasn't hungry. She touched her forehead. It felt hot. Could you take your own temperature that way? Becky didn't know. Odd that some kinds of sickness made the whole body heat up, even a little unnerving. Becky switched on the TV.

In the old days they were on the premium package, but now, economizing, they'd downgraded to superior cable, one step above basic. Superior cable meant ninety-eight channels, starting with PBS and ending with cooking. Becky clicked through. She watched a bit of a show about antiques, where a huge old sideboard turned out to be a cheap copy and the owner's smile faded fast; a weather report about big storms in the Rockies; and, on 98, a chef making honey-glazed ribs. Normally, Becky liked the cooking channel, but today there was something off-putting about food, so she clicked the DOWN arrow button, heading back to 97, home improvement. But by mistake, her finger brushed the UP arrow button instead, taking her to channel 99. Of course, there was no channel 99, just snow and static. And for a moment, snow and static is what she saw. Then, just as she was about to hit the DOWN arrow, a picture wriggled onto the screen.

Hey! Channel 99. They were showing a cartoon. From back in the premium days, Becky remembered 99 being Mexican soccer; they must have changed the lineup. She wasn't usually that big on cartoons—actually preferred Mexican soccer—but there was something about this one, like how beautiful it looked, for one thing.

A cabin stood in the woods, white smoke rising from the chimney. In the background, a stream flowed through the trees, its burbling sounds very clear. Birds wheeled around in a blue sky. Hard to tell if it was computer animation or hand drawn. The camera moved slowly in on the cabin, up to a window and through, the way cameras did.

Inside the cabin, a man sat at a computer, his back to the camera. He wore a lime-green suit and a yellow hat, colorful cartoon-character clothing. As he typed on the keyboard, the camera came alongside and showed his face. This had to be computer animation, the most advanced yet—the man looked so real. He had a thin face with a prominent nose and high cheekbones, but what caught Becky's attention was how his skin seemed like living skin, and how the way he breathed and appeared to be concentrating and actually thinking were just like a live human actor. Only his eyes failed to quite reach the same realistic standard: dark eyes, not as fine as real ones, lacking the brightness, the expressiveness, the sense of the person inside that made human eyes so interesting.

The camera circled back, focused over the man's shoulder on the screen. An e-mail popped up, addressed to malin@malinenterprises.com. The man opened it. The message read:

*Malin,*

*You've made a bad mistake. The kid has the code.*

*HQ*

The man, Malin, no doubt, spoke: "What kid?" he said, as though talking to himself. He had a deep voice and a slight accent Becky couldn't place.

Then came something that couldn't happen in real life: More words, the answer to Malin's spoken question, scrolled across the screen:

*Becca. What other kid could it be?*

"Becca has the code?" the man said, his voice rising in shock. The camera moved in to close-up on his face. Becky saw that in fact his skin wasn't quite right—a little too blue in the lips.

Back to the screen: *Don't make me repeat myself.*

"But how? How did this happen? It wasn't my fault."

*We'll sort that out later. Just do the necessary.*

"Should I use Greenie?"

*Whatever works.*

The screen went blank.

Malin rose. He was very tall, the top of his yellow hat almost brushing the ceiling, and impossibly thin, as only a cartoon character could be. He opened a cupboard, took out a bottle that read DEMON RUM XX in big letters, and drank. Then he turned to a small woven basket in the corner and said, "Greenie? Rise and shine."

The lid of the basket vibrated slightly, wobbled, shifted an inch or so out of place. For a second, two little eyes shone in the darkness of the basket. A snake rose up through the space between the lid and the basket rim, curled gracefully down to the floor, and coiled up, also with grace. Becky wasn't big on snakes—far from it—but this one, Greenie, was kind of cute, very small with a rounded head and a half-smiling mouth.

"Better take your medicine before you go, Greenie," said Malin. He took a red pill from one of those brown prescription medicine bottles and held it out. Greenie stuck out his little forked tongue—there were no fangs in his mouth, no teeth of any kind—and swallowed the pill. It made a funny bulge in his neck going down. Then Greenie slithered across the floor, up the wall to an open window, and out.

The camera followed Greenie. He—Greenie looked like a he—slithered through a garden filled with dried-out flower stalks, between some trees, and down to the burbling stream, his movements unhurried. He slipped into the water without making a ripple and disappeared.

For an instant, the TV darkened, as though a commercial was next. But no commercial came—Becky had seen that happen before, especially with reruns. Instead, the next scene of the cartoon started up.

A girl sat on the bank of a stream, lazily holding a fishing pole over the water, a line dangling down and a little white float bobbing on the surface. Like Malin, the girl looked very realistic, except for the eyes and that touch of blue on the lips. But what amazed Becky was how closely the cartoon girl resembled her. The face, the hair, the hands, the posture, it was uncanny. She sat up straight on the couch in the den. More than amazing or uncanny: Becky had no words to describe the resemblance. Was it possible the animators had somehow got hold of a photograph of her to work from? Either that, which seemed unlikely, or a complete coincidence, just a one-in-a-billion chance.

The girl glanced at the float. She kicked off a sandal, dipped her toes in the water. Becky slid the comforter aside, examined her own toes. Identical. Wow. She touched her forehead. Not quite as hot.

On the TV, the cartoon girl started humming to herself. Becky recognized the tune: "When I'm Sixty-four," a Beatles song, one of her favorites. Her dad had been a big Beatles fan. The humming stopped. The girl gazed into space, lost in thought, paying no attention to the fishing pole. The camera panned away from her, swept across the water, zoomed slowly in on the white float. It bobbed for a moment or two and then went still. Becky — how could she be so slow? — suddenly realized the girl must be Becca.

At that moment, the float got jerked down out of sight, which was what happened to floats when a big fish struck. That snapped Becca out of her reverie. She looked out at the water just in time to see it erupt with an enormous spouting roar, and Greenie — a greatly transformed Greenie, huge and thick with savage eyes and a wide-open mouth exposing enormous fangs — came flying right up the line, right up the pole, swallowing everything, and sank those fangs deep into Becca's hand.

Becky screamed in pain. She felt a searing in her own hand, white-hot and excruciating, the worst pain she'd ever known. She jumped up and bolted from the den in total screaming panic, hand swelling up, all purple. A small part of her was thinking, *Impossible*. But there was no way to disbelieve pain like this.

In the kitchen, Becky thrust her hand under cold water, held it there. After a minute or two the pain receded and the swelling started to go down. She got an ice pack from the freezer, the kind with Velcro straps, and wound it around her hand. Then she crept back toward the den, listened outside the door. She heard nothing.

Becky went inside. From the doorway, she couldn't see the screen, facing the couch. She circled slowly around it, took a quick glance. They were back in the cabin, Becca tied to a chair, Malin standing over her, one of those barber's straight razors in his hand and the straw basket in the corner, lid closed.

"I want that code," Malin said.

Becky sprang to the couch, grabbed the remote, pressed OFF. The TV stayed on. The camera showed a close-up of Becca working at the knotted rope behind her back. Becky pressed the OFF button again. And again and again and again, harder and harder. No use. She tried the DOWN arrow, the UP arrow. Nothing happened. The TV was stuck on channel 99.

The knots were coming loose. "Do you know how sharp this is?" Malin said. Close-up of the razor. The blade gleamed. "Imagine how your face will feel. Give me the code."

"I don't have any code," Becca said. "I don't even know what you're talking about." Her voice, her whole body, shook with fear.

"That won't work," said Malin, bringing the razor closer to Becca, closer to her eyes. "See how sharp?"

Becky dove across the floor, hit the POWER button on the TV, once, twice, three times. No use.

"I can't tell you what I don't know," Becca said, tears streaming down her face, a face now inches from Becky, right in front of the screen. A face so much like her own. And she, Becky, would feel that pain, the pain of the razor, on her own face, a certainty. She reached out and yanked the plug from the wall. No use.

"Just to be fair," said Malin, "before we begin, I'll count backward from ten. Ten, nine, eight, seven, six, fi—"

"I don't know anything about codes," Becca said. "I'm terrible at math."

"Funny joke," said Malin. "Will you still be witty when we're done?"

"But—"

"Where were we? Six, was it? No, five. Five, four, three—"

Close-up: razor.

Close-up: Becca's hands, not quite free.

"Two, one. ZERO!"

Malin slashed at Becca's face. Becky raised her own hand to ward off the blow, but at the same moment Becca dove off the chair. She raced for the cabin door. Malin flew across the room, his speed astonishing, and got there first, barring the way. Becca ran back, got behind the desk, keeping it between her and Malin.

"Stop playing games," Malin said. "There's no way out."

Becca picked up a paperweight and threw it at him—she was so brave—actually hitting him on the arm. His face got all twisted in fury. He took out the prescription bottle, fumbled with the cap.

"Greenie? You awake? I need a moment of your time."

"No, no, please," said Becca.

"No, no, please." Becky said it, too, all alone in the den of the little apartment.

The basket lid vibrated, wobbled slightly, shifted an inch or two. *Oh, no.* But at that moment, Becky had a thought, a last-ditch, emergency thought: *master switch.*

She tore out of the den, down the hall, into the kitchen, ripped open the fuse box. Becky had never been in the fuse box before, knew nothing of fuses or electricity, but she'd heard that term, "master switch." Which one was it? There were all these switches, nothing labeled. Maybe this one, the biggest? As she reached for it, Becky heard a faint scream, coming from the den. She banged the switch down with all her might.

The fridge went silent. The lights on the microwave went off. From down the hall, Becky heard nothing. She walked back to the den, every step cautious and slow. No sound came from the TV. Becky circled around, giving it a wide berth. The screen was black, power light off, show over.

Becky took a deep breath, sat on the bed. She looked at her hand. Back to normal. She felt no pain at all. "Brain fever." That was another expression she'd heard. Becky put the thermometer in her mouth, took her temperature. Ninety-eight point six. Back to normal. She drank some water. A horrible brain fever had passed through her, doing weird things to her imagination. She could prove that by switching the power back on, turning on the TV. Maybe later.

For now, she reached for the jam, spread it on a piece of toast. Raspberry jam, her favorite. After that, a close second, came strawberry, with blueberry in third place, and—

What was that?

A footstep in the hall?

"Mom?"

Becky rose. Footsteps, not Mom's, came closer. A shadow fell across the open doorway to the den. Then a man walked in, a very tall, very thin man in a green suit and a yellow hat: Malin. Only this was not a cartoon character, with not-quite-real eyes and too much blue in his lips. This was a flesh-and-blood human man, and his eyes were full of expression, all bad. He carried a little wicker basket in one hand.

"I'll have that code," he said.

Becky froze, so terrified she couldn't move an inch. "I don't know about any codes," she said. "This is insane."

"I'll be the judge of that," Malin said, coming closer. He stood beside the TV. "You'll give up the code, one way or another." He reached into his pocket, held up the prescription bottle. "Greenie?" he said.

"No." Becky tried to scream the word, but it came out all muffled and ragged. The basket lid vibrated. She had to do something, had to fight somehow, get out, down to the street. She had to be brave — brave like Becca, who'd had the nerve, the defiance to hurl that paperweight. Becky had no paperweight. Her best weapon was the bottle of Orangina. Becky grabbed the bottle of Orangina and threw it at Malin as hard as she could.

A terrible throw, ridiculously off target. It missed Malin completely, striking the TV dead center and smashing a big hole in the screen.

Malin saw what had happened. His eyes opened wide. And now he was the screamer, a scream quickly cut off. The next moment he was gone, and the basket, too, re-formed into two whirling spirals of blue light that soared around the den, swept right around her head and then got sucked at superspeed into the hole in the TV screen.

After that it was very quiet in the den. Becky bent toward the TV, gazed into the hole, saw nothing but TV parts, some broken. She went to the kitchen closet, found the flashlight, shone it inside the TV, and saw what she had just seen, a little more clearly.

A few minutes later, Becky had stopped shaking and her pulse had settled back down. Broken glass lay on the floor. She could clean that up, but how to explain the broken TV? Brain fever? Could brain fever make it all seem so real? Becky took her temperature again. Ninety-eight point six. Out in the hall, the phone rang, the only non plug-in phone they had.

Becky went to the hall table, picked up the phone.

"Becky?" said Mom. "Just checking in. How are you feeling?"

At that moment, Becky saw herself in the mirror above the hall table. Not quite herself. The face in the mirror wasn't right in the eyes, lacked that full sense of the person inside, and was a little too blue in the lips: the face of Becca.

"Becky?"

And in the pocket of her jammies, what was this she felt? Paper? She took it out: an envelope. And on the envelope was written: IGNITION CODE—BOMB #2.

"Becky? Are you there?"

# THE LEGEND OF ANNA BARTON

**Laurie Faria Stolarz**

The shrill of the phone ringing startles me out of sleep. I wake up with a gasp, my chest heaving in and out, and reach for the phone on my bedside table, accidentally tumbling over my glass of water. It shatters against the floor. The water spills out, picking up the deep molasses color of the hard oak wood.

For just an instant, it reminds me of blood.

"Hello?" I mumble into the receiver, only half asleep now.

No one answers, but there's definitely someone there. I can hear static on the other end, like maybe someone has a bad connection.

"Hello?" I repeat, almost detecting the sound of a voice, a soft, faraway giggle that cuts right through the fuzz.

"Macy?" I ask, wondering if it's my friend from next door.

The static sound gets louder and so does the laughter, a high-pitched menacing giggle that sends chills straight down my back.

The phone pressed up against my ear, I exit my room and move down the hallway. The sign on Macy's door reads MACY GREY: THE STYLIN' SOPHOMORE, NOT THE SOULFUL SINGER. I knock, and she answers not two seconds later, a wide and cheeky grin across her heart-shaped face.

"What's up?" she asks, supersize bags of Sun Chips and Cheez Doodles gripped in each hand. "I was just coming over."

I feel my face scrunch, still listening to the giggle on the other end of the phone.

"Who is this?" I insist, turning the volume up higher on the receiver.

The buzzing sound gets louder and changes pitch, almost like someone's trying to talk. "Can you hear me?" I ask, covering my opposite ear.

"I can't wait until you leave her alone," a female voice whispers. It buzzes out and cuts through the static, nearly making me drop the receiver.

A second later, the phone clicks off, followed by a dial tone, making my heart beat fast.

"Kayla?" Macy asks, taking a step out into the hallway. "Are you okay?"

I shake my head, completely weirded out.

"Who *was* that?" she asks.

Fingers trembling, I click off the receiver and peer up at Macy. "She said she couldn't wait until I left her alone."

"Until you left *who* alone?"

I shrug.

Macy smirks in response. "Obviously another prank."

I nod, telling myself that she's right. And maybe she is.

I mean, I *have* gotten my fair share of pranks this week—faux bloody rocks left outside my door; numerous prank phone calls in the middle of the night; and dozens of well-timed knocks on my door with no one on the other side when I go to answer.

It's all because of tonight.

Tonight is the one-hundredth anniversary of the death of Anna Barton, the girl who supposedly haunts our school. Anna Barton was a student here, but she ended up killing herself when she found out that her boyfriend was cheating on her—and with her best friend, no less.

Needless to say, Anna was beyond devastated, but when she went looking for a shoulder to cry on—for someone to console her—she found that no one wanted to get involved. And so, just before she killed herself, feeling completely abandoned, she wrote the words "You shouldn't have left me alone!" across her bedroom wall in dark red paint.

Legend has it that every twenty-five years following Anna's death someone on campus will die.

And it happens.

Seventy-five years ago, only twenty-five years after Anna's suicide, Maria Bradley was discovered drowned inside the school's swimming pool. The words "You shouldn't have left me alone!" were smeared across the wall in bright pink lipstick.

Fifty years ago it was Sarah Wheeler. Her body was found in the woods behind the school. People say that she'd been running, that someone was chasing her and that she tripped over some brush and smacked her head hard against a rock. It killed her almost instantly. Those same words had been scribbled right beside her in the dirt.

The girl who died twenty-five years ago was also discovered with that same phrase beside her bed. Her name was Rosemary Allegro, and they found her in her dorm room closet. She had slit both her wrists and written those words, in blood, across the inside of the closet door.

It's not that I'm some Anna Barton–murders guru or anything; I just happen to know some of this stuff. *Everybody* here at Schillington Prep (more commonly known as *Chill*ington or *Shrill*ington) does. Some kids, like my boyfriend, James, even come to this school *because* of the legend—because they love the idea of being scared. And they love, even more, to try to freak people out with their lame-o pranks—which is undoubtedly why Macy seems so unconcerned about my recent call.

I take a deep breath, reminding myself that, when it comes right down to it, there isn't a single soul at Shrillington who hasn't seen, heard, or tried to freak out one of their teachers with the infamous phrase or some variation of it. Some of my personal favorites:

"Don't dine alone!"

"Don't do it alone!"

"Don't leave me alone!"

"You really shouldn't have left me tonight!"

Pranksters at this school think it's absolutely hilarious to call you up in the middle of the night and blare these words into your ear. They also like to graffiti them on the walls in the locker rooms and scribble them across the chalkboard menus in the cafeteria.

But while pranks like that have become nothing more than a nuisance, I feel like this recent call is different.

Scarier.

A lot more menacing.

"You really don't think I should be worried?" I ask.

"Oh, please," Macy says, quacking her way into my room. She's got on her favorite pair of slippers—fuzzy ducklings that quack with each step. A chipper choice, in my opinion, for tonight's festivities. But I suppose they go with her hair, a happy fuzzy mass in itself, bleached-blond spikes that stick up straight all over her head. "I'll be surprised if that's the *only* weird phone call we get tonight."

Despite the uneasy feeling in the pit of my stomach, I tell myself that she's right, and then I fill her in on the rest of the phone call. "It was like the caller was making fun of me. She kept laughing at me—this creepy giggle."

"Right," Macy says, seemingly uninterested. She flops onto my bed and busts open the bag of Sun Chips. "Because that's what pranksters do."

"Do you think it might have been Georgiana?" I ask, still hesitant to drop the subject. For the record, our friend Georgiana is a self-proclaimed prankster. The girl's been known to sprinkle itching powder in people's beds, leave ransom notes in people's mailboxes (after stealing something like their favorite teddy bear), and contaminate the food of fellow lunch companions when they least expect it (like the time she added Pop Rocks to my chocolate milk).

"Negative." Macy sighs. "She went home for the weekend, remember?"

"*Everybody* went home for the weekend," I clarify.

It's true that aside from a handful of die-hard horror fiends, nobody in their right mind wanted to stay here this weekend.

Including me.

But James talked me into it, assuring me that everything would be fine, especially if we stick together. And since Macy was stranded here, too—her parents have some out-of-state wedding thing they're going to—I caved.

"When is James getting here?" Macy asks, wiping the chip dust from the corners of her mouth.

"Soon," I say, somewhat dreading his arrival.

James and I have been going out for almost six months now, but during the past couple of months it's been pretty much an endless cycle of fighting and making up. I hate that about our relationship. I mean, I'm not one of those girls who's all about the drama. And so I've found myself bending and yielding where I know I shouldn't.

Like tonight.

There's a reason he wanted to stick around this weekend. He thinks it's the ideal night to try to contact Anna's spirit, being the hundredth anniversary and all. And Macy, a horror dabbler on the side, seems fairly into the idea as well. I'm just going along to keep the peace—to make it five full days without getting into yet another fight with him.

"You're still freaking out over that phone call, aren't you?" Macy asks.

I shrug, not wanting to admit it, because honestly, it's not like the idea of ghosts scares me. I mean, even though everybody at this school is all abuzz about Anna Barton—even though they think it's fun to pull out the school annual from 1907, to post her picture, and come to tour my room (since I was unlucky enough to score Anna's old room)—I haven't really noticed much, spiritly speaking.

Even just last month, the producers of the SciFi Channel's *Ghost Hunters* series visited our campus for an upcoming show. People around here couldn't get enough, bragging about feeling cold spots on a regular basis, about noticing lights flickering and seeing sparkling, purplish globes floating toward them at all hours of the day and night. Meanwhile, I sort of hung back, because aside from icy-cold water in the morning for showers and a clunky old heating unit that makes a huge ruckus, I haven't really noticed anything all that dramatic.

"So, why don't you just dial star six-nine?" Macy suggests.

A good idea. I click on the receiver and start dialing. But nothing happens.

And so I know someone's on the other end.

"Hello?" I say, my voice quavering over the word.

"Do you want to die?" the voice whispers.

"Very funny," I say with a sigh of relief, recognizing the voice right away, despite his lame-o voice-changer tool. He bought it last summer at Spencer Gifts, this gag shop downtown.

It's James, and he's trying to freak me out.

I glance at the clock. It's a little after ten. "You're still coming over tonight, right?"

But he doesn't answer.

"James?" I ask, hearing the irritation in my voice. "This isn't funny."

"Do you want *to die*?" the voice repeats.

"Okay, are you *trying* to piss me off?"

The boy's a total dork, complete with the cheesiest collection of horror flicks lining the shelves of his room. He's even got pictures of just about every ghoul, vampire, and werewolf adorning all four walls, not to mention an Elvira blow-up doll.

"I'm hanging up!" I tell him.

"Okay, okay," he caves, in his normal voice now.

"You're such an ass."

"You know you love me."

"Sometimes I wonder," I say, glancing in the mirror at my dark bed-head hair. Before I nodded off, I had spent a good forty minutes working my mane into two perfectly frumpled braids, just like I had it during last spring's school carnival, when James told me how cute I looked.

But now it's a mess.

"Did you call before?" I ask.

"No. I called *now*."

"Wait, you didn't call a few minutes ago? You didn't pretend to be some girl crying? Were you on your cell phone? It was all fuzzy."

"Um, no."

"Seriously, James. Don't screw with my head."

*"Moi?"* he jokes.

"Come on," I insist.

"It wasn't me, okay? Why didn't you star six-nine?"

Because *you* called, dumbass, I want to say. But instead I bite the inside of my cheek and James promises to come by just as soon as he can sneak past security.

They've beefed things up for tonight, hiring extra cops to scout out the area and making us show our badges in the lobby upon entrance. Apparently there are a few other brave (or stupid) souls sticking around this weekend—at least that's what Raquel, my resident director, has told me. She's also called me at least four times today, checking that I'm okay, reminding me that there's Movie Night in the rec room (featuring *Psycho*, *The Blair Witch Project*, and *Friday the 13th*) with all-you-can-snack, skull-shaped popcorn balls for people who didn't go home.

"So, when's he getting here?" Macy asks, still munching her way through the bag of chips.

"Soon," I whisper, completely irritated.

"Let me guess: You're pissed at him again, right?"

I shrug, not wanting to go into it. The truth is that Macy's been telling me to break it off with James for the past couple months, reminding me over and over and *over* again how much he and I have nothing in common.

But I don't think that's true. I mean, just because I'm not into all the haunted happenings around this place doesn't mean that I don't appreciate a good scary movie once in a while.

I remind myself of this as I fix my hair, suddenly convinced that Bonnie, my hairdresser back home, was right. Not only do these auburn highlights add texture to my not-so-fabulous mousy brown tresses, but they also help to bring out the deep golden green in my otherwise olive-drab eyes.

"Are you sure you're okay?" Macy asks for the second time tonight.

I nod, feeling unusually unhinged. I look over at the radiator by my window—where Anna Barton killed herself. Word has it that she tied one end of a rope to a vertical pipe, the other end around her neck, and then hung herself out the window.

A few moments later, a banging sound comes from that same window, making me jump.

"Relax," Macy squawks. "It's only James."

I nod and take a deep breath, trying to get a grip. Since the school has this stupid rule about not letting boys in the girls' dorms and vice versa, James has become quite adept at scaling the side of the building. And luckily, I'm only two floors up.

Slowly, I approach the window, feeling a chill pass over my shoulders as I move past the radiator. I tug up on the sill just as James hoists himself onto the ledge.

"Hey, beautiful," he says, once inside.

"Hey," I say back, trying to force a smile. "I'm almost surprised you made it. Security's pretty tight tonight, no?"

James shrugs, commenting about how the new security is really just a bunch of rent-a-cops in uniform. Then he wraps his arms around me, remarking on how cold my skin feels. "Like ice," he whispers, running his fingers over the gooseflesh on my forearms.

I nod, pulling a sweater from the closet, suddenly overwhelmed by the feeling of being watched—and not by Macy or James. I glance out the window, wondering if anyone else is out there, imagining Sarah Wheeler as she was chased behind our school that night, fifty years ago, then as she tripped over some brush and landed down hard against a rock. People say that she scribbled those words in the dirt just before she took her last breath, that they found the dirt embedded under her fingernails.

The thought of it sends chills down the back of my neck.

I wrap the sweater around me and then lock the window back up. Meanwhile, James pulls a present from his backpack, almost making me forget his stupid phone call.

"I brought you something," he says.

"For real?" I perk up. I tear off the silver wrapping, producing a velvety black pouch with a purple drawstring. "What's this?" I ask, opening it up. There's a palm-size crystal inside. It's wide on top and pointed at the bottom, almost like an inverted cone. The crystal is attached to a long silver chain. James dangles it down in front of my eyes.

"Are you trying to hypnotize me?" I ask.

He smiles. His gray-blue eyes grow wide. "It's for our séance."

"Oh," I say, wondering how this is supposed to be a gift.

Meanwhile, James empties out the rest of his backpack. He's brought along a handful of incense sticks, a bunch of candles, a box of sea salt, and a square black handkerchief.

"I didn't know I was supposed to bring along my Ouija board," Macy says with a smirk. "Too bad I retired it back in fifth grade."

"Laugh if you want," James says, setting everything up on the floor. "But this is going to help us contact Anna."

"And what if I'm having second thoughts?" I ask, watching as he places down the handkerchief. He sprinkles sea salt along its perimeter.

"The salt will help keep evil spirits out," he explains, ignoring my question.

"Since when is Anna Barton's spirit not evil?" Macy asks.

James pauses, like the question never even occurred to him, but then he quickly resumes his setup. He lights the incense and candles and then wafts the smoke from them over the handkerchief, as though that's supposed to bless the space — or so I'm guessing.

"James?" I say, still trying to get his attention.

"Hey," he says, finally glancing up at me as he positions a

few of the candles around the room, "did I leave my watch here last night? I can't find it anywhere."

I shake my head, annoyed that he isn't really hearing me. "I think I might be having second thoughts," I repeat, a little louder this time.

He and Macy exchange an eye-roll—like I can't see them—and then James flicks off the overhead light, leaving only the candles and the tiny reading lamp over my desk to illuminate the room. "Relax," he says. "This is supposed to be fun."

"I know." I shrug. "It's just that maybe I don't feel quite right about this. Especially tonight."

"Since when are *you* scared about all this ghost stuff?" he continues.

"I'm not," I say, silently caving.

"Good." He crosses the room to give my cheek a cold peck. "Then let's get started."

I nod and glance back over at the radiator, wondering what color it was when Anna lived here. Or how the room was decorated—white walls or moss green, like now? Was her bed positioned opposite the dresser like mine, or did she kitty-corner it to the door? Did she scribble the words "You shouldn't have left me alone!" across the east wall, like everyone says, or by the window, where the paint never seems to stick?

"Are you ready?" James asks, snapping me back to attention. He's sitting on the floor by his setup now, dangling the crystal at me.

I nod some more, suddenly feeling a little nauseated—and the musky scent of the incense isn't helping. Still, I join him, and so does Macy, and we listen diligently as he explains the directions.

"It works like this," he begins. "We each take a turn with the crystal. We close our eyes, concentrate hard, and ask Anna a question."

"And how do we get the answer?" Macy asks.

James demonstrates, telling us to position our hands palm down on the handkerchief. He holds the end of the chain in one hand and then drops the crystal from the other, the point dangling downward toward our hands. "If the crystal moves from left to right, the answer is yes," he explains.

"And if it moves from front to back, the answer is no, right?" I ask, remembering some similar practice I heard of before—something about determining the sex of a baby, front to back for a boy, side to side for a girl.

James nods, reminding us that we'll need to phrase our questions so they have only a yes or no answer.

"So, let's get started." Macy rubs her palms together and then places them in the middle of the handkerchief. I follow suit (minus the palm rubbing), noticing how the reading light over my desk keeps flickering.

"Are you okay?" Macy asks, noticing my spaciness, maybe.

"Yeah," I say, trying to refocus by staring at the chipped pearl polish on my thumbnail.

"So, I'll go first," James says. "Anna, are you here tonight?"

He drops the crystal and it dangles downward, wavering from left to right over our hands and making him smile.

"Let *me* ask it something," Macy says, taking the crystal from him. She closes her eyes to concentrate, a happy grin inching up her lips like she's really enjoying this, too. "Anna," she whispers, "is it true that someone is going to die tonight?"

At that the flickering light over my desk goes out completely, turning my bones to absolute ice.

Macy lets out a gasp.

At the same moment, I hear a banging noise come from inside my closet, like maybe a shoe box tumbled off the shelf.

Macy leans over to snatch a candle from atop my night table. She positions it in front of us for added light.

"Holy shit!" James shouts, totally beaming.

Meanwhile, I remain still and quiet, bracing myself for something else to happen. When nothing else does, James gets up to inspect the light.

"It's Anna." He grins, unscrewing the dead bulb.

"Or maybe it's a coincidence," I say, perhaps trying to convince myself. "That bulb's been flickering all night."

The crystal, still dangling in Macy's grip, shifts from left to right. "Check it out," she whispers.

"So it's true!" James says, practically drooling. "Someone is going to die tonight."

"And why do you look so happy about that?" I ask, wondering how accurate the dangling even is, especially since Macy moved to reach for a candle.

"It's not that I'm happy," he says, running his fingers through his shaggy dark hair. "But maybe we can find out who the next victim is."

"We can stop the death before it happens," Macy pipes up.

"Right," James says, joining us back on the floor. "So, let's name some people. Who's staying on campus this weekend?"

"No!" I shout. "I don't want to know."

"Why not?" James asks. "We could be helping someone."

"He does have a point," Macy says, continuing to defend

him. "Maybe if someone had warned those girls, they wouldn't have died."

I glance at my closet, thinking about the snippets I've heard about Rosemary, the third girl who died after Anna. People say that she was pretty and popular and perfectly happy. Apparently, she played lots of sports and participated on the yearbook and newspaper staffs and volunteered at the library on Sunday afternoons.

No one ever imagined that she'd do it—that she'd kill herself.

Though neither of the other deaths really make any sense, either.

Maria Bradley, the girl who drowned, was Schillington's champion swimmer. When the coroner examined her body—for a blow to the head, or something toxic in her bloodstream, anything that might have explained the reason for her drowning—they became even more perplexed, because she checked out perfectly fine.

In Sarah's case, no one was ever able to discover who or what had been chasing her that night. There was only one set of footprints—her own—but she had to have been running pretty frantically because when they found her body it was covered with scratches from having broken through branches and brush the entire way.

I look at James, wondering what he's thinking. He and Macy are laughing at a joke he told, something about Norman Bates and something else I wouldn't understand. At least that's what they tell me. James tops the joke off by picking up a candle. He positions it under his chin. The shadow of the flame dances against his face, illuminating his wicked expression, like Halloween come to life.

"You're such a spaz." Macy laughs, throwing a Cheez Doodle at him.

James goes to catch it in his mouth, but he's interrupted by a noise.

We all are.

It's coming from the closet—a weird scratching sound.

"What the hell is that?" James whispers.

Macy stands and takes a step toward it.

"Maybe it's a rat," I suggest, somewhat for my own benefit.

James stands, too, angling his ear to listen harder. "It sounds like someone's in there."

"There's no one in my closet," I assure him. "I was just in there to get a sweater."

But the noise is unmistakable, like someone's clawing at the wood.

"You know," James begins, "that Rosemary girl, the one who slit her wrists, word has it that she was locked inside her closet when she did it—she was trapped."

"No way," Macy says, like this is the first time she's hearing of it.

It's the first time I'm hearing of it, too.

"It's true." James nods. "When the police entered her room that night, they had to bust the closet door open. Her fingernails were all bloody; she'd damaged the hell out of them trying to get out. Nobody knew how she even got in there, but someone must have done it because the door was locked from the outside, meaning she either had to have had the blades with her at the time of entrance . . ."

"Or maybe Anna slid them under the door," Macy suggests.

"Bingo!" James says, flicking on the overhead light.

I shake my head, fighting the urge to cover my ears. People say that the ghost of Anna is what drove those girls to die. They say she chooses her victims carefully, picking girls who have one very important thing in common—they've all had secret relationships with someone else's boyfriend. People believe it's Anna's way of getting back at her best friend, that just before they wind up dead she prompts her victims to write the words "You shouldn't have left me alone!" as a sort of tribute to herself, so she's never forgotten.

"Anna, is that you?" James whispers, edging closer to the closet door. He grabs the heavy silver picture frame from the corner of my dresser, the one with the snapshot of me and my grandpa, and positions it over his shoulder, like a makeshift mallet.

The clawing sound continues, getting more urgent, causing my heart to thrash around in my chest. James extends his hand to the doorknob. And in one quick motion, he whips open the door.

Macy lets out a gasp in response. And so do I, standing up from our séance spot.

James rushes my closet, grappling through my clothes, my shoes, the boxes on the overhead shelf.

But there's nothing there.

And the noise has suddenly stopped.

"That's totally messed up," Macy whispers.

James nods, taking a step back. Finally, he turns to us. "That was Anna," he beams, as though thoroughly amused.

"Or Rosemary," Macy suggests. "Of course, if it were *really* Rosemary, it would make a lot more sense for her to haunt

Janice Acher's closet on the fourth floor. You know, since that's where she died and all."

"Maybe she's lost," James jokes.

"And maybe all that scratching noise was just an echo from one of the other rooms," I say, my voice shaking over the words. "You have to admit, the walls in this place *are* pretty thin."

"*Denial,*" James sings.

"Maybe," I say, noticing how my head keeps spinning. "Or maybe I don't feel so well." I take a deep breath, wondering if Raquel would mind if I stopped by her room for a bit. Sometimes she lets us take a rest on her spare futon. She has a peppermint-scented pillow that never fails to ease me.

"Take some Advil," James tells me, clicking the light back off. He reignites the candle—the one that Macy blew out—and takes a seat back on the floor.

Reluctantly, I join him, curled up on my side in a fetal position, using my arm as a pillow and wishing I could just block everything out.

"Come on," James urges. He grabs the crystal, eager to resume like nothing happened. "Don't ruin it for everybody. This is just getting good."

"Maybe *you're* the one who's ruining it," I venture, suddenly feeling bold.

"What's that supposed to mean?"

"It means you knew I didn't want to do this tonight," I say, sitting back up.

James's face twists up into a giant question mark. "What are you talking about?"

"Maybe I should leave," Macy says.

"No," I insist. "Nobody is going anywhere." I take yet another deep breath, trying to keep my cool, knowing that whether I believe in all this séance stuff or not, there's one question I just have to ask. "Let me go next."

"I knew you'd get into it eventually." James smiles.

He hands me the crystal and I concentrate hard, really imagining myself talking to Anna's spirit—if it truly even exists here. "Was that *you* who called me earlier?" I whisper. Fingers shaking, I drop the crystal, wishing it to move from front to back.

But instead it shifts from side to side, causing my stomach to churn.

"Um, no offense, James," Macy says, "but I think this crystal idea is a load of crap. It only moves in one direction."

"Wait!" I insist, somewhat surprised by my urgent tone. "Maybe we should ask it a 'no' question—something we already know the answer to."

"Good idea," Macy says with a wink. "Does James have even the slightest clue about how to contact spirits?" She grabs the crystal and drops it from its chain, purposely forcing it in a front-to-back motion.

"You can be such a downer-bitch, you know that?" James says to her, completely setting me off.

We end up in a huge argument, one that segues into the real problems between us. How James is completely insensitive, how he only thinks about himself, and how he consistently fails to see all the sacrifices I make for the sake of our relationship.

"I'm outta here," Macy announces somewhere in the midst of it all. And then James and I just keep on fighting, arguing to the point of exhaustion, until my voice grows tired and hoarse.

Somehow at the end of it all, he ends up apologizing, wrapping his arms around me and saying that he loves me and doesn't want to lose me.

But for once I don't say anything back.

We fall asleep shortly after. But then, around 3 A.M., I wake up with a start, remembering Macy.

I'd meant to go and get her right after the fighting ended.

"What's the problem?" James asks, turning over in bed, pulling the covers up over his ear to block out any answer.

I grab the phone and move out into the hallway to Macy's room. I try knocking, but no one answers. I try pounding, calling her on the telephone, and shouting her name.

Still no one comes, even after five full minutes.

"What the hell is going on?" Raquel asks, finally coming to my aid. She's dressed in her robe and slippers. A security guy follows close at her heels.

I try to explain, but I can't get the words out—how I need to get in there; how Macy, James, and I were supposed to stick together tonight.

The security guy unlocks Macy's door and lets us in.

And that's when we see it—the open window and the curtains flapping in the breeze. And the words "You shouldn't have left me alone!" scribbled across the mirror in dark red lipstick.

Sitting atop the dresser is James's watch, the one he said he lost, enabling me to put the pieces together—all the private jokes and all the secret glances, and the way Macy was forever trying to get me to break it off with James.

My stomach churns. My hands start to sweat. And that menacing giggle—the one from the phone call earlier—begins to play in my mind's ear.

I take a deep breath, trying to get a grip, noticing how one end of a rope is tied to the radiator while the other end trails outside.

Raquel clenches my hand as the security guy approaches the window. He doesn't even flinch when he sees her, hanging there. He just turns around and nods to us, tells Raquel to call 9-1-1.

And that's when I know for sure.

That Macy is dead.

But the legend of Anna Barton lives on.

# SAVING FACE

**Christopher Pike**

"I want to be you," my twin sister said. "You have to die."

"Jane. Shut up," I replied with a laugh. Jane often said off-the-wall stuff. That last remark didn't scare me. Not until she brought out a knife. It was part of a set I had bought her the previous Christmas for her apartment—a Cutco carving knife.

The blade was big, shiny, very sharp. She toyed with it as my laugh died in my throat, not looking at me, not now, just at the knife, fingering the metal, testing the tip. She pricked her finger, probably on purpose. So I could see the blood and better imagine what my own blood would look like.

Jane sighed as she spoke next. "I always hate it when you tell me to shut up. And you do it anyway, you don't care. Tons of crap that bugs me—you just do it and then smile like that's going to make everything all right. You think because you're a famous model and everyone likes you that I like you, too." Jane looked up and stared at me. "But I don't, Jill, I don't like you at all. The truth is, I've hated you for years. Only you were too stupid to realize it."

I forced a smile, although I was beginning to feel anxious. This turn in our conversation had come out of nowhere. Minutes ago we had been "just hanging" in Jane's new apartment — she had moved from our parents' house only last month — eating Chinese and trying to decide which DVD we were going to watch.

It had been a while since I had spent time with Jane. My schedule was demanding. The evening had not looked particularly exciting, but I figured it would be pleasant enough. Especially when Jane brought out a homemade chocolate cake for dessert — which she knew I loved — and whipped up a special brew of herbal tea to drink with it.

The tea had been the only thing unusual about the evening — that is, before she started talking about murdering me. The truth was I had never seen Jane drink herbal tea. She was a straight Coke girl, unlike me, who seldom drank soda. As a budding model — I was not famous, not yet, but I had done a few covers and had finally landed a real New York agent — I had to watch my weight. Jane usually ran fifteen pounds heavier, although in the past few months she had dropped down to my size.

*To* exactly *my size,* I thought.

My guts rumbled from the tea — the stuff had tasted lousy. Only the sugar in the cake and the vanilla ice cream she had heaped on it had allowed me to drink the stuff without making a face. Yet that made me wonder all the more. Had she been trying to disguise the taste of the herbs?

I stopped smiling.

"Why are you saying all this stuff?" I asked. "I'm here, right? Isn't that what you wanted? We're having fun. Why bring up this junk about hating me and how stupid I am? When you think about it, we're identical twins; we're genetically the same. If I'm dumb that means you're dumb." I paused. "Put that knife away."

Jane ignored me and sucked at the drops of blood that formed at the tip of her right index finger. The knife was in her left hand. Unlike me, Jane was left-handed. "I wasn't dumb enough to drink the tea," she muttered.

"What's that supposed to mean?" I demanded, putting a hand over my belly. The rumbling was turning into nauseous waves. I wanted to run to the bathroom and throw up. At the same time I felt weak, like I wouldn't make it without help. I was about to ask my sister for assistance when she caught my eye. I realized she knew exactly what I was feeling.

"It doesn't matter if you throw up or not," she said. "You swallowed a whole cup. It's been in your system thirty minutes." She added, "You're already screwed."

"I don't understand."

"It means you're going to die."

"Stop talking like that!" I snapped. "I'm feeling real sick." Besides the nausea and overall weakness, I noticed I was sweating heavily. It was an oily kind of sweat; it seemed to suffocate my pores, maybe my lungs as well. It was an effort to talk, to breathe.

Jane nodded. "You feel like you're smothering."

"What was in that tea?" I whispered.

Jane shrugged. "Leaves. Twigs. Bark. I don't know all the details of the concoction, but I know it's poisonous. With the dose you drank, you'll be dead in an hour. Probably within thirty minutes."

I raised my arm to wipe away the sweat that was pouring into my eyes. It seemed as if the limb took an hour to reach my face. Everything felt as if it was happening in slow motion.

"Call nine-one-one," I mumbled.

"Call them yourself."

"Jane, I'm serious. Call for an ambulance."

My sister shook her head and said nothing.

I tried to stand. I managed to straighten my legs and get to my feet. But then something happened to my knees. They disappeared. My brain was no longer connected to them. No knees, no walking to the phone and calling an ambulance. I saw myself fall more than I felt the fall — until I hit the floor. My nose shattered on impact and sent out a spray of blood.

The red liquid pooled around my eyes and might have blinded me if Jane had not rolled me over. How tall my sister looked right then, standing over me, the knife still in her hands.

"Why?" I gasped.

Jane knelt by my side. "The simplest reason would be the most honest. Because I can. Our parents hardly see me anymore, and when they do, you're never around. You must have noticed that for the past year I've gone out of my way not to be in the same room as you. Except for the last month, and that was just to sucker you back into my life so we could have tonight."

"Why?" I mumbled again, not understanding. Jane moved her head closer and it looked as large as the Goodyear blimp.

"You're not listening, Jill. It's easy to become you, to have your life, and still be me at the same time. Since we graduated from high school last year, no one ever sees the two of us together. We're both nineteen and we both live on our own. I can play both roles and enjoy the best parts of the two lives and no one will be any the wiser. I'll get to model, make all that cash, live in that swanky apartment of yours, drive your Carrera." She paused. "Best of all, I'll get to make out with Henry."

"No." It was the only word I had left.

"Think how much better it's going to be for us. We both know how uptight you are about sex. Henry and I have talked about it. The guy is a walking frustration. But as of tonight he's going to go to sleep smiling and wake up grinning." Jane smiled. "If you do love him, you have to admit it's for the best."

"No," I heard myself repeat.

Jane brought her knife close to my face and sighed.

"I wish you weren't passing out so fast. I wanted to have a little fun with your face before you left the world. I know how attached you are to it. You think you're prettier than me. If you must know, that's the one thing that made me decide to go ahead with my plan. It was your vanity. Two minutes ago you said we're genetically identical, but you don't believe it. I bet you've never once looked at me and thought how beautiful I was. Have you?"

I tried to answer but could not.

My jaw was numb, my tongue frozen.

But the answer would have been no.

I had never thought Jane was beautiful.

Not like me.

I felt a sudden warm sensation on the side of my face. Ralph, my black cocker spaniel, was licking my face. I'd brought my dog over to my sister's house because he sometimes got lonely when

I was away too long. I was very attached to my dog. Henry often joked that I liked Ralph more than him. I didn't think that was true, but I sure did love my dog. He was, like, my best friend.

He was the only friend I had right now.

Ralph groaned in pain as if sensing my pain.

Jane set down the knife and stroked him lovingly.

"Don't worry, I'll take good care of Ralph. I'm sure in a few days he won't be able to tell me from you. Like Henry, he might even prefer me."

What could I say when I could not speak?

Jane picked up the knife and pointed it at the tip of my nose.

"The poison has probably numbed you up some, so you're not going to feel this the way I'd like. But I want you to know I'm going to mess you up real good. I'm going to poke out those bright blues and carve away those high cheekbones. I'll take off your lips, too. You can deny it all you want, but I know you talked Dad into letting you have collagen injections. Why do you think I had to go and get them, too?"

I stared. My eyes were frozen open. All I could do was stare.

Jane grinned again and leaned over with her knife.

She began to cut, and it was true, I didn't really feel it. Too numb, I suppose. But I felt it inside, oh, yes, deep inside, as she began to tear away my flesh and feed it to my dog. That was the last thing I saw before I lost consciousness. Ralph eating pieces of my face.

When I woke up I felt as if I was on fire. The weird thing is, besides the burning sensation, I *heard* flames. The crackling of wood. The smell of smoke.

Then I opened my eyes and saw a campfire. It was four feet away. I was lying on my right side, close to it. There were only three medium-size logs in the center of the pyre but they gave off a lot of heat. Still, it did not match the burning sensation radiating from my face. It was as if someone had peeled off my skin. . . .

The thought was enough. I remembered.

Jane had carved up my face before she killed me.

That meant I was dead, and this was what? Purgatory? I felt bad enough to be in hell. It was dark, away from the fire; everything was a dim blur.

"Don't try to sit up," a scratchy voice said behind me. I immediately disobeyed. Twisting around, I tried to see who was talking, but two dusty hands came out of the dark and gently pressed me back down. The female voice added, "Rest. You have to regain your strength."

"Where am I?" I mumbled, and it was no ordinary mumble. I was missing parts of my anatomy needed to form clear words. My lips, for example.

"You're in the middle of nowhere," she said.

"Who are you?" I asked.

"Name's Arleen."

"Why are you here?"

"Be happy I was here tonight, child. Or else right now you'd be in the belly of a gator."

The Everglades. Jane must have dumped me in the swamp. Did this woman rescue me?

"Did you see her?" I asked, feeling a drowsiness sweeping over me. An angry note entered the woman's voice.

"Not clearly. But I saw her drag you to the water and roll you in."

Tears burned my eyes, and I wanted to sob loudly. But the weariness continued to grow in strength, and besides, there was something wrong with my vision. I could not focus properly. My depth perception was off; my tears were flowing on only one side of my face.

It was then I realized I was missing an eye.

I closed my one eye. I wished I were dead.

"How do I look?" I whispered.

The woman sighed. "You're alive, child. That's all that matters."

*Not true,* I thought as I passed out again.

The woman's full name was Arleen Tabbit. She was forty, a gypsy of sorts, who lived in a hut deep in the Everglades. She said she had friends in the woods, but I never met any of them the whole time we were together.

Arleen had been gathering roots for a stew she was cooking when she chanced upon Jane and her unique burden. She stumbled upon my sister before Jane had finished wrapping me up. Arleen described how my sister had fitted two trash bags over me, one over my head, the other around my legs. Before sealing them with duct tape, she scooped in rocks. The instant she rolled me into the water, I sank. It was only because Jane left right away and Arleen moved fast that I was still alive.

"You should have let me die," I groaned as I sat on a stool outside Arleen's shack while she applied what she called an "ancient healing paste" to my face. The formula was remarkably soothing. If not for the woman's skill with herbs, I would have been in horrible pain. As it was, my face and head throbbed but it was not unbearable.

"Nonsense," Arleen said. "Nothing wrong with you the best plastic surgeons in Miami can't fix."

I brushed away her hand. "Nothing they can't fix? Look at me! I have no lips! The skin has been scraped off my face. If you look real close you might notice I'm missing an eye. Tell me which surgeon is going to fix me up with one of those and I'll go see him this afternoon."

Arleen brushed aside my outburst. She had cleaned her fingers to apply the paste, but otherwise she was buried under years of soot. The filth made her face hard to describe—as did my missing eye—but I could tell she had exotic features. Her coloring was dark, although her skin was more olive than black. There were streaks of white in her brown hair, which she wore knotted under a woolen cap, but there were few wrinkles around her lustrous eyes. The latter shone as if from a great depth, despite being as dark as coal. If she cleaned herself up and put on nice clothes she could be pretty.

But I figured that was the last thing Arleen cared about.

She chuckled as I wept about my missing eye.

"Why, child, you can still see, can't you?" she said. "That's all that matters. As far as your empty socket is concerned, there are doctors who can fit a glass eye in there that looks no different than the other one. Then no one's going to look at you twice."

"Yeah? What about the rest of my face?"

Arleen shrugged. "From what you've told me, you've got money. Get your face fixed up as best you can and get on with your life. No sense worrying whether you're pretty enough to be on the cover of a magazine. No one reads those kinds of magazines anyway. They just buy them 'cause everyone else buys them. There ain't no fun stories to read in them."

I kicked the ground in frustration. "You don't understand! I can't go back to my life! The life I was living! I have a boyfriend, Henry, and if he saw me like this he'd dump me. The same with my friends. They'd never hang out with a monster like me."

"If this Henry really loves you, he won't care what you look like," she said as she continued to apply the ointment. She had an odd accent. At first I assumed she was from the Caribbean islands, but the more she talked the more I heard European tones. Not one but a strange mix of accents. She added, "If he leaves you because of what's happened to you, then you've lost nothing of value."

I snorted. "You don't live in the real world."

That amused Arleen. "Are you saying you do?"

I gestured to her shack and the swamp.

"This place stinks," I said.

Arleen stopped applying the paste. "This place is my home." She added, "You need to get home to your family. They'll care about you no matter how you look."

I hesitated. "I didn't tell you. That girl who cut me up and dumped me in the water—that was my twin sister."

For once, Arleen was shocked. She sighed and shook her head.

"Maybe you shouldn't go home, girl," she muttered.

Of course, Arleen was not serious when she said I should avoid home. She told me to call my parents right away, that they would be worried about me. I explained that as far as my parents knew, I was doing just fine. When Arleen heard the full scope of Jane's plan, she gasped in wonder.

"That girl's got an imagination, you gotta grant her that," she cackled.

"That girl made a mistake when she didn't see you," I replied. "She's going to pay for that mistake."

Arleen gave me a long look. "Best you go to the police and let them take care of the nasty end of this business."

I shook my head. There were two things that made it impossible to return to my old life: my hideous face and my desire for revenge. Even if Jane went to jail, I thought, what kind of satisfaction would that bring?

I was the one who would have to live in a walking prison until the day I died. I hadn't been lying when I had told Arleen that my friends, Henry included, would dump me the second they saw me. In my world, looks were everything. They were everything to me.

If I could not have my face back the way it had been, I at least wanted Jane to suffer. But to hurt her I had to come up with a plan, and to do that I needed to stalk her until I could figure out how to make my move. I said as much to Arleen, who naturally disapproved.

"You're underestimating what them fancy doctors can do," she said. "Why, I read about a woman in Europe who had a brand-new face sewn on. Imagine that!"

I grumbled. "She had the face of a brain-dead woman transplanted on. After the surgery, she didn't look anything like she used to. She looked like the other woman."

Arleen shook her head. "So you want revenge. I can understand that. I'd probably want the same if someone tried to feed me to the gators. But you've still got a life ahead of you to live. You have to give thought to that."

I didn't reply. My future was the last thing I wanted to think about.

My face healed, slowly, painfully. If not for Arleen's help, the process would have been unbearable. She was weird but kind. She often hitchhiked into town to buy bandages, rubbing alcohol, antibiotic ointment. She even managed to find me a black patch for my empty eye socket.

But although she was wise enough to embrace what modern drugstores had to offer, it was her knowledge of herbal teas and pastes that helped the most. When it came to soothing my pain, the Tylenol and aspirin she gave me did not come close to the brews she made out of the bark of trees and the leaves of bushes that grew in the Everglades. She never told me the names of the ingredients, but whenever I drank the teas, my pain would recede to a distant ache. Then I would be able to sleep like a child.

But each morning I awakened more determined than ever to have my revenge. At my insistence, Arleen brought me a mirror, and after I got over the initial shock—after two nights of crying—I swore that no matter what it took, Jane was going to look worse than me.

A month after Jane buried me, I hitched into town. I went back to my old neighborhood, to the apartment I rented the day after I graduated from high school last year. I was third in my class and had been voted homecoming queen the previous fall.

Jane had dropped out of school early. She took the GED test and didn't go to the homecoming dance, although several guys had asked her. I remembered how she had smiled, even back then, and said if she couldn't go with Henry, then she didn't want to go at all.

Jane was not in my apartment when I arrived. She didn't know where I kept a secret key. She didn't know a lot of things about my life. Once inside I was able to go online to my e-mail account and read all the mail Jane had been unable to access. I saw she had managed to make contact with my modeling agent and had in fact gone on several jobs. The man wrote that she was doing a wonderful job.

Jane did not know my ATM password and as a result she had been unable to drain my account. That had not stopped her from writing checks on my account, but she had not made any cash withdrawals. Without the password, she could not see exactly what I had in the bank. But I doubted she was worried about grabbing everything in my bank. After all, what was the hurry? She thought I was dead.

Yet her inability to directly view my balance gave me an advantage. I could withdraw money without her knowledge. I did just that when I sent a wire for ten thousand dollars to a new account at a different bank. I needed to rent an apartment and a car, but I didn't want to take so much that I raised suspicions. I could never drain the account so low that she bounced a check. Then she would know someone was on to her. Jane knew I had money in the bank.

Before I left the apartment, Jane came home—with Henry.

I got trapped in a garden area off the master bedroom. There I found Ralph, my dog. Thank God he recognized me and didn't bark once. I petted him and whispered soothing words in his big ears while Jane and Henry made a beeline for the bedroom.

I had to sit outside the screen door while they fooled around.

It made me hate Henry almost as much as I hated Jane.

Eventually they left, and I staggered into the bedroom and collapsed on the rumpled sheets and wept out my remaining eye. Ralph followed me inside and licked my tears away. He seemed so happy to see me, I knew in my heart he understood that my sister was an impostor.

Again, I vowed to make Jane pay.

But what was my plan? To be honest, I wasn't sure. I would stalk her to establish her routine. I had to know when she was alone, when she was vulnerable. I also knew I needed a weapon of some sort. But I didn't know what I wanted to do to her.

There were spare debit and credit cards plus a copy of my driver's license in a shoe box at the rear of my closet. The chance that Jane was aware of the duplicates was close to zero. I took them, left the apartment, and went in search of a place to live.

Even with all the bandages on my face, renting a studio proved easy. I just had to wave the cash and the agent asked me to sign on the dotted line. But he looked at me with such pity and disgust that I wanted to break his nose. However, all I did was weep when he handed me the keys and left me alone in the empty apartment. I was hideous. I was going to have to get used to it.

Renting a car proved more difficult. I didn't look like the girl on my license. It was not until I answered a dozen questions about my personal life — my Social Security number, my mother's maiden name, and so on—that they let me drive off in a four-year-old Camry. The car was a big step down from my Porsche, but I wanted inconspicuous wheels for my stalking hours.

My new apartment was three blocks from the old one. I could walk over and look at my sister whenever I wished. But I preferred to stay inside the Camry and follow her to photo shoots or to Henry's house. I would even sit outside in the dark and listen while their laughter echoed out to my lonely ears.

My detective work taught me several surprising things. Jane was a harder worker than I was. She was doing twice the number of shoots I had been doing. She had also completely faked out my parents. When I trailed her on a shopping trip with my mother, I saw she had my mannerisms down pat. Mom didn't notice a thing.

Jane spent almost no time being Jane Clayten. She had quit her job at the music store. The few times she returned to her apartment—the place where I had been poisoned—she merely made a few calls and checked her e-mail. She preferred my place, which made sense. It cost three grand a month. Her dump cost only seven hundred bucks.

Jane never drove her old Honda. She was addicted to my Carrera. She was a speed freak. Three times I saw her stopped by the cops. Only once was she given a ticket. The other times she just smiled at the officers, told them how sorry she was, batted her big blues, and got away with it.

Stalking her gave me the details of her life but did not tell me how to end her life. I lacked inspiration. I even began to wonder if I lacked the guts to destroy her. As the days turned into weeks and into months, my wounds healed, yet I continued to bandage my face. It was better to be a recovering patient,

I thought, than let the world know I was a horror. For the first time, I seriously contemplated killing myself.

Jane had wanted to be me. Now I wanted to be her.

Every mirror on earth silently cursed me.

I was UGLY! I could not bear it!

Then, one night, while sitting in the Camry outside my old apartment, listening to Henry and Jane enjoying a movie and buttered popcorn, I had a revelation. I don't know why the idea had taken so long to come. My only excuse was I had undergone a major trauma and wasn't thinking clearly.

I began to think back to the night Jane had attacked me.

She had given me a poisonous herbal tea. A concoction, she said, "of leaves, twigs, and bark." Yet Jane knew nothing about herbs, and her poison had not killed me, it had only knocked me out. Once Arleen had rescued me from the water, I recovered rapidly.

It was only because of Arleen that I was still alive. It was only because the woman had "just happened" to see Jane roll me into the water that I was still breathing. What a coincidence, I thought, that she had been at the right place at the right time to save me. What a coincidence that Arleen was also a master when it came to herbs.

It occurred to me that I might be stalking the wrong person.

I had only been back to see Arleen twice since returning to town. Both times she had been living in the shack, the same as I had left her, eating her strange diet of herbs and fish, hiking through the swamp late at night, and talking to the stars. There was no doubt she was a genuine gypsy, but was it possible she was something more?

I returned to the swamp and stalked her. For several days

she kept to her usual routine. As she had during the time I spent with her, she awoke at dawn and fished until noon. She tended a still she had set up deep in the swamp. Then she collected flowers and herbs and stored them in burlap sacks outside her hut.

But after a week she had a visitor.

The man arrived in a black Mercedes. He was Chinese, old but alert. Wearing an immaculate blue suit and a red tie, he climbed out of the car. It was he who bowed when they met, not Arleen. I had only to watch them for a minute to see that she was the boss and he the servant.

He had with him a white poodle that Arleen fawned over excessively. She treated the dog the same way I treated Ralph. She let the animal lick her mouth, and she hugged it as if it were a child, not a pet. I was jealous of her relationship with the dog. The time I had spent with her, she had treated me kindly, but she had never showered me with affection.

It was obvious the poodle was the love of her life.

I was not surprised when Arleen climbed into the Mercedes and drove away with the man. It was fortunate I was parked nearby. I was able to catch up with them, and I followed them to Palm Beach, where the stars and jet-setters had their mansions. Arleen had a palace of her own. As they pulled into the driveway, two dozen employees lined up outside. She was given roses as she stepped from the car. Her servants all smiled in welcome. A few had tears in their eyes. It was like they worshipped her!

"Who the hell is that woman?" I said aloud.

I did not know. But one thing I realized as she disappeared inside was that she had been behind Jane's attack. That Arleen had been behind it from the beginning. Alone, my sister would never have had the nerve to carry out such a bold scheme. But strength of will was clearly a quality Arleen did not lack.

Plus, she was so damn rich. With money, one could do anything.

But *why* had Arleen helped Jane? I had to discover the answer to that riddle before I could figure out what to do next.

Easier said than done. Stalking Arleen, when she was at her mansion, proved to be more difficult than following Jane. The woman never left her palace without an entourage, and never without wearing the latest fashions. Jewelry, too. She had one diamond necklace that must have been worth ten million. In her hands, she always carried the beautiful white poodle.

When she stopped at a store to shop, her people entered and cleared the place before Arleen put a foot inside. Her precautions were elaborate—they more closely rivaled those of a head of state than a world-famous actor. It was as if the woman lived in constant fear of being assassinated.

But not when she returned to the swamp, which she came back to regularly. In the Everglades, covered with dirt and wearing her rags, she seemed carefree. It was amazing how she could swing from one lifestyle to the other. She was more at home in the swamp. It was the only place I saw her smile.

Then one day I caught her and Jane together, in a shopping mall in downtown Miami.

For once Arleen was without her entourage. And for once my sister looked uneasy. To remain unseen, I had to keep a distance. Consequently, I had no idea what they talked about. Yet the whole time I could see Jane was nervous. She kept nodding and fidgeting. Twice Arleen pointed a finger at her, practically scraping the tip of Jane's nose with a sharp fingernail.

Their meeting raised more questions than it answered. At the same time, when I saw them together, I knew I had to kill them both.

I took another two grand in cash out of my new account and visited the underbelly of Miami. There I bought a snub-nosed Colt revolver and a switchblade. The guy who sold me the goods threw in the ammunition free. He was the first person I had met since my disfigurement who seemed to appreciate my scars, even through my heavy bandages. He gave me his card, told me to call anytime I wished, day or night.

I practiced with the gun outside of town. Blew away a dozen Coke bottles in honor of my sister.

I took Jane hostage easily, on a Thursday night, when I knew she was home alone, and when I knew Arleen was spending the week in the swamp. Jane almost fainted when I burst through the door, my gun held ready. It was clear Arleen had told her nothing about saving my life. After getting over her initial shock, she tried reasoning with me, but I took out my blade and drew a red line across her chin.

It was wonderful. She began to beg. I loved it!

I made her drive my car. I sat in the backseat with Ralph, let the dog cuddle with me, and kept the gun on the back of my sister's skull. She could not stop trembling. The blood from her chin was all over her shirt.

"Where are we going?" she asked.

"Same place you took me."

Jane shook her head. "You'll never get away with it."

I smiled. "I don't need to get away with it."

"Jill, please, listen to me. I know what I did was totally evil, but I can make it up to you. I'm making much more than you were. I can afford the best surgeons in town. They're doing amazing work these—"

"Shut up!" I said, belting her on the back of the head so hard she almost swerved off the road. "Just drive."

When we reached the swamp, I wrapped Jane's hands and mouth with duct tape. We crept through the trees toward Arleen's hut. I was pleased to find the woman sitting alone beside a fire outside her shack.

When she saw us, even when I held out my gun, Arleen did not flinch. That worried me. Putting Jane between us, I scanned the woods but heard no one. There was just me, Jane, Arleen, Ralph, and Arleen's poodle.

I had never seen the dog in the swamp before. I had assumed Arleen considered the animal too special to wander the dirty place. I found it ironic that the dog seemed more scared of me than its master did. It had large black eyes—they fastened on me and never let go, while Arleen acted as if I had shown up with my folks and a box of pizza.

I pointed my revolver at Arleen. "Answers," I said.

"Do you plan to kill us both?" she asked.

"Yes."

Arleen shrugged. "Then why should I tell you anything?"

I shifted my aim toward her knee. "There are many ways to die."

Arleen studied me. "When you're through taking your revenge, it's not going to be enough for you."

Arleen had lost her thick accent.

I snorted. "It will be plenty, believe me."

Arleen shook her head. "I know you better than you know yourself. Your desire for revenge is strong, but it's not as strong as your feelings of loss. When you're finished with us, you'll finish with yourself."

*The woman is a sorcerer,* I thought. She had read my mind better than I could. It was true, I had no intention of leaving the swamp that night. With my face in ruins, there was no point.

Nevertheless, I sneered at Arleen. "Tell me why," I demanded.

Arleen looked at Jane, who was weeping quietly, then at me. She sighed. "Each of us is given a single life to live. That life is granted to us by nature or the universe or God, whatever you want to call it. Many people speak of life as a gift, and over the years I have learned this is true. But for many that gift is short-lived. People die before their time, cursing whatever forces put them in their grave. Others live for decades, but they're miserable and they curse the world just the same." Arleen paused. "A long time ago, as a child, I used to puzzle over this enigma. Why are we given only one life when it is so nice for some and so terrible for others? It did not seem fair." She paused. "Do you understand?"

I snorted. "I haven't a clue what you're talking about. Why did you help Jane to ruin my life?"

Arleen held up a hand. "Before I can answer that question you have to understand these points. First, that life is a gift. A single life is given to a man or woman to live as he or she sees fit. This is the nature of life on this planet. We are born and we die. But, like I said, even as a child I used to question if this rule could be broken. Did a person have to live just one life? Could he or she not live a series of lives through different bodies, if the people inhabiting the other bodies decided to give up their gift of life?" She paused. "It was a question I dwelled upon as I grew into adulthood and began to travel the world. It became the all-consuming goal of my life to answer this riddle."

I grew impatient. The gun shook in my hand. "Arleen, if you don't start making sense soon, I'm going to start shooting. And it's not your heart I'm going to put a bullet in first. You're going to discover what it feels like to have a kneecap explode." I paused. "Answer my question about Jane!"

"But I *am* answering your question about your sister. I'm discussing your life, and Jane's life, and my life, and Sira's life."

I blinked. "Who's Sira?"

Arleen stroked the poodle. "This is Sira."

"That's a damn dog," I said.

Arleen shook her head. "No. She just appears to be a dog at this time. Sira is not an animal. She is as human as you and me."

"You're mad," I said. Yet my voice shook; I did not know why.

"Listen, then decide if I am crazy or not." Arleen continued her story. "While I was trying to discover if it was possible to live more than one life—to pass our soul from one body to another—my sister became ill with what is now called cancer and began to wither away. Sira and I were very close. We were not twins, like you and Jane, but she was only a year younger, and it was as if we were joined at the hip. We did everything together. There was nothing incestuous about our relationship, and yet, I will go as far as to say she was the love of my life. It was this great love we shared that made my quest for a solution to death that much more vital. For I could not accept that our love should one day perish, even as Sira's cancer continued to spread and she began to die." Arleen paused. "But she didn't die."

"What happened?" I whispered.

"I saved her."

"How?"

"By finding the answer to my riddle." Arleen stared at the dog with affection. "You would have trouble imagining how long ago that was. But I suppose it doesn't matter when all this happened, just as long as you understand it was more than one lifetime ago."

I hesitated. "I don't believe it," I whispered.

The odd thing was, I was lying. There was a power in her words, in her voice, that made me believe her. Yet that did not mean I understood her.

"You know more than you're willing to admit, Jill. Try to think as I thought in those days. Follow my reasoning. If life is indeed a gift, then it can be accepted and cherished like any other gift one might receive. Or else it can be rejected. It can be scorned and sent back." Arleen added, "When that happens one is no longer worthy of the gift. One loses all rights to it, so to speak."

A glimmer of insight began to dawn inside.

"Can the gift of life be stolen?" I asked.

"Yes and no. It cannot be stolen in the ordinary sense of the word. But it can be taken by another, especially when it has been relinquished by its owner."

I cocked the hammer on my revolver. "Whose life did you

plan on taking? Mine? Jane's? Who did you plan on giving it to?"

Arleen petted the poodle. "The answer to your last question is Sira. I need a human body for her. We've needed it for some time now. But it has not been easy to find a proper body, much less arrive at a situation where the person inside the body no longer wanted it."

"But I want to live!" Jane suddenly cried, having pulled the tape from her mouth.

I belted her with the gun. "I'm asking the questions here!" I turned back to Arleen and spoke in a quieter voice. "You're saying you and Sira have been able to live throughout the ages by finding people who no longer appreciate the gift of their own lives?"

Arleen nodded. "That is correct."

I glanced at Jane, then back at Arleen. "If that's true, then neither of us can be of any use to you. Sira won't want my body. I'm half blind and badly disfigured. Even little children run from me. And Jane may be a murdering bitch, but she's telling the truth when she says she wants to live."

Arleen shook her head. "There's seldom been a worse example of someone who rejected the gift of life than Jane. She refused to be who she was born to be. She wanted to be you. She was willing to murder to become you." Arleen paused. "Jane has forfeited all rights to her body. The gift of life that was given to her at birth can now be taken away and given to another."

"No," Jane whispered, crying. "I'll go back to being Jane. I'll tell everyone what I did to Jill. I'll go to jail if I have to. Only, please don't kill me."

I found it interesting, since I was holding the gun, that Jane was begging Arleen for her life. It increased my suspicion that there were people in the swamp waiting for Arleen's call. But try as I might, I could hear no one else in the immediate area.

Arleen shook her head at Jane. "It's too late for tears, child," she said. .

"No!" Jane wailed.

"Would you please shut up!" I screamed at her before turning back to Arleen. "I follow what you're saying, and I don't know why, but I believe you. At the same time I don't understand where I fit in this picture. I mean, I was happy with my life; I had no desire to give it up."

Arleen nodded. "In the beginning, we used you to get Jane to forsake her right to her own life. We needed you to convince her to commit murder—another sin I long ago discovered caused one to lose the right to their own body."

I felt excited. "But if I'm innocent, and Jane has forsaken the right to her body, then I should get it!"

Arleen lifted up the poodle and placed it in her lap.

"Then what is to become of Sira?" she asked.

"If you can transfer me over to Jane's body, I'll help you find Sira another body," I swore.

Arleen sighed. "It's taken us many years to find a pair as perfectly suited as you two. Sira's waited a long time to be human again. It's not fair that my sister should have to wait any longer."

I snorted. "The hell with your sister! If you don't help me, you'll die, you'll all die. Including your precious Sira."

Arleen was unmoved. "That's not going to happen."

There was a sound behind me. I stood quickly, keeping my

gun aimed at Arleen. I shouted into the woods, "If you rush me, I'll shoot!"

No one responded. It was possible there was no one there.

I stared down at Arleen. "You said it yourself, I'm innocent. I don't deserve to be a part of your plan. I didn't ask for it. You have no right to take away my life!"

There was a note of sorrow in Arleen's voice when she spoke next.

"We did not take away your life, your sister did. We merely gave her a package full of herbs and a few instructions. As far as she knew, when she came to dump you in the swamp, you were going to die. She knew nothing about my plan for her body."

"But you maneuvered her into ruining my life!" I shouted.

"We helped her do what she wanted to do," Arleen said. "We're not at fault when it comes to your life. But you are."

Her last remark caught me off guard. "How can I be at fault?"

Arleen pointed to my face. "You woke up out here, after your sister attacked you, and you were perfectly healthy. True, you were wounded and your looks had been ruined, but there was no reason you couldn't have gone to a plastic surgeon and had your face fixed."

There was nothing but bitterness in my voice. "I could have had my face fixed, yeah, so I didn't look like a monster! But I was never going to be beautiful again!"

Arleen set down the dog and rose to her feet, standing across the campfire from me. "True, you would no longer have been beautiful. But you could have had a life. You could have married and had children. You could have gone to college and become a teacher. There were many things you could have done. But because you could not be beautiful, you decided you had only two options — the same two options Jane settled upon when she forsook her right to her body."

"That's nonsense!" I snorted.

"No. It's the truth. Just because you were no longer beautiful — just because of your *vanity* — you decided you had to commit murder and then suicide." Arleen paused. "No, Jill, you are not the innocent one here."

Her words struck deep. I heard the truth of them.

But that did not mean I was going to give in to them.

I aimed the gun at Arleen's face. "I may not be innocent, but neither are you. You're not going to walk out of this swamp alive."

Arleen shrugged. "I planned from the start that you would figure out I had a role in what Jane did to you. But as you stalked your sister, my people stalked you. We knew you would bring Jane here tonight."

As she spoke, a dozen men in dark clothes came out of the swamp. They were armed — their weapons were all pointed at me. The Chinese man was with them. He carried a high-tech rifle equipped with a laser sight. I felt rather than saw the red dot on my forehead.

Yet I acted like I didn't care.

"I've got four pounds of pressure on a five-pound trigger!" I cried. "Even if you shoot me in the head, my finger will twitch. Arleen will die."

Arleen spread her hands. "I can't give you Jane's body. That belongs to Sira. But I can give you back your life. You can walk out of here and no one will harm you, Jill."

Tears burned my remaining eye. The gun trembled in my hand.

"I can't live like this," I whispered.

Arleen was sympathetic. "Then tell me what I can do for you."

I stared at Sira and I thought, what a pretty poodle. She seemed smart, too, the way she sat beside Ralph, not making a sound. She was like my own dog, very well behaved. I bet the two animals could have been friends.

Arleen seemed to read my mind again.

"Maybe there is something we can do for you," she said.

I lowered the gun. "Really?" I whispered hopefully.

Arleen smiled and nodded, and then her gaze fell on Jane. The mysterious woman scowled. "We can do something *with* Jane, as well," she said.

Henry felt sick at heart as he stood in the mental hospital and stared at his girlfriend. She was tied to the bed. The nurses and orderlies had left just after sedating Jill with some kind of shot that was just beginning to take effect. Jill's eyelids were closing over their empty sockets. She'd had another one of her attacks. She had tried to grab a pen from one of the nurses and scribble on the hospital wall that she was not really Jill. That her name was Jane.

Of course, since the brutal assault three months earlier that had killed her sister, Jill was no longer equipped to think or write coherently. Besides the severe emotional trauma that had caused her to identify with her dead sister, Jill could not see what she was writing. Her assailant had taken both her eyes and cut out her tongue as well. Henry often felt it was her inability to communicate properly that had thrust her into such a deep psychosis.

It was a pity the police had been unable to find Jane's body. Perhaps if they had, the sight of it . . . no, the *feel* of it might have convinced Jill that her sister was gone. As it stood, with half her senses stripped away, the girl was trapped in a nightmarish realm where even her sense of self had been obliterated.

Occasionally, Henry wondered if Jane was truly dead. But the police seemed sure of their facts. The crime scene had been soaked with blood, too many pints of blood for Jane to have survived. The DNA tests said the blood must have come from Jill's sister, and since that was the case, it followed that Jane must be dead.

But no body. *How strange,* he thought.

Henry knew the mystery would haunt him until the day he died.

With tears burning his eyes, Henry knelt to kiss Jill goodbye. It was then her own eyelids popped open and he had the uncanny sensation that she was staring at him, although there was nothing but gruesome scar tissue where her beautiful blues had been.

She moved her mouth. Her lips were gone, too. The monster had taken it all. Yet, somehow, Henry recognized the words she was trying to say.

"Jan . . . Iggg . . . Jan . . ."

Jill was trying to say, "I am Jane."

A minute later she was asleep.

His heart breaking, Henry left the hospital.

When he got home, he was greeted by a cheerful sight. Jill's cocker spaniel, Ralph, and a beautiful white poodle Henry had discovered outside his door not long after the attack on his girlfriend, were both sitting on the couch watching TV. Or at least it appeared that way. The two dogs looked so comfortable, they could have been enjoying a movie together.

Then Henry noticed it was only the poodle that was focused on the set. Ralph wagged his tail and came running over to lick Henry's hands, but the poodle remained seated. It did not give him a welcoming bark until there was a commercial.

Henry had seen the poodle behave the same way before. It always weirded him out a little. He wondered if it was because the dog chose to watch the same shows Jill used to like. It was uncanny, really. The poodle had *exactly* the same taste as his girlfriend.

# THE LITTLE SACRIFICE

**Joyce Carol Oates**

"Where is our sister?"—the cry went up among us, who were her older sisters and brothers on the morning after the little one was discovered missing. We were a large farm family, and our farm was not very prosperous, and so we children were obliged to share rooms and beds; but our youngest sister still slept alone in a corner of our parents' bedroom in a bed hardly bigger than a crib. "Oh, where is she? My daughter, my baby? Who has taken her from us?" So our distraught mother cried, for Momma knew that the little one would not have wandered off by herself, but must have been abducted. (Father, too, was upset; but it was typical of Father to turn away in silence, as if in shame; for Father could not forgive himself, his farm was less than prosperous no matter how hard he and the rest of us toiled.)

All that day we searched for our little sister, and all that week, and all that month and year we would search for our little sister; and never would we abandon our search for her, for the remainder of our troubled lives. Had cruel fairies carried her off into the Underworld? Had a wild beast made its way through an open window as we slept, and borne her away into the woods, in his jaws? Or had our little sister simply vanished, as dew sparkling like gems will vanish on the grass with the inexorable rising of the sun, transforming the comfort of night to the starkness of day.

In fact, our little sister had been abducted by fairies. But with Father's consent. (In exchange for our little sister, the fairies promised Father an abundant harvest, after several years of drought.) Only later would this fact be revealed, when we were grown and gone from home and scattered to the corners of the earth; and yet remembered vividly our little sister as she'd been on the eve of her disappearance: a delicately boned child of four, with a small, oval face, somber, cobalt-blue eyes, pale silvery-blond hair of unusual fineness. We would learn that our sister had not been taken to the Underworld, for her fate was more mysterious, and yet more cruel: The fairies bartered her to a wealthy noble family who lived on a great estate on a promontory above our village, their ancient name synonymous with high rank and devout religious belief and the solemn responsibilities of such.

"Momma! Momma, help me!" Our little sister woke to find herself crudely gagged and wrapped in a blanket, hoisted aloft by fairies whose faces she was never to see. At first, it seemed that our little sister was carried up a steep embankment; and then our little sister was carried into the earth, to be "freed" in a dungeon below the nobleman's great estate. She would be given just enough food and drink to sustain her, and just enough candlelight for her to see dimly, as undersea creatures with their rudimentary eyes. At the outset of her confinement she wept and called for her mother; she wept and pleaded with her invisible captors to release her, but her captors were but servants of the noble family, and dared pay her no attention. And so the child might have been pleading with the blank granite face of the mountain, as with such individuals. She might have been pleading with great Jehovah himself.

It is said that the noble family came to glimpse our little sister, through a grating in the dungeon door, only a few times. It is said that they were led by a priest, appointed to oversee the noble family's private chapel within the high walls of the estate. To serve as a priest in such privileged quarters is a position of great esteem, and the priest was conscious of his worth in assuring the family that the "little sacrifice"—for so our sister was known to them, lacking any other name—was safely confined and suffering no pain. The priest advised his patrons: "She is a peasant child and lacks the sensitivity of our kind. You can see, she is still alive and reasonably healthy. She eats, greedily. She will lap up water like a dog. She no longer walks in this confined space, but she can crawl if she wishes. She has grown more dull-witted with time. Her vision is poor, but she has so little to see, how can it matter? She has ceased crying for her mother. She has ceased pleading to be released. Like the others before her she will forget, in time, the world beyond her dungeon that is now her home."

In this way the noble family was assured that the little sacrifice was a success.

"She is our measure of what God will allow. Without her, how could we gauge the wickedness in our hearts? And, in our hearts, in the heart of mankind? How could we gauge our own good fortune, blessed by God?"

The noble family looked upon their own offspring with joy and gratitude.

These were good, generous, God-fearing folk. Except for their single aberration, they were upstanding human beings. You would be excited and flattered by their good opinion of you, as by the most casual nod of the head, a warm greeting from such aristocrats in your direction. Sometimes the noble family descends from their promontory to attend church services in the village, on especially holy days. They are seated in the very front pew of the church and they never fail to rise for Communion, one by one, in their splendidly tasteful clothes. They are known to tithe their considerable income and to give directly to the poor, in some instances. They are never without smiles and blessings for others less fortunate than themselves. Seeing, from time to time, in the village church, the grieving, broken parents and family of the little sacrifice, they are especially kind.

# IF YOU KNEW SUZIE

**Heather Graham**

Years had gone by, and sometimes Derek Fallon thought that he was crazy himself.

The world knew Suzie Kenner.

But not like he did. And not like he *didn't*.

Most of the time, he didn't think about the past. He had shoved that final year of high school into a box in a place in his mind called "secret and best-forgotten memories" or "sheer, unadulterated imagination devices."

But then that morning, the last day of October, when he'd been married to Rebecca for several years, had two great sons of his own, and designed video games for a really decent living, it all came back.

Because Rebecca had been reading the paper.

"Derek! Your old friend Suzie . . . she's listed here as one of the Hollywood A-list celebs running for office. She plans on being governor, and she says here that there's no reason a woman can't be smart and beautiful and politically on top of it all. So, I'm assuming she eventually plans on running for president."

That chilled him. Right to the bone. But he had never really told Rebecca about Suzie.

Rebecca looked up at him, smiling, with a curious little twist to her lips. "Weren't you two one of the hottest items going in high school? Although the rumor mills have it that she was an absolute bitch back then. But she changed—after a tragedy. You were close then, right?"

Those words brought about an inner shudder.

He loved Rebecca. Everything about her. She wasn't knock-dead gorgeous like Suzie, but she was better. She was lithe, and pretty, and she laughed so easily, and she met every challenge with courage, and she would never hurt another living soul. She was honest, and she did have the most beautiful and open blue eyes anyone had ever seen. She trusted him as he trusted her. Sometimes, simple silence between them said so many things.

Luckily, he had met her after the whole thing with Suzie.

"Hot stuff, huh?" Rebecca teased.

"Once upon a time," he said.

"You broke it off with her before college, right after your friend Marianne Helming died, right?"

"Something like that. Trust me, I would never vote for her. Seriously, I don't know her anymore."

"She mentions in the interview that she has a dear old friend living here. You?"

It was a question, but one that really brought a shiver streaking along his spine. "Maybe. Who knows?" he murmured.

"I would like to meet her," Rebecca said seriously. "I mean, think of it. It seems that one day she could be president. Actress to Congress to White House. Hey, the time might be right."

He shrugged. *Had he dreamed it all up? Could it have been real? And if he explained his sheer horror at seeing the woman again, would his own wife have him locked away?*

"You don't want to meet Suzie. I'll be in my office. I have to work. And, hey, don't you have some new sketches to do for the almost Mrs. Mitchell?" Rebecca designed custom wedding gowns. He was very proud of her. One day, he knew she was going to be famous. She was intuitive and talented. And smart.

*Suzie was smart! There was no denying that. And to think, all through high school, she'd been a gorgeous, busty blond. Cruel, because she knew the power of her own beauty.*

*Then, of course, she'd made that change. . . .*

In his office, Derek booted up the computer. There was a glitch in his newest game for the preteen crowd. He loved his work, creating games. And he needed to work.

But he couldn't concentrate. He sat back in his chair.

He closed his eyes. Rebecca's words came back to him, and he couldn't forget what she had said. Suzie was running for governor.

*Hawthorne Street.*

He'd lived there as long as he could remember. It was a pretty cool street to live on. The neighborhood had been around since World War II. The houses weren't huge, but they were nice. He wasn't a rich kid. He wasn't a poor kid.

Most of the kids around had known one another forever. But he had known Marianne Helming longer than anyone. She lived two doors down. They'd played together as far back as he could remember. It was tough sometimes. Marianne had suffered from a mild case of polio; she was one of the rare cases when the vaccine backfired. Still, it wasn't all bad. She was pretty enough, with long brown hair and big, long-lashed eyes. And she was just about a genius; she helped him through many a math class. But she walked with an awkward lurch.

And some of the kids made fun of her.

It all started, though, he thought, the summer of their junior year.

When he first started seeing Suzie Kenner.

Suzie . . .

What wasn't there to like?

He was doing well enough in school, albeit Marianne helped him a lot. He was the star quarterback for the football team. And there was Suzie. In her tight little shorts and her sexy little cheerleader halter tops.

With a crush on *him*.

July Fourth, they were at the old rock pit. The city discouraged kids from going there. It was, after all, a rock pit. Could be dangerous. One city council had gone through a whole big thing to make it safe for the kids to swim, but considering all the stuff on the bottom, it was almost an impossible task. The rock pit was one of the coolest places around. There were old junks down on the bottom, abandoned cars. They liked to make up stories and look in them, certain they were going to find some kind of murder victim down there. Of course, the authorities, police divers, had been down. There were no bodies to be found. But it was still fun to explore the old cars. At the deepest point, the water was about forty feet. Mostly, it was around twenty feet deep.

It wasn't a new place, though. It had been created hundreds of years earlier by local Indians. There was a mound or a hill on the eastern side of the pit. Kids liked to believe that the Indians had practiced human sacrifices to their gods there. There were lots of legends about the place. And they might well be true—they were studying it all in school. Supposedly, the Indians practiced magic, with blood sacrifices. They could transport their minds and their souls, levitate, and take themselves to astral planes.

All the legends just made it a really cool place to be. Lots of guys managed good make-out sessions once the sun started to fall. It was a little creepy, the girls would get scared and want to be close, and from there on, a guy could get real affectionate.

Pines surrounded the pit. Kids found little empty spots to park their cars, and in the midst of the pines, they could bring their blankets, sometimes books to read, and sometimes, in the summer, the girls could even get their precious tans.

He'd come with Marianne, Ted Byner, and Jack Gaines. They all lived on Hawthorne Street. Marianne was going on and on that day about her interest in their latest subject in American history, the local tribe of Native Americans. It was cool enough stuff, and he was interested when they were at school. Marianne was obsessed. Fascinated with the practice of magic, astral projection, and blood rituals and sacrifice. He listened to her with half an ear as he enjoyed the day. She was trying to get their teacher to arrange a field trip to some of the caverns. There were excavations going on in their area.

They had an ice chest full of sandwich stuff, sodas, and beer, compliments of Jack Gaines. When they started setting up their blankets, Suzie arrived with some of the cheerleaders.

She wore a bikini really well. Seeing her, he couldn't care less about the past.

"Hey!" She was so nice to everyone at first, greeting them all. In a matter of minutes, she was sitting next to him on the blanket. She kept touching him. Hell, he was human. Hell, he was a high school boy with a libido running rampant.

"Hey, we're going to win the next game, right, Derek?" she demanded, eyes wide on him.

"We're going to damn well try," he assured her.

"Hey! I could swear I saw a body part in one of the cars down there the other day," Marianne said.

Suzie didn't look at her when she replied, "That's just stupid and childish. The cops check this place out. Derek, want to take a swim with me? Alone?"

She was being mean to Marianne, and Derek should have said something. It was the bikini Suzie was wearing. It was a string.

They went off to the water, played and splashed around. And fooled around. Suzie liked to kiss and tease. Derek figured he couldn't help but go along. There was no reason he shouldn't give in to being seduced by Suzie.

But, eventually, he broke away from her.

"What's the matter?" she asked him. "You're hot, I'm hot." She laughed. "Quite honestly, I am the hottest."

"I came with Marianne and the others. I just want to check on them."

"Why? Do you think they might drown?"

"I need to get back."

She smoothed back her sleek wet hair. "That little gimp has a crush on you, Derek."

"She's just one of my best friends."

"Well, you really shouldn't hang around with her. She'll just drag you down. Derek, you can be with me, or . . . well, you can be a loser who hangs around with a geeky, unbalanced gimp, and that's the way it is."

Derek got an odd sensation he'd never be able to explain. He looked up. Marianne had come to the edge of the pit. And not alone. Several of their friends were there. Everyone heard the words said about Marianne.

And Marianne just turned away.

He would have gone after her. But Suzie pretended she hadn't said anything or seen anything and she cried out, "Jump on in, guys, game time! Water tag. And, ladies, wherever they tag us, it'll be free game."

Every guy there jumped in. The cheerleaders giggled and followed.

Somehow Marianne got a ride home that day.

He found himself out all day with Suzie. He tried to tell himself that he wasn't about to be her puppet in any way. But Suzie was . . . Suzie. She hadn't lied. She was the hottest thing around.

She was unbelievably popular. And it was strange, because she wasn't just into herself, she was cruel.

Throughout the summer, he spent all his time with her. Then school started up again, and Marianne called him, wanting to know if he still wanted help.

He did.

He saw her the first Tuesday afternoon they were back in classes. They'd made a study date.

"I didn't think you'd actually make it," she said, letting him in. "Suzie let you off her string for an afternoon?"

"Hey, we've had study dates forever," he said lightly. "I wouldn't break our dates. We're friends."

"Friends," she murmured. "Well, I'm glad you can still be friends with such a geek."

He flushed. "Marianne . . ."

"Believe it or not, she's as mean as she is because she's jealous of me."

Derek was startled. "Oh, yeah?"

"She's stupid."

"Well, she doesn't have your grades," he told her.

She stared at him. "I have always had a crush on you, you know."

He wanted to run. He felt awkward. Cruel himself. "Marianne, we're friends. I just don't . . . I mean, we're really, like, best friends."

"I love you, you know!" she said softly. "One day I will have you."

He stared at her, stunned.

She started to laugh. "It's okay. I'm joking. Just joking." She nodded, studying him. Then she shrugged. "Let's work, huh? Get your math out. Work the problems, then I'll go over them with you."

He worked. He hated math, but he loved being on the football team, and, hell, he did want to go to college. As he worked, though, he noticed Marianne. She had a book about the Tehillihano, the native tribe who had once lived in the area. The folks who had supposedly committed the blood sacrifices at the rock pit.

"You doing an essay?" he asked her.

She shrugged. "There's a dig going on near the rock pit."

"I didn't know you were *that* into archaeology."

"You know that it has all fascinated me forever," she said with a wave of her hand. "I'm into the Tehillihano," she said. She was excited, and brought her book over to him. "They were into the power of the sun and the moon, the day and the night. And they had a harvest festival, and a night of the dead. Like Halloween—All Hallows' Eve! They practiced all kinds of rituals, and the stories about their blood sacrifices are true. Their magic is true. They fed the earth, gave to the power of their gods through the blood of others. When they made sacrifices, they had the power of the ancients, of the gods themselves!"

"Great," Derek murmured. But she was so excited.

"Want to see the dig?"

"You have to be . . . like you, like a genius, I imagine."

"Oh, I hope not. Remember last year? I was trying to get a field trip up and going. Now, I'm applying to the scientists running the dig, hoping they'll do a special project for our class."

"Well, cool, we'll see, huh?"

Days passed. Derek spent them with Suzie. He played football; his team won. He was popular; his friends were good.

Suzie was better.

Except that she continued being horribly cruel to Marianne. In history class, Marianne talked about the archaeologists and the Indians.

"Field trip!" Tom cried out. "You go, Marianne!"

"Into a stupid hole in the earth," Suzie said with a yawn.

"Hey, it is a field trip," Derek said.

"We can go down on Halloween," Marianne said. "Dr. Benton, the head of the current dig, has said that we can actually go on Halloween. It will be great. Spooky."

"It will be in a hole," Suzie said.

But despite their love for Suzie, the class liked field trips. It was arranged. Marianne was ecstatic about the whole thing, flushed and excited.

Dr. Benton, an archaeologist, had no problem with the kids dressing up in costumes as they usually did—the high school allowed it. So on the thirty-first, it was an unusual busload that headed for the site.

Suzie was a princess. And she looked like one.

"Ah, Cinderella!" Marianne said to her.

"Sleeping Beauty, stupid," Suzie said.

"All the better," Marianne told her.

"And what the hell are you?" Suzie demanded. Marianne was in a most unusual costume. She wore a leather jacket and something like a loincloth. She had a headdress that fell almost to the floor, made of magnificent feathers.

"High priest Fiathol," Marianne told her.

"Who?" Suzie demanded, giggling. "Did you say Fidel Castro in drag?"

Naturally, the class laughed. But not Derek. He was concerned. He knew Marianne had made the costume.

They reached their destination. Dr. Benton greeted the school bus with a few of his assistants, grad students there to make sure the high school riffraff didn't ruin any artifacts.

"Welcome, welcome, people and creatures!" He was a skinny man, an academic whose work was his life. He was one of those people who wanted to be funny and charming but just fell flat. "Well, let's go down. Mind the handrails!"

Once they had descended, many in the class were awed. They were in a graveyard of the Tehillihano. The people had practiced a form of mummification, and there were a few open graves. There was a table where the dead had been prepared, and cups, bowls, weapons, and decaying clothing could be seen.

"They were a superstitious people," Benton announced to the class. "They took enemies in war, and they believed that when they sacrificed a warrior, they gained his strength. The language was similar to an Apache tongue, and one of their rituals has been translated: 'Death in flesh is never death in soul; death to you who would harm me. And it is I who come atop and within, and it is I who survive. Woe to the enemy who would harm me.' "

He talked a little longer, but he was nervous, afraid that the kids would take something. As Derek walked around, he was startled to hear Suzie cry out.

He was instantly at her side. As was Benton. And the others. She was standing in front of a life-size image of the high priest Fiathol. Marianne's costume was very good—when she stood perfectly still, she looked just like the statue that had been made of a strange kind of plaster. The statue's furs and feathers were amazingly preserved.

"What happened?" Benton demanded with a note of panic in his voice.

"The statue thing here stabbed me!" Suzie said.

The class was silent. Then someone began to giggle.

"I'm serious! I'm bleeding!" Suzie said. She spun around and stared at Marianne. "It was probably Miss Bozo here who did it!"

"I'm nowhere near you," Marianne said. But she seemed perfectly calm, and amused.

I took Suzie's hand. There was a cut on her palm. I frowned.

"I went to touch it and . . . I don't know. It . . . stabbed me." She stared at Marianne. Costumed as the high priest, Marianne carried a knife like the one in the statue's grasp.

"I'm way over here!" Marianne protested.

"They did believe in astral projection," Ted said, laughing.

Derek was startled to find himself pulling her back when Benton went to get a first-aid kit. "Suzie . . . you shouldn't be so cruel."

She jerked away from him. "I'm not cruel. I'm me. And other people don't get to be me. Leave me alone, Derek."

"Suzie, I . . ."

"You're being a geek. Quit standing up for that ridiculous cripple!"

She jerked away. When her hand was bandaged, she came back. "Meeting at the rock pit tonight? Ted has scored a few kegs of beer. It's the place to be."

He was still angry. She turned and headed for the stairs and the bus. He felt Marianne come behind him. He had to admit that with her limp, he couldn't have missed her arrival.

"So, you're going to the rock pit?"

He looked at her. Ever since they'd all been old enough to escape their parents and trick-or-treating on Halloween, he and his friends had spent the evening at the rock pit. This year would be no different.

But he felt uneasy. He hesitated, then he told her, "If you want to do something else this year, I'll go with you."

She smiled. "Oh, no. The rock pit will be fine."

They were actually laughable, Derek decided later. And he didn't have to be an adult to realize it, even that night. They were all in their costumes. They built a few bonfires. They had the kegs of beer, and snacks, and their parents all thought that they were at a dance the next town over.

At first, everything was okay. It was fun. They danced in the woods. They told ghost stories. But then Suzie just couldn't let it go.

She grabbed Marianne by the hand. She drew her to the bonfire, on top of a little rise. "Hey, why are we fooling with ghost stories when Marianne can tell us about real murders? Come on, you want to talk all the time. Scare us, Marianne. Hey, I've got a deal, you scare the hell out of us all, or you jump into the rock pit."

Derek was surprised when Marianne just shrugged and agreed. "They are here; don't you know it, can't you feel them? The Tehillihano. Be quiet; listen. Turn off the music. Close your eyes. You'll feel them!"

As she spoke, the wind picked up. It was like they could hear a moaning in the breeze.

"Feel the air, feel the souls of those sacrificed! Listen to them, listen to them scream and cry!"

It was more than a breeze then; it was a serious wind, and it sounded as if, indeed, a howling came from it. The branches and leaves of the trees began to bend and bow. "Ted! Look out, a warrior behind you!" Marianne cried.

"Where, what?" Ted demanded, and he gasped and staggered, as if he had been hit.

Derek could hear a strange whooshing sound. It appeared as if black shadows were flitting from tree to tree. It felt as if the earth beneath their feet rumbled.

"Marianne, enough," he said. "Come on, you beat us all, I'll take you home!" He realized that he was almost screaming to be heard above that sudden wail and moan of the wind.

But she smiled.

Atop the mound, she began to chant, "'Death in flesh is never death in soul; death to you who would harm me. And it is I who come atop and within, and it is I who survive. Woe to the enemy who would harm me.'"

The wind seemed to scream. The kids were ducking, cowering, holding on to one another.

*"Run, get the hell out of here!"* Derek screamed.

But no one listened.

Marianne kept chanting. The wind didn't touch her. She looked like the high priest she portrayed. It was frightening.

*"'Death in flesh is never death in soul; death to you who would harm me. And it is I who come atop and within, and I who will survive. Woe to the enemy who would harm me.'"*

Abruptly, the wind ceased to blow. There was no sound. No moaning. Nothing.

"Wow," someone whispered.

"Oh, what a crock!" Suzie cried out.

Derek would never forget that moment. Never. Because Marianne stared at Suzie, and it was as if time stood still.

Then Marianne smiled. "Well, okay. I've failed. I guess I'll jump in the rock pit! Come, make sure I do it! *And do it with me!"*

She stepped from the mound, lifting her hand. She carried a knife like the high priest, and she raised it.

Derek's heart was in his throat. He thought that she meant to stab Suzie.

But she slashed her own hand.

As Suzie's had been slashed.

And then she grabbed Suzie's hand.

"Come on, watch me go in!"

Suzie was strong; Marianne was slim and . . . well, somewhat crippled, in truth. But she was a fury of power that night, dragging Suzie through the trees. Everyone followed.

"Hey, Marianne!" Derek called, trying to catch them both, trying to reach her. "Stop it, it's just Halloween, it's just fun. You don't have to jump in!"

When he reached the rock pit, Marianne was posed at the edge. She offered him a strange smile.

"Let me go!" Suzie cried in panic.

"Stop!" he screamed. She could swim, but it was night, and it was dark, and it was cold.

Marianne teetered, and then she was in. It was a graceful swan dive. She was there, and then she wasn't.

And Suzie was gone, too.

"Marianne!" Derek shouted her name, and plunged in after her. Then others started jumping in, trying to find those beneath the surface. Every geek and jock in the school was in the water, and so was every cheerleader and not-cheerleader and anyone else there.

But Marianne could not be found.

And at first, Suzie couldn't be found, either.

When her body was dragged out, someone shouted that she was dead.

But by then, the police and fire rescue had arrived, and Suzie was brought up, and when the EMTs worked on her, she spewed out a ton of water, and then she started to breathe again. She was taken to the hospital.

Marianne wasn't found until the following day. The police

diver who brought her up was mystified. "It was as if she lodged herself into one of those old cars on purpose," he said.

Derek was numb.

At her funeral, in her coffin, Marianne was, at last, beautiful. The undertaker had given her such a serene smile, it was almost as if she would awaken any minute.

He didn't go to see Suzie in the hospital. He was too angry.

In fact, it was almost a month later when she came to his house one day.

By then, her reputation had grown. She was still popular. Still beautiful. She'd gotten a modeling contract. And, his mother told him, having heard it from her mother, she'd also gotten a personal manager. Apparently, Suzie had a plan. She believed she needed to do all the right things to accomplish her goals. First, she wanted to be really famous. Then she wanted to be powerful.

Like a senator.

Or even president.

She needed her name seen in the paper, apparently. She had started visiting nursing homes and arranging sales to benefit soldiers and she'd just about turned into a perfect and beautiful Mother Teresa. Because she was so beautiful and working so hard for others, her manager could get her on all the talk shows.

"Why don't you ever come to see me now, Derek?" she asked him.

He shook his head. "I'm sorry. I can't."

"Because Marianne is dead?"

*You killed her*, he wanted to say. He didn't.

"I'm sorry, Suzie. I just . . . I just can't see you."

She lowered her head, then looked up and smiled at him. "I have such a crush on you, Derek. One day, I will have you," she said softly.

*There was something about her words, something about the way she spoke, something, even, about the sound of her voice. . . .*

"I will survive," she said, and smiled. "The world is out there. And someday, I will have you." She laughed. "I'm patient. I can wait. I don't mind getting really famous first."

She left, as if accepting what couldn't be, as if understanding.

That night, he was plagued by nightmares.

He saw the statue of the high priest on the mound, and it was as if the ancient Fiathol had come back to life. He was ranting about blood sacrifices.

*Death is never death of the soul. . . .*

He saw Suzie's cut hand.

And Marianne's cut hand. And he even thought about Marianne's funeral.

And then, as time went by, he tried very hard not to think about it.

*You killed her,* he had thought. *But just who was it who had died?*

"Derek!"

He must have fallen asleep. He was startled awake by the sound of his wife's voice calling to him.

"Yeah?"

"Derek, turn on the television," Rebecca said, walking into the office. "She's on the news right now, talking about her campaign. There's something about her that's . . . unsettling."

He picked up the remote and swiveled his chair around. The small TV in his office went on.

And there she was. Suzie on the news. A pretty newswoman held a microphone and asked, "Now that your appearances for the day are done, how do you plan on spending your evening? It is Halloween."

"Ah, well, I have an old friend in the area I intend to look up," Suzie said. "I've heard through mutual friends that he has two young sons. And a lovely wife. I need to convince my friend that he does need me . . . in office, of course."

It was strange. It was as if her eyes were looking straight at him. With amusement. As if she were silently reminding him that she had always intended to have him.

*In office, my ass,* he thought.

"Get the boys. We're out of here *now*! We'll do Halloween at — at your folks' house in Arizona."

Rebecca stared back at him. He was afraid that she would protest. That she would stare at him as if he were totally insane and say, *"Arizona?"*

But she didn't. She just looked back at him gravely.

"Trust me," he said softly, "if you knew Suzie like I know Suzie . . ."

He didn't finish. He didn't need to.

She was Rebecca, she was his wife. She trusted something that was in his tone, or maybe even in his eyes.

"A trip to Arizona. Great. The boys will love it," she said simply.

He had a wonderful wife.

And he meant to keep it that way.

Within an hour, they were ready to leave the house.

As he locked up, he nearly tripped over something. He reached down, frowning.

There was a doll on his porch.

A doll.

It was the image of the Tehillihano high priest Fiathol.

The wind picked up, and he heard laughter.

*Suzie's laughter.*

He ran for the car, but he wondered if he could ever run fast enough.

There was still laughter on the wind.

And he could have sworn that he heard a chant.

*Death in flesh is never death in soul; death to you who would harm me. And it is I who come atop and within, and I who will survive. Woe to the enemy who would harm me.*

*Death in flesh is never death in soul . . .*

"Derek! Come on," Rebecca called.

He stopped running. And he stared at his car.

"Rebecca?" he whispered.

And the wind rose.

# SLAM DANCE

**Bentley Little**

The portrait of St. Millard hung at the front of the classroom between the clock and the flag, a ragged horrific figure standing before a crowd of huddled peasants, an emaciated, nearly naked man with wild hair and piercing demonic eyes that glared out of the painting and down at the six rows of neatly ordered desks and the twenty-three students busily working on their math assignments. Anna, as usual, had finished her worksheet early. She had turned over her paper on the desk so no one else could copy her answers and was now staring up at the portrait, curious. The portrait stared back. She could never seem to reconcile the hate in the eyes of this harsh and terrifying visage with the Christianity preached by Jesus, that meek and gentle martyr she learned about in chapel. They seemed like two opposing entities with absolutely nothing in common.

"Anna!" someone whispered.

Her eyes dropped from the ragged figure of St. Millard to the calm figure of Sister Caroline, reading peacefully and obliviously at her desk, before searching out the source of the whisper.

"Anna!"

She turned to glance behind her and felt the square hardness of a book being shoved into her left hand. Her fingers closed around the object, and she nodded to Jenny McDaniels, acknowledging receipt of the item. Jenny turned quickly back to her assignment.

Anna kept her eyes on Sister Caroline as she slowly and surreptitiously maneuvered the book from her lap to the top of her desk. *Slam Book*, it said in felt-pen letters on the cover, and Anna felt a thrill of forbidden excitement pass through her as she read the words. She glanced back at Jenny, but her friend was staring down at her worksheet, busily writing.

Anna's gaze returned to the bound volume before her. Slam books had been all the rage at St. Mary's for the past semester, and though she and Jenny had tried their hardest to lay their hands on one, neither of them had seen, much less held, one of the famous and dreaded items. Father Joseph had declared last October that slam books were not allowed at the school, promising that any student caught with one would be punished, but the ban really had no effect. If anything, the books grew in popularity after Father Joseph's decree.

How in the heck had Jenny gotten ahold of one?

Anna carefully opened the book to the first page. "Gerard Starr," it said at the top in neatly printed script. Beneath that was a list of personal information: height, weight, age, favorite color, favorite musical performer, favorite movie, favorite food. Below the statistics were the comments. All unsigned, of course.

*What a babe! I love his hair!!!*

*Sooooo cool! I want to marry him.*

*Dork.*

*Probably a fag. Gay haircut.*

*Fairy.*

*What a hunk!*

Anna smiled. The comments were pretty much divided along male-female lines. Still, the good observations outweighed the bad. And even the slams were generic and not all that cutting.

She skipped over Sandra Cowan's page and all the pages of Sandra's cheerleader friends until she found Jenny's entry. Her eyes skimmed the stats and went straight to the comments.

*Too shy. Too quiet.*

*Not bad-looking. Average.*

*Plain Jane.*

*Would be alright if she didn't hang around Anna Douglas all the time.*

Anna's heart raced, her pulse pounding. Her face grew hot as she reddened with embarrassment.

*Not much to look at, but she seems OK.*

*Nice but doesn't talk much.*

*She's fine except for her retarded friend, Anna.*

Afraid to look but needing to know, Anna turned to her own page. She noticed immediately that her name and statistics were sloppily written. Most of the information was wrong. Holding her breath, she read the comments:

*A scuz.*

*I hate her.*

*If I was its owner, I'd shave its ass and walk it backward.*

*Severe problems. Major damage. She should be locked in her house until she dies so the rest of us don't have to suffer.*

*Snoopy, come home!*

*She smells. I don't think she bathes or knows about deodorant.*

*Puke! Barf! Puke!!!! Baarrfff!!!*

*She'll grow into a lonely old lady and die alone. Who wants her?*

An arrow pointed to this last one, and a black scrawled arrow led to another, connected comment: *She should do us all a favor and kill herself.*

Heart thumping, Anna turned the page, looking on the back for more comments. There was only one, in Jenny's small, neat handwriting: *My best friend. Very smart, very kind, very special. I'm lucky to know her.*

Anna looked gratefully toward Jenny, but her friend was still working on the math assignment.

Anna turned back to the page again, her gaze returning to the cruel comments below her name. The criticisms were harsh, unnecessarily so, and she knew without looking that no other person in the book would have such hostility directed toward them.

And this was only one slam book in one class. There were probably dozens more floating around the school.

She wondered what the other books had to say about her.

No.

She didn't wonder.

She already knew. She'd known before she'd even opened this book.

Anna glanced up at St. Millard standing before the peasants, that look of twisted hate on his haggard face. He was undoubtedly preaching about Jesus. But Jesus preached peace and understanding. He exhorted everyone to love their neighbors.

Her neighbors didn't love her, though.

It was Jesus who taught that she should turn the other cheek, but even his disciples had not always been able to live up to that standard. She had the feeling that the saint before her now, the one at the front of the classroom, would not stand for such softness, such . . . submission.

She stared at the ragged figure, meeting those demonic eyes.

The figure stared back.

"Molly Caulfield."

Anna finished writing the last name and closed the book. She put her pen down and flexed her fingers. They were starting to cramp. Picking up the volume, she examined its cover. It looked almost identical to the slam book she had read this morning. She smiled. This would show them. She would write her own comments, disguising her handwriting, then pass the book around. *They* would know what it felt like to be unpopular for once, to be the butt of the jokes. *They* would know what it felt like to be hated.

She put the book down and opened it to the first page. "Sandra Cowan." Anna stared at the blank page for a moment, then wrote: *An airhead.*

A strange tingle passed through her, a rush of forbidden pleasure. Always, when Sandra had made fun of her, Anna had lowered her head and hurried past, trying to ignore the laughter, trying not to let it hurt. She had never had either the strength or the guts to fight back and stand up for herself. Now, in one minute, she had passed judgment on Sandra Cowan. Writing from on high, a voice of anonymous omniscience, she had dismissed the girl and decreed her stupid.

Anna laughed, feeling a thrill of sudden power. She picked up another pen and, changing her handwriting, wrote: *A bitch.*

She read the sentence and giggled, glancing quickly around to make sure her mother or her sister weren't standing over her shoulder. She was feeling brave now. She could say anything. She could be as cruel to Sandra as Sandra had been to her.

*She's a whore,* Anna wrote. *She'll do it for a dime.*

Moving on to the next name in the book, Sandra's friend Brittany, Anna wrote: *A godless witch.* The phone rang out in the living room, and Anna waited for a moment to see if the call was for her. There was a seven-second lag, then her mother called, "Anna!"

She put down the pen, closed the book, and ran to the living room, wishing not for the first time that her parents would let her have a cell phone or, at the very least, get an extension of her own. She took the receiver from her mother's proffered hand. "Hello?"

"Guess what?" It was Jenny. Her voice was breathless, excited, something that came through even with the cheap mobile connection. "Sandra just got arrested! By the police!"

"What?"

"I saw it! Right here, right this second. In front of the mall."

"Where are you?"

"By Nordstrom's. I can't talk much longer. My mom's on her way out."

"Well, what happened?"

"I'm not sure. I came just at the very end. But it looked like she was trying to, you know . . . sell herself to some guy. Only the guy turned out to be a cop!" Jenny let out a loud, disbelieving breath. "I never liked Sandra, but I never would've thought she'd do this."

Anna was no longer listening. She was thinking of the slam book in the other room. *She's a whore,* she had written. *She'll do it for a dime.*

Anna was suddenly certain that the cheerleader had offered her services for ten cents.

"Gotta go," Jenny said. "My mom's here. I'll call you when I get home."

There was the sound of a dial tone, and Anna hung up the phone.

"Who was it?" her mother asked.

"No one. Just Jenny." She walked back to her room in a daze. This was too bizarre to be just a coincidence. She *hated* Sandra Cowan, and even *she* didn't believe Sandra would do such a thing. She didn't even think that Sandra, despite all her talk, had ever had sex. Or wanted to.

Until now.

Anna looked at the slam book on her desk, feeling slightly afraid of it. She knew she should throw the book away or, better yet, burn it, but it suddenly occurred to her that if she did so, all of the people listed on its pages might . . . die.

She took a deep breath, filled with fear and weighed down with responsibility. What had she done? And how could she put a stop to it?

*Did she want to put a stop to it?*

That was the real question, but even as she asked it of

herself, Anna knew the answer. She thought of that harsh, wild saint at the front of the classroom. *He* wouldn't back down, she knew. He would see this through to the end.

Slowly, carefully, she picked up the slam book and one of the pens lying next to it on the desk. First things first. She needed to find out if this was really happening. She glanced up at the clock on her dresser. Four thirty-five. Late but not too late. If she could get Jenny to call her . . .

Anna made her way back out to the living room, checking first to see where her mother and sister were. Her dad wouldn't be home for another hour at least, so she was safe there. Luckily, her mom was in the bathroom, and her sister was in the bedroom with her iPod. Anna quickly dialed Jenny's cell number and told her friend to call her back immediately.

"I'm in the car with my mom!"

"It's an emergency," Anna said. "I'll explain later. Please?"

"Okay."

Jenny hung up and called back after a few minutes. Anna let it go two rings so everyone could hear, then shouted out, "I'll get it!" She answered the phone, thanked Jenny for helping her, then hung up, promising to tell her friend everything tomorrow at school.

"Mom!" Anna called down the hall.

Her mother was just emerging from the bathroom. "Yes?"

"Jenny just called back. She forgot her math book at school. We're supposed to do twenty questions at the end of the chapter—"

"If she wants to come by, that's fine."

Anna felt a split second of panic. "No, she wants me to go over there. She's . . . grounded. She can't leave the house. I'll just speed over. I'll be back way before dinner." She spoke quickly, hoping her mom wouldn't notice the nervousness.

Her mom didn't.

"You have forty-five minutes, young lady. I want you back here by five-thirty. And if you're late, *you'll* be grounded."

"Thanks, Mom." Anna ran back into her room for the math text, placed the slam book beneath it, and hurried out the front door.

Where to go?

Liz McAlwaite, Sandra's chirpy little toady, lived closest, on the next block over, so it was to her house that Anna went. She had no concrete plan, assuming she would think of something on the way over, but when she reached Liz's driveway and still hadn't come up with a viable idea she decided to throw caution to the wind and just go for it. Flipping over the math text and opening the slam book to Liz's entry, she took out her pen and wrote: *Sandra would like her better if she wasn't so buddy-buddy with Anna.*

She walked up to Liz's door.

Knocked.

"Anna!" Liz threw open the screen and hugged her like a long-lost sister. It was all she could do not to cringe.

"Hey," Anna said.

"You should've called and told me you were coming! We're just getting ready to eat."

"That's okay. I was on my way to Sandra's and thought I'd stop by."

"Sandra's? Oh, my God! She wouldn't . . . you're not . . . you're joking, right?"

Anna shook her head. "She asked me to come over."

"Sandra?" Liz looked stunned. "I can't believe it."

Anna opened the slam book to the page marked by her finger and clicked her pen.

"What's that? A slam book?"

*Liz is a lez*, she wrote. *She's in love with Sandra.*

"What are you writing?"

"I know about your crush on Sandra," Anna said. "I'm telling her."

Liz looked stricken. "Anna!" She burst into tears.

"Everyone's going to know."

"No!"

Anna turned away, closed the slam book, and walked down the driveway toward the sidewalk, ignoring the cries of anguish behind her.

She smiled to herself.

It worked.

After dinner, Anna sat in her room, door shut, staring at the closed slam book on her desk. She'd told her parents she was going to be doing homework, though her real plan was to write in the slam book. But instead she just sat there, thinking.

Returning from Liz's house, she'd been elated. The slam book really did have power. She could do whatever she wanted to *whomever* she wanted. She was queen of the world!

What had she actually learned, though? That Liz had a thing for Sandra and that she didn't want anyone to find out about it? Both of those could have been true irregardless. The fact that she'd written about them in the slam book might very well be coincidence. Wasn't it logical that a girl as fanatically devoted to Sandra as Liz was might have a secret crush on her? And of course she wouldn't want such information to get out.

Even Liz's friendliness was a matter of interpretation. After all, her parents had been home, probably standing right behind her, so of course she would be on her best behavior. And maybe Liz wasn't so bad outside of Sandra's influence, maybe she just acted like a bitch at school because of peer pressure.

Then again, maybe not.

There was no way to know. That was the problem.

What Anna needed was a more definitive answer, concrete proof that the slam book could do . . . what she thought it could.

Another test.

It had to be something both serious and concrete, something that could not occur any other way, something that happened instantly. It also had to be something verifiable, something she could see with her own eyes. Tonight.

And it had to involve Sandra Cowan.

That was the most important part, wasn't it? That was what she really wanted—to *see* what happened to Sandra. It wasn't enough to *make* it happen; she wanted to *be* there when it did.

Anna glanced up at the shelf above her desk, her gaze falling upon the spine of an E. B. White book, one of her favorites from childhood. An idea suddenly came to her. She looked down at the cover of the slam book.

And grinned.

The street seemed scary at night.

It wasn't really that late. And it was a suburban street in her own quiet neighborhood. But Anna had never sneaked out of the house before. She was a good girl, and the fact that she was going behind her parents' backs, doing something she shouldn't, made her feel guilty, gave a darker, more malevolent tinge to everything.

Up the next block, on the opposite side of the street, a man was walking a dog. She could see only his silhouette, but he appeared to be moving much slower than he should, as though he were casing houses. Or waiting for someone else to come along, someone he could attack.

She clutched the slam book to her chest, prepared to use it.

The man and his dog turned the corner onto First Avenue.

She relaxed a little. Sandra's house was only two blocks up ahead, and she quickened her step, praying that neither her parents nor her sister would get up to go to the bathroom, peek into her bedroom, and discover that she was gone. If she would just be allowed to get away with this one transgression . . .

*She could write an entry for her family in the slam book, make* sure *they didn't find out.*

Anna pushed that thought immediately out of her mind.

The Cowans' house was two stories, with a two-car garage. Anna stood on the sidewalk staring at the darkened home, trying to determine which window was Sandra's. This was the part of her plan that was flawed. If she'd had a cell phone, she could have called the cheerleader and told her to come out. Or if it was earlier in the evening, she could have simply rung the doorbell and asked to see her. But as it was, the best idea she could come up with was to throw rocks at Sandra's window until she opened it.

She was about ready to try to sneak around the side of the house to the back when a car came up the street. Anna feigned casualness as she stood on the sidewalk waiting for the vehicle to pass by. But it didn't. It pulled into the Cowans' driveway, triggering motion-detector lights that illuminated the entire front yard. Seconds after stopping, the car's doors flew open.

"Not another word out of you, young lady," her mom said angrily, getting out.

A beaten Sandra emerged from the backseat, saying nothing.

The prostitution arrest! Anna had forgotten all about it. She watched from the shadows as Sandra's briefcase-carrying dad and perfectly coiffed mom herded her toward the front door. It must have taken her parents this long to bail her out of jail.

Anna's plans were all screwed up. There was no way she'd be able to do what she had planned, so she quickly opened the slam book to Sandra's page and under the cheerleader's name and stats wrote: *She is a rat.*

It was something that had always been true metaphorically, but that was not how she meant it this time. And that was not how the slam book took it.

The change happened instantaneously. Sandra's pretty face pushed forward, suddenly covered with fur, whiskers twitching above huge front teeth. Still in her cheerleader outfit, she dropped on arms and legs that were thin, hairy, and clawed.

Mrs. Cowan screamed to wake the dead. Mr. Cowan tried to grab his madly scrambling rat daughter, crying, "Oh, my God! Oh, my God!"

Anna watched the scene from the sidewalk.

Then ran home as fast as she could.

* * *

It had been a long, hard night. She had not slept at all but had written and crossed out, written and crossed out, until she heard her father's alarm clock ring at five. Natalie Tyron had been given the head of a cow, then the head of a dog, then her own head back. Bonnie Behar had been killed in a bathtub accident, then brought back to life. Lynn Fitzgerald, perhaps the prettiest girl at St. Mary's, had been hideously deformed, then her looks had been restored. Anna had liked punishing those people who had punished her, and the feeling of revenge had been sweet. She had even, during one brief, crazy, power-mad moment, considered writing in Jenny's name. Jenny may have been her best friend and may have written the only nice comments in the slam book from Sister Caroline's class, but Jenny was also the one who had handed her the book. She had known what she'd see; maybe she had even *wanted* her to see it.

She immediately dismissed the idea of doing anything to Jenny, though, shocked and suddenly scared by the fact that she could even conceive of such a notion.

She thought of that ragged horrific saint in the portrait at the front of the classroom, then thought about the gentle loving Jesus she'd learned about in chapel.

This morning, she had finished writing one comment for each person and had then hidden the slam book at the bottom of her dresser drawer.

And that is where it would stay.

Before class, Anna went into the chapel and prayed, offering her thanks and her love to that benign martyr above the altar, and when she reentered the school hallway she was greeted with salutations of "Hi!" and "Hello, Anna!" from students who had never before spoken to her. She was given three slam books to write in, and when she looked at her own pages they were filled with complimentary comments.

She was popular.

Jenny met her outside Sister Caroline's room just before the bell rang. "What is going on?" her friend asked wonderingly. "Everyone's being so . . . nice."

Anna laughed. "It's like we died and went to heaven."

"I know. Everything seems so different today."

"Except us."

"Except us."

They walked into class, took their seats. Sister Caroline began talking, but Anna didn't listen. Instead, she stared at the frightening figure of St. Millard at the front of the room. The twisted face was staring down at her with a mixture of hate and disgust, its demonic eyes boring into hers.

She met the gaze, held it.

Then triumphantly looked away.

DARKNESS

# A TRICK OF THE LIGHT

**Chet Williamson**

**MySpace.com**
**A Trick of the Light**
**Current mood: expectant**
**Category: Dreams and the Supernatural**

I could just as easily have put this in Romance and Relationships, or maybe even Travel and Places. But I figured here was best. That way I can let other people know, and maybe they can do something to help.

But what I *don't* want you to know is who I am, and that's why I'm going anonymous. My name isn't Andy, and my girlfriend's name isn't Kyle, and everybody else's name is changed, too.

But I have to let people know, because it's really important, more important than you can guess. When you get right down to it, it's the most important thing of all, the darkness and the light.

Nighttime was when I noticed the shadows in the hospice. And when I saw the lights, too. At first I thought they were just a trick of the light, since I had tears in my eyes a lot when I was there, and tears can do funny things to your vision.

I had good reason to cry. Kyle was dying. I think I loved Kylie ever since we were little kids. When we played at recess, her blond hair was so bright I thought the sun had gotten caught in it. Sometimes—not very often—I'd get close enough to her so that I could smell her hair, a cross between lemons and fresh strawberries. And when Kylie laughed, well, it wasn't like other girls, high-pitched and squeaky, but like wind chimes, honest to God.

But it wasn't until this past year that she really started to notice me and we started going out. I knew she was having problems, but I didn't realize how bad it was until she went into the hospital.

It was something with her blood, and she'd been on meds for years, but they didn't work anymore, so she had to get transfusions, and then she started getting them more and more often, which sucked. She was great right after getting one, but in a few days she'd start looking pale and get tired real easy. Her veins started getting screwed up too, and they put this port thing in her chest around her collarbone so the doctors could get blood and give her transfusions without digging for a vein, which really hurt her.

She got an infection right after that, and went into the hospital. It was okay at first. She talked and smiled, and we played some games that fit on her bed tray, like Yahtzee, which she really liked, and card games. But she went downhill fast, got weaker, barely responded when I talked to her, and finally the doctors said it was acute leukemia. They couldn't do anything else for her, and they sent her to this hospice. To die.

I couldn't believe it. Just a few weeks before she'd been fine, been my Kylie, my *girlfriend,* who I'd finally gotten together with that fall after loving her so long. We watched DVDs together (a lot of sci-fi), went to movies and football games and the mall, and when she'd see something she really liked, like a cool tee or a neat cap or something, I'd get it for her, just because I was so happy to be with her, and she'd laugh and thank me and give me a hotter kiss than usual when I took her home, and now she was in a hospice, not eating, barely drinking, just waiting to *die*. Life just wasn't fair.

Death wasn't either, so let me get to that part of it.

The hospice was nice. If you had to die, I guess it was a pretty cool place to do it. On the outskirts of town, about a mile from the biggest shopping mall in the county, so I could drive over there and get a cappuccino when I needed a break. Even though there were only eighteen patient rooms, the building was big, with two wings and gardens and all these other rooms where you could go and meditate and stuff. There was a big kitchen and a TV room in each wing, and you could bring in your own food and even cook (there was a microwave, so I used that sometimes).

Kyle's room was stupidly awesome compared to the hospital—a really nice big bed that went all different directions to make her comfortable, two easy chairs, a big couch that I slept on a lot, a cabinet with a TV and VCR, a bathroom with all the medical equipment in it so we didn't have to look at it all the time, and an alcove with a table and chairs and a window seat that looked out onto the garden. There was even a patio with those French doors, but it was too cold to go out there.

The people were great too. Holly was the neatest. She was

one of the night nurses, a little younger than my mom, and I talked with her a lot. See, I was there with Kyle more than anybody else. Her dad walked out a long time before, and her mom has two jobs. She came over when she could, but the medical bills were adding up and she had to work as much as possible. It wasn't that she didn't want to be with Kyle, because she loved her and all, but by the time Kyle went into the hospice it was like she didn't know who was there and who wasn't. She had a lot of pain, so they kept giving her morphine, which was good, but it made her dopey and she slept a lot. Even when her eyes were open it was like she was sleeping. I held her hand a lot of the time, but she didn't squeeze back.

Christmas vacation had started, and since I didn't have school to worry about, I just stayed there as much as I could. A few of Kyle's friends came in to visit—Annie and Drew and Liz and Mike and even Rick, who dated her for a while—but the whole dying thing creeped them out and none of them came back a second time. That was okay with me. I just wanted to be with her alone as much as I could. And I didn't like Rick around anyway—he was dating Kyle before she started going with me, and I was afraid he was still jealous, since Kylie zoned in on me pretty quick after they broke up. My mom and dad were okay with my being at the hospice. I guess they knew it wouldn't be long.

Late one night I was half lying, half sitting on the couch, wondering whether or not to close my eyes and try to sleep. I was starting to turn my head toward the back of the couch when I caught something out of the corner of my eye. It was like a white light that hadn't been there before, close to Kyle, right above her bed. I expected it to vanish when I looked directly at it, but it *didn't*, not right away. It stayed there for maybe three or four seconds, and then it just kind of winked out.

But what weirded me out even more was the shadow. I hadn't noticed it when the light was there, but once its brightness was gone I became aware of what seemed like a crouching, waiting darkness in a corner of the room, just a puddle of shadow that seemed to *shiver*. I shivered myself when I saw it. Then it dissolved like smoke.

I swallowed hard, then stood up and walked over to where I'd seen it. There was nothing there. I looked above the bed where I'd seen the light, but that was totally gone too.

*"Hey . . ."*

I jumped about three feet in the air. When I came down I saw Holly standing near the door. "You startled me," I said.

"Sorry. I just came on shift, thought I'd see if you were here. You okay?"

I nodded. "Just had a little scare."

"What?"

"Oh . . . it was dumb. Just a trick of the light, or an afterimage or something." I told Holly what I'd seen and she didn't say anything, but she looked funny, like she was trying to see inside me, and I thought maybe I hit on something, so I said, "That wasn't, like, *the* light, was it?"

"*The* light?" she said, like she didn't know what I meant.

"You know. The one that people are supposed to go to when . . . they die." I still had trouble with the whole *dead* thing too. I guess I thought if I didn't say it, it wouldn't happen.

"I'm not sure, Andy," she said. "It probably was just an afterimage, like you thought."

Still, I saw the light again, maybe once or twice a night,

always around Kyle, and always when I looked away. When I looked back, it disappeared. The shadow was there too, or at least it seemed like it. It was harder to be sure, because it was, well, a *shadow*.

Christmas came, and Kyle's mom spent most of the day with her, so I had the holiday with my family. It wasn't all that great. I'd done some shopping for my mom and dad and my older brother, Chris, who was back from college, and my presents from them were cool, but to tell the truth I was glad when the day was over and I could get back to the hospice. It had started to snow, and I think Kyle's mom was relieved to be able to go home. She was pretty tired. The way she worked, she was *always* tired.

The snow really kicked in after she left, and I stood at the window for a long time and watched it come down. Then I realized that Kylie had stopped breathing. It wasn't because I had supersenses or anything, it was just that her breathing had gotten pretty loud, and when it stopped I noticed it. It happened all the time now. I went to her and just stood there looking at her. I knew there wasn't anything to do. She was here to die, and they wouldn't try to resuscitate her. But after maybe forty-five seconds or so, she hitched in a breath that made me jump, and started breathing again.

I should have been used to it, but it still freaked me out, like she was dead and then came back to life again. The nurses had told me it was apnea, like people have when they snore, or maybe Cheyne-Stokes breathing — I get the two mixed up — but it's what happens when people get close to dying.

Then I heard something else, a clicking in Kyle's throat, like dice rattling in a Yahtzee cup, and I'd never heard that before. I pushed the button to call a nurse, and in a minute or two

Lucinda, one of the night nurses, showed up. I told her about the breathing, and she listened to it and shook her head. "I'm sorry, Andy," she said, "but I don't think she has much time. Maybe less than an hour or so."

I swallowed hard. "Is Holly around?" I asked. For some reason I wanted Holly to be there.

"She should have gotten here by now, but the snow . . . the roads are really bad." She paused. "Do you want me to stay with you, or leave you alone with Kyle?"

"I'm okay alone," I said, and Lucinda put Kylie on her side so she could breathe easier, and then she left.

Kylie died ten minutes later.

It was like a movie. Her throat was rattling, and then it just stopped, and a breath came out so long and so soft, and then there was nothing. I waited and waited, but she didn't breathe again.

That's when I saw the light.

It was right over her head, a small white light, and something from Kyle, a gleaming shadow, came up and out of her body and went into the light, and the light dimmed and vanished. I was all alone. Kylie was gone.

And I knew that something was wrong. Something bad had happened, but I didn't know what. I didn't feel any peace, just the opposite.

Then Holly came into the room. Her coat and hat were still on and were wet with snow. Her boots were dripping as she crossed the carpet to me. "Is she gone?" she asked. I nodded, and she saw the look on my face. "Into the light?" I nodded again, and Holly's face puckered up. "*Damn*," she said softly. "I wanted to be here. I tried, but the snow . . ."

"It wasn't right, was it?" I asked. "The light?"

She shook her head. "Sit down, Andy. I have to talk to you."

Holly took off her coat and hat, and we sat across from each other at the small table in the alcove. She looked at me so hard I thought her eyes were going to cut right through me. "You *know,*" she said. "You've seen the light and the shadow. And you knew something was wrong with the light. Andy . . . you're one of us."

"I don't know what you mean," I said. Kylie was dead, and I should have been crying, but instead I felt like I was on the edge of something big and scary and exciting, and I was mad at myself for feeling that way.

"Did you ever see anything like that before, Andy? Think back. Think *hard.*"

I did, and I remembered. "My grandpa," I said. "My dad took me to see him in the hospital. My mom didn't want him to. I was sitting there when Dad was talking to him, and I saw . . . a shadow in the corner. I cried, and Dad took me out. Grandpa died that night."

She nodded. "I can see them too. I wanted to get here so I could be with Kyle when it happened and warn her away from the light, guide her into the shadow. That's what we do."

"'We'?"

"The ones who see. And know. There are more of us than you'd think, some in every hospital, every hospice, every place people die. We know each other, but nobody else knows us, and that's how we like it. They'd never believe us. They'd think we were crazy."

"I don't . . ."

"People say go into the light when you die. No. That's the worst thing you can do. People think the light is good, but when you die it's the *darkness* that's good. It's comforting and soothing, and you have to go through it to get to whatever's on the other side."

"And . . . what is?"

Holly shook her head. "I have no idea. Never been there. But I *do* know what's in the light."

"What?"

"Nothing good. It fools people, sucks in their spirits, takes the ones who are desperate to stop suffering but who are still afraid to die. And in the light, they don't ever die, but they keep *dying*. Their pain goes on, and the light blinds them and burns them and keeps them forever." Holly paused and gave a little shudder. "Some of us think it's how the idea of Hell got started. And the more people it pulls in, the more powerful it gets."

"Are you saying . . . it's like an *entity*?"

"Might as well call it that as anything else. But what it boils down to is that the shadow, the darkness, is true and peaceful death, and the light is nothing but torment. You can see them both, Andy—you can see the edges—so you're one of those who has to know the truth so you can help."

"Help who? Help *how*?"

"Become one of us, and try to save the dying. Urge them away from the light and into the darkness. Places like this are where we work, because the light is stronger here. It's absorbed so many dying people over the years."

This was crazy. "Look," I said, "my girlfriend just died, and if what you say is true, she's been sucked into some kind of monster, and all you can think about is recruiting me to be a . . . a nurse for dead people?"

"We call ourselves soul catchers."

"Well, good for you, but, I mean, I want to help *Kylie*, not somebody else! I want to get her *out* of . . . wherever she is!"

She held up her hands to quiet me, and I closed my eyes and tried to take it all in. "You *can* help her," Holly said. "But it's not going to be easy." She looked scared, and her next words told me why. "You've got to go in after her. Into the light."

I shrugged. "Okay."

"Not so fast. Let me tell you what you're up against. It's hardly ever been done. There has to be a strong emotional link between the person going in and the person they want to save. Most soul catchers don't have that, so once they're in the light . . . well, it's like looking for a needle in a haystack. You might get lost and never get out again."

"Screw that. I've got a link. So what do I have to do?"

"You have to find Kyle . . . feel your way to her, and then bring her back to the edge of the light and take her out. Then, finally, guide her into the darkness."

"Fine."

"No. Not so fine. It's incredibly dangerous. You don't make it, you're trapped in the light forever. I've never done it myself—hardly anybody has—but it's bad in there, really bad. And even if you make it back . . . things might not be the same again."

"I don't care." I wasn't brave, really. All I could think about was Kylie, who I loved so much, trapped inside that light, its brightness burning her, feeling the pain of dying forever.

I couldn't keep living knowing that I had let that happen and hadn't tried to do something about it. "What do I do?"

I did what Holly told me. I sat next to Kyle's body and held her dead hand and just thought about the light. I did what so many people want the dying to do—*go to the light, go to the light.* I thought hard, and before too long I began to see it. It was as if I had called it and it came. I don't think it even suspected that I was trying to cheat it. I don't think it even cared one way or another. I think it was just hungry and thought it might get fed again.

Soon it was bright as the sun and right in front of me, just above Kyle's head. I took one last look at her face, her dead eyes partly open, her mouth wide, and then I went into the light.

It was easy as falling off a cliff. My mind just slipped into it, and I was surrounded by blazing light on all sides. I could hardly see, but the first thing that struck me about being in the light wasn't anything I saw. It was the smell. We don't smell death much. I know the only time I ever smell it is when a mouse dies inside a wall in the house and it takes a couple of days for that sweet-bitter, sickening odor to go away.

This was a hundred times worse—a thousand. It was like everything that had ever died had crawled up into my brain through my nose. The whole world seemed made of rotting flesh, cells breaking down into pus, this thick, viscous liquid that coated my skin like water after rain.

And then it seemed like *I* was dying too. I could feel my body breaking down, the flesh becoming soft and slipping off my muscles, the muscles sliding off my bones, my eyes drying up inside my skull, my guts starting to liquefy and burst, the juices leaking out of me through every hole in my body.

I tried to catch a breath, even to breathe in that foul, stinking air, but my decaying lungs were filled with fluid, and I heard the clicking and bubbling as I struggled to pull in oxygen. I could feel my mind slipping away as my heart worked harder than ever before to pump blood up into my brain, but I could feel it failing, shrinking like a sponge being squeezed dry so that there was no blood in my dying brain, and my thoughts started escaping, my mind dribbling away, everything slithering into utter hopelessness.

And then I felt Kylie. With what lousy senses I had left, I *felt* her, knew she was here, and that knowledge, weak as it was, brought me back. *I'm not dying,* I thought to myself. *I'm not!* But everyone else around me was, and I started moving through them toward my Kylie.

You know how in the *Lord of the Rings* movies you've got these rows upon rows of CG orcs and monsters? It was like that, as far as I could see, these vast ranks of the dying standing and lying and writhing on . . . it wasn't ground, exactly. I don't know *what* it was, but it was wet, and it stank just as badly as the things that lived—or died—there. And it wasn't flat like the ground. It curved up and around, like I was inside a huge globe, but a globe as big as the earth. Still, with the light all around me, I could see everything, way across on the other side above my head. It was freaky as hell, and if it hadn't been for Kyle being there I probably would've lost it. I had to keep it together for her, and that's what I was going to do.

I tried to call her name, but when I did it felt like my mouth was turned inside out and was pouring out of my head, my tongue slopping down over my jaw. So I called her from inside myself, and I felt an answer. I stumbled through these slimy, groping, eternally dying things that crawled and shambled all around me, trying to get closer to Kylie, telling myself that it was okay, that my body wasn't dying, that pieces of myself weren't really dropping off with every move I made, that I was sitting back in the hospice next to Holly, and outside the snow was falling and it was dark and cool and safe, not hot and bright and blinding and stinking like the contents of a slaughterhouse left in the sun for weeks.

Still, with every step I felt my bare feet sink into the sweltering ooze that was both the ground and the bodies that I walked on. In some places you couldn't tell one from the other—the landscape seemed made of the dying. Heads and hands and arms rose out of it like tree branches from a swamp. Only branches didn't twist and clutch and writhe in agony. And they didn't look up at you with eyes that blazed like the light that imprisoned them.

I kept moving, kept thinking *Kylie . . . Kylie . . . Kylie,* but there were all these other things that were trying to get into my mind, thoughts and visions and memories that weren't mine. And I finally figured out that it was from coming into contact with all these dying people, that somehow what was in their heads was creeping into my own. It was like I was part of a mass mind, like a zombie Borg-collective, if you're into *Star Trek* like I am.

The worst part was that so many of their thoughts were about their dying, and so many were the same, because all these people in this particular light had died in the hospice, so their deaths were long and painful. That's all I want to say about it. But if anybody ever tells me, oh, nobody knows what it's like to die, I can say that *I* do.

In spite of all these alien thoughts battering away at my

mind, I felt Kylie growing nearer. Even in all that stench of death I could suddenly sense the lemon-strawberry scent of her hair, and before I realized it I was right beside her.

She was naked, and it was the first time I'd seen her that way, but it wasn't sexy at all. Her body was like a skeleton with skin stretched across it, and it scared me, but she was still Kylie and I had come to save her, so I grabbed her hand.

I don't know which was worse—the fact that her hand seemed to melt into mine like they were both made of pudding, or what I felt coming into my mind from her own. It was like I knew everything that she knew, like all her memories and thoughts were an open book to me.

I knew that she never loved me, that she loved Rick, and that Rick *had* seen her naked.

I knew that Rick had broken up with her right after she got sick, and that was when she started pretending to like me, because she wanted somebody who would love her and take care of her and not leave her to die alone.

I knew what she was thinking when she was kissing me, and I knew that she held her breath when she did so that she wouldn't smell my bad breath, and she closed her eyes so that she wouldn't see the zits that I brushed my hair to cover.

I knew that she thought my hand was sweaty when I held hers.

I knew that she thought the sci-fi DVDs we watched were stupid.

I knew that Annie and Drew and Liz teased her for dating a nerd.

I knew that she hated them for doing it.

I knew that she didn't love me, not at all.

For a moment I thought about leaving her there, but I couldn't. In spite of everything, I still loved her. I had come in there to save her from the light, and that's what I was going to do.

I don't know exactly how I was able to get her out. It was twice as hard getting back to the edge of the light as it had been to get to Kyle in the first place, but after what seemed like hours I knew we were there. I could see the room in the hospice like it was through deep water, and I wrapped my arms around Kyle, felt her body *ooze* into mine, and I pushed out of the light. It was as though the light made one final effort to hold us and blazed up, blinding me, so that when I could see again I was sitting in the chair by the bed in the hospice, Holly beside me, Kyle lying dead, her eyes still open.

"Andy?" Holly said, and I looked up at her and smiled. "Are you okay?"

"I'm fine," I said, and my voice sounded funny to me. "I've got her. I saved her."

"Where . . . where is she?"

"In here," I said, touching my chest. "She's safe in here." And she was. I could feel her soul inside my mind and my body, warm against my heart, within my brain. I looked above the bed, then all around the room. "It's gone," I said. "The light. I think I kicked its ass."

Holly laughed uncomfortably. "I guess you did." She took a deep breath. I looked down at my hands, happy that they were solid again. "Are you ready to let her go?" Holly asked. "Into the shadow?"

I nodded.

"Then let's bring it back," she said. "Start to let Kyle out, but watch out for the light." That was all it took. As I began to let

Kyle's spirit slip out of me I started to see the shadow, forming like a thick cloud of darkness in a corner of the room, about eye level. I heard Holly gasp, but it wasn't at the shadow. It was at the sight of what was pouring out of me, a gleaming, iridescent ribbon made of air and light.

She watched it start to go into the darkness, and then I gave a cry of pain, and Holly's gaze snapped back to me. When we looked at the shadow again, the ribbon was gone, and in another moment so was the shadow.

"That was amazing," Holly whispered, "what you did. I never knew anyone who went into the light and came back. What was it like?"

I told her. Everything.

"She didn't love me," I said. "I thought she did, but she was lying all along. Just to have somebody to be with her . . . when she died."

Holly's face was pale. "My god, Andy. When did you learn that?"

"As soon as I . . . touched her."

"And you brought her out anyway." She shook her head and smiled at me. "That was incredibly generous. And very brave."

"Yeah, whatever." I looked at Kyle's dead face. "Should we let everybody else know? That she's gone, I mean."

"I'll take care of it," Holly said as she stood up. "I'd tell you to go home, but I don't think anybody's going anywhere in this weather. You want to wait in the lounge, or—"

"I'll just sit here for a while," I said. "If that's okay."

She looked a little surprised. "Sure. Sure it is. You take as long as you like, and then I'll get some of the others and we'll . . . take care of Kyle. And Andy?" I looked up at her. "Don't take this too hard. You've got a gift, a very special gift, and we'll talk more about it and what you might want to do with it. But you're also a very special guy, and I promise you that someday there's going to be a girl who will love you, just for yourself. Okay?"

I nodded and put on a brave smile. Holly left me alone and I sat and looked at Kyle's body.

Then I looked at—and right into—her spirit, still inside me.

Holly was right. There *was* going to be a girl who really loved me, and it was going to be Kyle.

I'd decided what to do on the way out, fighting my way through that nightmare, that hell that I'd gone into for her. I had let Kyle slip partway into the shadow, but then I'd made that noise to distract Holly, and when she looked at me I yanked Kyle back, like pulling in a fish all at once. Misdirection. Like sleight of hand, but really sleight of mind. Holly thought that Kyle had gone into the shadow, but she was really tucked away inside me.

She still is. And that's where I'm going to keep her until the day that she loves me for real. She says she does, but she's just saying that to get out, so that she can go into the darkness. I know she's lying. I know everything in her mind and her soul. She can't lie to me, not this time.

So that's about it. My main reason in posting this is to let people know—*don't* go to the light or tell anybody else to go there. Tell them to go to the shadow and they'll be okay. Or as okay as you can be when you die.

I said at the beginning it was important, and it is. So spread it around, post it on your own blogs. Because I want people to know. I want to help save them. I mean, I'm not a bad person, even if Kyle thinks I am. She thinks I'm really bad right now, but I'm not. And soon she'll see that. Soon she'll love me.

She'd better, for both our sakes.

# ERASED

**Jane Mason**

Isabel stared at the crackling bonfire and let the hubbub of her friends' conversations wash over her. It was just getting dark, and the sparks from the burning driftwood swirled in the air above the dancing flames. Her sweetie, Jacob, had a muscular arm slung over her shoulder. Isabel eyed him in the firelight and felt her heart flicker with the flames. She loved the way his curly dark bangs hung almost into his green eyes, but didn't quite. Actually, she loved a lot of things about Jacob.

"Are you warm enough?" he asked, turning away from his best friend, Samuel, and pulling her closer. She could feel his heartbeat through his shirt.

"Toasty," Isabel replied as he leaned in for a kiss. He smelled of beer and wood smoke. Delicious.

"This isn't a motel, guys," Isabel's best friend, Annika, griped. She reached her own arm out and hastily pushed Isabel sideways onto the sand.

Isabel eyed her friend and brushed the tiny camel-colored

grains out of her hair before giving Annika a retaliatory shove. "What's your problem, girl?" she asked.

"Nothing," Annika replied. "I'm just a little tired of the constant PDA." Isabel rolled her eyes. Annika could be so . . . testy. It wasn't as if she and Jacob were making out or anything. Cripes.

Beyond the giant fire Isabel could see the waves lapping on the sandy shore, and beyond *that* the blackness of the lake. A giant ore boat was slowly making its way out of the harbor, bound for the Atlantic. Isabel stared at the dark water, illuminated only by the moon and the ship's lights.

The next thing she knew she was on her feet and skimming her lips over Jacob's. "I'll be back," she whispered, turning and walking toward the water. She slid out of her jacket and pulled her T-shirt over her head, revealing a bikini top underneath. "Time for a swim!" she called over her shoulder. "Anyone want to join me?"

"You're crazy, Iz," someone shouted. "The water is freezing."

"Lame-ass," Isabel replied as she stepped into the lake. It *was* icy, but the air was warm for September. Isabel held her breath as she walked into the gradually deepening lake. Then, when it was up to her waist, she dived.

As her body was engulfed by the frigid water, Isabel felt at once utterly shocked and amazingly calm. Every inch of her skin was instantly covered in goose bumps, and as she began her freestyle she gasped desperately for air. Then, as she swam, the black iciness of the lake welcomed her. She kicked away from shore, feeling the rhythm of the waves and her strokes as they became more and more synced, until they felt as though they were in perfect unison.

Isabel swam. She could hear the distant calls of her friends back on the shore and mentally dared one of them to come in after her—they wouldn't make it in past their calves. She dived down and stayed under for a few seconds, staring into the blackness that surrounded her.

*I should turn around,* she told herself after she'd surfaced. Her hands and feet were getting numb. But the water was so quiet, so cold, so still. . . .

Isabel turned on her back to look up at the sky. The moon was higher now, and full. An endless array of stars twinkled above her. She lay perfectly still, following the line of a shooting star as it grazed the black curtain overhead. The sky looked cozy, like a giant blanket. Isabel closed her eyes and took in the silence.

Her motionless frame bobbed on the surface of the giant lake, then, very slowly, began to sink. Her feet drifted downward, then her butt, her arms, her head. . . .

Suddenly, Isabel jolted awake—and saw nothing but blackness. She was totally submerged! Flailing her arms and legs, she sucked in water. Then her legs remembered how to kick properly and she began to move toward the moonlight above the surface. Desperately pushing the water aside with her arms and feeling like her lungs were about to explode, she burst through the surface into the night air.

*Holy shit,* Isabel thought as her heart thudded maniacally in her chest. She'd almost drowned. All of a sudden she was desperate to get back to shore, to the fire, to her friends. Turning, she scanned the horizon. She could see her old elementary school, the parking lot, and the massive, grass-covered dune. But the beach itself was empty.

Isabel shivered. Her legs were numb from the knees down. She'd better get moving before she couldn't feel anything at all. Stroking slowly so she wouldn't exhaust herself any further, she began to make her way back to shore. After what seemed like forever she was walking in shallow water, then dragging herself onto the relatively warm sand. She looked around for a sign of her friends, but the beach was dark and quiet. And empty.

"Damn you, Jacob," she grumbled. She'd told him she'd be back, hadn't she? Where the hell did he, and Annika and everyone else, go? If this was a prank, it wasn't funny. At all.

Isabel pulled her shivering form to her feet and began to walk. Each step sent a jolt of pinpricks through her legs, but she kept putting one foot in front of the other until she reached the pile of burned driftwood near the dunes. She had to find her clothes before she shivered to death. But when she held her hands over the charred driftwood she immediately realized that it was cold. Her clothes were nowhere to be seen. "Thanks for nothing, assholes," she whispered furiously.

Isabel sat down on a driftwood bench, then immediately got back onto her feet. It had been one weird-ass night, she was dangerously cold, and she needed to find her clothes and her friends. The sooner she got to Jacob's house, the better.

Isabel moved as quickly as she could toward the sidewalk. Jacob lived just up the street, thank God.

A few shivery minutes later she was standing on Jacob's doorstep. She didn't bother to knock—the door was always unlocked and the music coming from the basement was so loud that nobody would hear her anyway. Pulling Jacob's leather jacket off the coatrack in the hall, Isabel slipped into it and felt warmer before she was halfway to the door that led down to the basement.

Isabel's bare feet gingerly walked down the carpeted stairs. Someone had turned the music down, and she could hear Annika laughing. She paused on the bottom step, not sure what to do or say. The room was pretty crowded with kids from Central. She suddenly felt like a freak, standing there half naked in her boyfriend's basement.

"Hey," she called to Jacob and Annika, who were sitting together on the couch talking. But they were so engrossed in whatever they were talking about that they didn't look up.

Isabel took a breath and stepped off the stair, closing in on her best friend and boyfriend. "You two look cozy," she said, trying to sound casual.

Jacob looked up at her but didn't smile. "We are pretty cozy," he replied, putting an arm around Annika and pulling her close.

"Yeah, right!" Annika teased, whacking him playfully on the knee. But she was smiling. Isabel waited for her to ask her if she was okay, to say she was sorry for not waiting on the beach, or drag her into the bathroom and tell her she looked like a wet rodent. But she didn't say anything to Isabel at all. She just kind of sat there. . . .

"Hey, is that my jacket?" Jacob suddenly blurted.

"Yeah," Isabel said with a nod. It was a pretty stupid question, since Isabel wore it all the time. "I was cold. Freezing, in fact. You know, after I got out of the lake and discovered that the bonfire was out and that my friends and clothes had all disappeared."

Jacob eyed her for a second, then shrugged. "Bummer," he

agreed nonchalantly. Isabel felt the blood drain from her face. What was going on? Were they pissed? Annoyed? What the hell had she done to *them*?

Isabel struggled not to lose her cool, which wasn't easy. "Can I just have my clothes?" she asked quietly.

Annika stared at her like she was delusional. "Don't look at me," she said.

"I don't have 'em," Jacob added.

*Jesus Christ*, Isabel thought. *They're* my *goddamn clothes!* But she didn't want to make any more of a scene—people were already looking at her like she was a sideshow. Even Caleb Whitney, who was the usual oddball, was looking at her like she was a carnival reject.

"Whatever, people," Isabel hissed as she whipped around and headed back up the stairs. She didn't have the energy to play games. She didn't have any energy at all.

"Hey, I want my jacket!" Jacob's deep voice called after her.

Isabel made a beeline for the front door, keeping the jacket and not looking back. Fifteen minutes later she was stumbling up the walkway to her house. She felt around her neck for the key she kept on a chain, but it wasn't there. *Swallowed by the lake*, she thought with a shudder. She had nearly been swallowed, too.

Shaking her head, Isabel rang the doorbell. She was going to catch hell from her parents, coming home ultra late, soaking wet, and half naked. Shit.

It took forever for her mom to answer the door. She was wearing her nightgown and a bathrobe Isabel had never seen before. Isabel was about to start in with excuses when her mom's eyes widened. "Oh, my God, child," she said, eyeing her bare legs and feet before pulling her into the kitchen and sitting her down at the table. "Don't move. I'll be right back."

"I must really look like hell," Isabel mumbled as her mom reappeared with a thick fleece blanket and flutteringly wrapped it around her shoulders, then floated away again to fill the kettle with water and put it on the stove. She was being oddly . . . evasive, as if she had no idea what to say to her teenage daughter who had come home half frozen and looking like a half-drowned rat.

Isabel eyed her mom warily, trying to get a read. Was she furious? Too worried to remember to be furious? Still half asleep? It was hard to tell, but Isabel knew that if she didn't start talking she'd miss her chance to get a word in edgewise.

Just then her dad pushed open the swinging door and stepped into the kitchen.

*Crap,* Isabel thought, tightening the blanket around her shoulders as if it were some kind of protective armor. *It's gonna be in stereo.* And yet there was something weird about the expression on her dad's face. It wasn't the all-too-familiar what-the-hell-were-you-thinking look she got whenever she blew off her curfew. No, the look was . . . blank.

"Mom, Dad, it's not my fault," Isabel blurted. Lame, but better than nothing.

Isabel's mother looked perplexed for a moment, then crossed to the table and sat down across from Isabel. "We're not your parents, honey," she said slowly.

Isabel leaned back in her chair and shot her mom a look. "Funny, Mom, real funny," she retorted.

Her mom didn't flinch. "Would you like us to call your parents for you?" she said gently. "They're probably worried."

"Ha-ha." Isabel rolled her eyes. "You're a regular comedy act. But I'm freezing and exhausted, so if you're going to punish me, go ahead. I want to take a shower and go to bed."

Isabel saw her parents exchange glances. "We're not your parents," her dad repeated. "We're not anybody's parents."

Isabel looked at each of her parents in turn, trying not to freak. They looked the same, she suddenly realized, but also different. Older, somehow. More tired. Or was it less alive? And the kitchen . . . where were the pictures on the fridge, the boxes of sugar cereal that usually lined the counter?

"But I'm your daughter," she said, trying to keep her voice from shaking. "Isabel . . . Isabel Earhardt. The kid who drove you crazy in preschool with the constant questions. The one who fell out of the tree house and broke her arm in third grade."

Isabel's mother placed a comforting hand on Isabel's arm. "You must be exhausted," she nearly whispered. "We don't blame you for being confused."

"I'm not confused!" Isabel yelled, lurching to her feet. What was wrong with everyone? "Here, I'll show you." Turning, she raced out to the front hall and up the stairs, ignoring the shouts behind her. She just needed to get to her room, to her stuff. She was vaguely aware of the fact that the wooden letters that spelled her name weren't on the door, but she threw it open, anyway . . . and gasped.

She was looking at a sparsely decorated, ultraorganized home office. She raced to another room and threw open the door—an impeccably decorated guest room. *The bathroom. I've got stuff in the bathroom,* she told herself frantically. But the all-white hall bathroom was spotless and clearly unused. She looked around the upstairs hall. Where was the floral wallpaper? The family portrait? A loud sob escaped Isabel's throat, and she felt hot tears spill down her cheeks. There was not a single sign of teenage life, her life, anywhere. It was as if she had been erased.

Her parents were standing at the top of the stairs, looking at her like she was a caged wild animal.

"But you're my parents," Isabel insisted.

Her father shook his head. "We don't have any children," he repeated.

"Why don't you take a hot shower and get into some dry clothes?" her mother suggested. Isabel nodded numbly. Yes, a hot shower would be good.

Her mother disappeared for a minute and came back with a pair of jeans, some underwear, and a shirt. She pulled a bleached-white towel out of a cupboard in the bathroom and handed it to Isabel. "We'll be downstairs," she said kindly.

Isabel took the clothes and the towel and nodded again before closing the bathroom door. Turning on the water full blast, she stepped under the warm spray. She stood there, letting the warmth thaw her brain and her body. By the time she was getting dressed she almost felt normal. But as soon as she opened the bathroom door everything came crashing back.

"She's clearly delusional," she heard her mother say. "We'll have to call the mental hospital if she can't tell us who her parents are."

*You are my parents!* Isabel screamed in her head. But she couldn't wait around for them to believe her—if they ever would. And she sure as hell wasn't going to some loony bin. Not waiting to hear any more, Isabel pulled on Jacob's jacket and silently crept down the stairs. She shoved her feet into a pair of flats, and silently opened the door and stepped into the night.

Isabel hurried away from her house, sure her parents were going to come after her with pitchforks and torches. But there was no sound behind her. There was only the silent night air.

Before she even knew where she was going, Isabel found herself back at the lake. In the distance she could see a bonfire burning—the brightest light on the beach.

Isabel wrapped Jacob's leather jacket more tightly around her and started toward the fire. As she neared she saw Annika standing close to Jacob, laughing. Then he pulled her in front of him and wrapped his arms around her, kissing her neck.

Isabel stopped dead. Her boyfriend was kissing Annika, her best friend. A lump rose in Isabel's throat and she turned away from the fire, kicking off the flats, jeans, jacket, and shirt. Silently, she slipped back into the water. If she didn't exist to these people, to anyone, she may as well not exist at all.

Isabel ignored her frozen, throbbing head, the goose bumps, the ache in her heart. She swam hard, away from shore, until she knew she was essentially invisible, a speck in the water. Then she lay back and let the chilling calm of the lake overtake her. She closed her eyes. Soon she would be free.

Suddenly, a loud bellow thundered through the air. A ferryboat had come out of the harbor and was bearing down on her.

*Jesus Christ!* Survival instinct kicked in and Isabel rolled over and swam. This was not how she wanted to go, run into the deep by a ferry. Her arms and legs pumped hard as she gasped for air between strokes. Her limbs ached but she didn't pause. When she finally stopped to tread water she was well out of the ferry's path. As the multitiered boat chugged past her, Isabel realized just how fucking freezing she was. That, and that she was not ready to check out. Not yet. She could see the bonfire in the distance and started toward it. But she was so tired it was hard to keep moving. Her eyes on the fire, Isabel did her best to make it to shore.

The next thing she knew, Jacob and Annika were pulling her out of the freezing lake. Isabel gasped for air, then threw up a bunch of water.

"God, Isabel," Annika said. "Are you trying to kill yourself, or what?"

Jacob took off his leather jacket and wrapped it around her. *When did he take that back?* Isabel wondered. "You're freezing," he said gently.

They helped her to her feet and walked with her to the fire. "Move over," Jacob told Samuel and some guys from the football team. "This girl needs some heat."

Isabel shivered with cold and uncertainty. "You were out there a long time," Jacob said, standing close. "I was really starting to worry." Isabel waited for him to wrap his arms around her, but he didn't. A few feet away, Annika was warming her hands by the fire and watching them closely. Isabel thought she saw her and Jacob exchange a look, but couldn't be sure.

Isabel stepped a bit closer to the fire, holding her hands out as well. She soon felt the painful, prickly sensation of frozen limbs warming up. Beyond the bonfire, she could see the waves lapping on the shore, and beyond that the lake. There was no ferryboat in sight . . . only the giant lumbering ore boat making its way across the dark water.

# EMPIRE OF DIRT

**Amelia Atwater-Rhodes**

The office is of medium size, with a desk and chair set, two love seats, a bookcase, and a coffee table, all in nonthreatening earth tones. Inside, a young teenager leans forward in response to a question. His tousled, black-coffee hair falls forward to shadow his blue eyes as he asks, "Have you heard the story about the three umpires?"

"No, I haven't," a woman replies. "Why don't you tell me?"

"Well, three baseball umpires are talking about their jobs.

"The first one says, 'Some are balls and some are strikes. I call 'em like I see 'em.'

"The second one says, 'Some are balls and some are strikes. I call 'em like they *are*.'

"Then the third one says, 'Well, some are balls and some are strikes, but they ain't nothing til I call 'em.'"

"Is this an answer to my question, Sassy?"

In a rose-colored pantsuit, with her hair cut in a short but flattering style, the woman is both motherly and professional.

She jots down a note without even seeming to look at the clipboard in her lap.

"The story," the boy explains, "is supposed to illustrate how reality is different for different people. It was told to me by a psychologist."

"People have different understandings of reality, yes," the doctor replies, "but that doesn't mean everything is open to interpretation. For instance, there is a book on the table." Their gazes fall to the book, a large hardcover anthology about compulsive behaviors. "If you believe that the book isn't there, that doesn't make it go away."

"I fail to see the relevance." He shoves his hair out of his face again, regretting that he hadn't brushed it that morning.

"Sassy . . ." He watches her consider and then decide not to engage with him on the topic. Instead, she asks, "Can you explain to me why you felt the need to tell Nurse Sanford that your regular doctor hit you?"

"Oh. That." That had, of course, been the original question, but it had not interested Sherwood James Kash, better known by his nickname Sassy, any more a minute ago than it did now. He pulls at a loose thread dangling from his torn jeans, which are so well broken in they look more like felt than denim. "My doctor here told my parents I was a compulsive liar and had an oppositional defiance disorder. He seems like a nice enough guy, so I thought I'd let him know he was right."

"You nearly got him fired."

He shrugs. "And now Nurse Sanford has learned to read her patients' charts more carefully. In my eyes, I performed a public service."

He is pretty sure the doctor is stalling as she flips pages in her notes. He has a lot of practice in looking casual and can recognize it when other people do it. "I'd like to try to talk about something you said at your last hospital."

"The bit about the panda?"

"No, the—"

"Oh, you mean the kidnapping?"

"Sassy." He quirks a brow, but silences and allows her to continue. "You are creative and witty," she says. "Most of your stories sound reasonable enough that you have at different times fooled half a dozen professionals. You are rational, and intelligent enough to know what is believable. And then *this*." She taps her clipboard authoritatively. "This is the story that doesn't fit in. According to Doctor Parma, you had been cooperating fully in the conversation, opening up, and then felt the need to tell him that you are a werewolf, a lie you know is so ridiculous no doctor is going to believe it. Why is that?"

"Hyena," he corrects, under his breath. He pauses, looking deeply contemplative. "What an excellent question. You should consider that. Ask again when you have an answer, because I'm sick of trying to spell it out for everyone."

Doctor Madison shakes her head and glances at the clock. Their hour is almost over. "Are you going to come to group today?"

"Probably." His attention has turned to a scuff on the side of his battered sneakers. He hopes he looks and sounds as disinterested as he intends to. He is usually very successful in such façades. Lies are easy to sell. The truth is the only thing that is ever hard.

"Are you going to be disruptive again?"

He half smiles, an expression between a frown and a smirk. "Also probably. Erin's a funny girl, you know."

None of the doctors has told him anything about Erin, though the other patients have shared some interesting stories. Apparently, she has been around the ward for much longer than the twelve days he has been, but she has spent most of that time in isolation.

"You upset her a lot yesterday."

"She upset me, too."

"How was that?"

There is no reason not to tell the truth. People don't believe the truth, anyway.

"She saw me."

*"The Doctor C. L. Simon Ward for Troubled Teens is a small, intimate facility, dedicated to providing personal care and treatment for high-risk teens whose needs haven't been met by larger hospitals."*

Sassy had listened in, not really caring, as a doctor gave his parents that pitch two weeks before. Even then, he knew that all it meant was that the ward would have locks on the doors and nurses quick to administer a shot to quiet down any of its suicide-risk, "history of violent behavior," long-term patients.

The most fascinating of those other patients, in Sassy's opinion, is Erin Misrahe. As Sassy leaves Doctor Madison's office and steps into the common room, Erin is hunched on the couch, gazing blankly at a paperback book but not actually reading it. Her eyes are half shut and unfocused, and she doesn't seem to notice that her long brown hair has fallen over her shoulder to pool on the surface of the page she is supposedly reading. She has stared at the same spot for a long time before Sassy clears his throat to get her attention.

*She doesn't look like someone who should be here,* Sassy ponders as Erin looks up. She flinches when she sees him, and the nurse across the room makes a valiant but ultimately unsuccessful effort not to give Sassy a dirty look. *And she certainly doesn't look dangerous.* Also according to the rumors, the nurse isn't assigned to protect Erin from anyone else, but to protect other patients from Erin.

"Am I intruding?" he asks.

He expects her to say yes, but instead she shakes her head.

"I'm sorry," she says. "About yesterday. Group."

"I had a bad session," he explains haltingly. He doesn't apologize a lot, and it shows. "The doctors here are just so full of sh—" He cuts himself off, though he knows it's a little funny that he who has been arrested for swearing a blue streak at a cop makes an effort to be polite when he has already been committed. "They just don't know what they're doing. And they don't care. No one cares that maybe they aren't *right* all the time." He realizes he is beginning a tirade that is not only entirely beside the point but is starting to make Erin's eyes unfocus even more. "Never mind. I'm sorry I took my bad mood out on you yesterday is what I'm trying to say. But, what you said—"

"Are you right all the time?" she asks, making him bristle.

"You saying I'm not?"

"*I'm* not," she points out. "They give me a dozen different drugs, and I still hallucinate. I wake up and I'm not where I last remember being. Half the time I insist I'm someone else. I'm the last person who will call you right or wrong."

"I . . . thank you." That's something else he doesn't say often. "You don't know what that—"

"I think I tried to kill you," she interrupts him, awkwardly trying to make her own apology. "That's what they told me."

*That's what they told me.* He heard that, too. "Disassociative identity disorder" is the label on Erin's charts. For the lucky duck who hasn't spent the last months learning doctor language, her diagnosis is simple: split personalities.

"Oh. That. Well, some of my doctors might have thanked you for it," Sassy says, discomfort making him retreat behind his more familiar glibness. "I understand that it wasn't you." She shrugs. "You said something—before you disassociated and tried to tear my throat out, I mean."

Wrong words, probably. Erin blanches. Voice tight, she replies, "I don't remember."

"Please, you have to." If he can just find one person, just *one*, who understands . . .

"I don't remember!" she snaps, with a great deal of force considering the tranquilizers in her bloodstream. The shout is enough to prompt the nurse to separate them, ending the conversation with Sassy's question still unanswered.

*He strode into the room angry and ready to take that anger out on anyone who got in his way. Group therapy. He had told them, again and again, that he wasn't crazy. He wasn't supposed to be here. Now they wanted to put him in a room full of other needy, whining, psychotropically dependent emo-kids and have him share his "feelings" with them?*

*He didn't want to share, and he wanted even less to listen to other people's problems.*

*If he could just get outside . . .*

*"Cat got your tongue?" he snarled when his mere entrance made a girl across the room whimper and drop her head in her hands.*

*She looked up at him.*

*Really* looked.

*Clearly, distinctively, she replied, "More like a scared little hyena."*

Another building blocks the view of the sky from his window, but he knows that out there, hidden from him, the moon is full.

He can feel it. His skin crawls from it. His muscles twitch, and his bones ache. He knows that, if he can just get outside . . .

"Checks!" The cheery night nurse, the same one who was devastated to hear his tearful confession a few nights prior, pokes her head in the door. "Sassy, you should get some sleep."

"I can't," he answers. Not while the moon is up, but hidden away from him. Not until he can feel it on his skin, his *right* skin. He rubs his hands along his arms, smoothing imaginary goose bumps and real scars.

"I'll talk to Nurse Reynolds," she says kindly. In other words, she will see about getting him a shiny little pill that will supposedly *make* him sleep.

"I'll lie down," he says quickly. Every time they sedate him, they have to use something stronger, because his tolerance builds so fast. He doesn't want to know what the next drug will be. "It's okay. Mostly I sleep fine."

She makes a *tsk*ing sound but relents for the moment. "I'll check on you later."

Lying on the sterile bed does nothing to alleviate the crawling of his flesh. If he could shed his skin, he would put on his real body and run, but here he is trapped. Trapped like a rabbit in a stinking hole in the ground. Trapped in his skin, trapped in this room.

If only he could get *outside*. He had to get out, *had to*. . . .

"Checks!"

Then, "Sassy!"

"I'm sorry," he whispers. "I'm sorry, I can't . . ."

"Sassy, look at me. *Look at me!* Sassy, do you hear me?"

"Hello again, Sassy. How are you today?"

"Drugged," he mumbles. "Can I have some water?"

"Of course." Doctor Madison provides a small cup of cold water, which helps the dry mouth a little, but not nearly enough. "Do you want to talk about last night?"

"Go to hell." His head aches. So do all the muscles in his arms and legs. Partially that's from struggling against restraints; partially it's just from fighting drugs and moonlight.

"Sassy . . ."

"And if you could refrain from saying my name and sighing, that would be *great*." He gulps down the water in a few swift swallows.

"Okay. Is there anything you *would* like to talk about?"

"No," he barks, staring at the paper cup and regretting that the liquid is gone. His mouth still feels like he gargled talcum powder.

She goes quiet, probably intending to wait him out. That's fine. He likes the quiet. He scratches idly at one of the new bandages on his arms.

"Do those hurt?" Doctor Madison asks.

"They itch. That's all."

She stands, refills his water cup, and then sits in silence again. He takes another small sip of water, swishing the liquid around in his mouth before swallowing.

"I hear that you and Erin had a conversation yesterday," she prompts, probably fishing for some kind of trigger for his attack the night before.

"We did." At first he intends to leave it at that and then decides there might be something worth saying. "She made me think, actually. About – well, about maybe I could be wrong." The doctor's fingertips almost tremble, as she resists the instinct to write down another note and instead keeps all her attention on him. "Or maybe you could be. Or maybe it doesn't matter so much whether one of us is wrong. I mean, what does it *matter*? There is a book on the table or there isn't. I . . ."

"Sassy, look at your wrists."

Her calm voice cuts into the rising energy of his tirade, transforming his fury into the helpless rage that has been his constant companion for months. The bandages wrapped around his wrists are not the first, nor are the stitches beneath them. There were no weapons in the ward, even so much as a plastic knife, but teeth could still rip flesh.

He shoves himself to his feet. "You say it's a ball. I say it's a strike. The crazy part isn't that we disagree, but why I'm still arguing." There is a brittle, hysterical edge to it that gets sharper as he continues to speak. "Why is that? That's not a rhetorical question," he adds, when she seems to be waiting for him to continue. "If I could just believe you. If I could just accept that the world is the way you say it is, maybe I would be happier. . . ." His voice cracks here, and he hates hearing it do that, but the words keep flowing. "More 'well adjusted.' So why can't I do that?"

"I don't know," Doctor Madison says, her voice soft and compassionate. She reaches over and touches his hand, trying to guide him back to a seat, but he wraps his arms across his chest instead. "But if you'll work with me, I can help you figure that out."

"If I could just get outside . . ." He trails off, because as soon as he says the words, the optimistic light in her eyes becomes guarded again. He goes back to the beginning. "If I genuinely, absolutely believe what I tell you, and I am wrong, then isn't it your job to *help* me? Not just call me a liar?"

Of course, he *was* a liar. He had admitted it just one session ago. But he had only started lying because no one seemed to believe the truth, anyway.

"Okay, then, Sassy. Why don't you sit down and start at the beginning?"

"Why do you even *have* that clipboard," he snaps, "if you are just going to have me repeat everything?"

"Sa—"

"No," he interrupts, before she can say it. "Let me outside. Let me outside, tonight, while the moon is up, so I can see it and feel it and—" He breaks off before he starts ranting again and takes a deep breath. "Bring as many guards as you want. Just let me outside, and if nothing happens, I will agree that you are right and swear I'll . . . I'll . . . I'll try that medication you wanted me to, how's that?"

He sees her prepare to refuse and then stop to consider. "I would need to talk to your regular doctor and your parents. I can't make any promises. Even if I can get permission, it will probably take a few days."

*A few days* won't help. In a few days, the moon won't be full anymore, and he won't be able to change so he won't be able to convince them of anything. "It needs to be tonight. Or tomorrow," he says. "Please."

He doesn't apologize often, and he *never* begs.

"I will do what I can, but—"

"If it isn't while the moon is full, it won't make a difference!" he snarls. Why doesn't she understand that?

"Can we compromise?" she asks. "I cannot get this kind of request through in a day or two. But maybe, if you cooperate and convince your doctors that you are serious about accepting our help and that you will not try to run away, we can go outside *next* month?"

His hands move, expressing his anger, before he can think about it. Doctor Madison barely manages to duck in time to avoid a flying book about addiction and dependence. "Damn it! I am *not* taking your pills, and I am *not* going to go share my feelings in group, and I am *not* going to play with paints in OT, and I am—"

"Sassy, please try to calm down."

"—*not* going to listen to your psychobabble, all on account of your promise that *next* month you'll 'try.' Next month, it will just be another excuse. 'Oh, it didn't work out this time, but maybe . . .'"

He isn't sure if his shouting brought attention or if Doctor Madison has some kind of button she can press to trigger an alarm, but he doesn't get any further before two larger-than-nurses push into the room, telling him to calm down but not waiting on it.

*He walked into school like it was any other day. He exchanged books at his locker. He didn't say hello to friends, because they had long ago become too frustrated to stick around. He disturbed them.*

Truth hurts, doesn't it? *he found himself thinking as he watched one of those fair-weather friends pass by him with his gaze pointedly averted.*

*The bell rang while he was in the bathroom, but it was only a ten-second walk down the now empty hall to his classroom. He shouldered open the door as a dizzy spell hit him.*

*"Sherwood, you're late," the teacher said, before even looking.*

*Then she* did *look.*

*"Oh, my God . . . Sassy! Someone call 9-1-1. Oh, God . . ."*

*He woke up in his first hospital. Between the bottle of prescription painkillers he had swallowed at the water fountain, and the two wrists he had slit in the boys' bathroom, the doctors were shocked to find him still alive.*

*He wasn't shocked. He just wasn't pleased.*

He wakes up this time to find a child's toy by his bed. He reaches for it and knows by the way he stares at his arm, the beautiful arch it makes on the way to the table, that whatever they tranquilized him with is still in his system.

It takes a long time to reach the bedside table and curl his fingers around the stuffed animal there. The wolf's fur is gray-brown, and as he touches it, he realizes it is made of that new, ultrasoft material that didn't exist when he was a baby.

Purple. Oh. He reaches to the bedside table when he notices a note there, written in slightly trembling handwriting with a purple crayon on a piece of construction paper.

*Hope you can read this. My handwriting sucks. This batch of drugs makes my hands shake. Eating cereal is a real adventure. Breakfast looks like a rainbow crash-landing. Froot Loops flying everywhere.*

He chuckles at the slightly macabre attempt at humor, then goes back to reading.

*Be glad you have a little pathological problem instead of psychosis. Want to trade? Sorry, I don't mean to make fun. Well, I do. Never mind.*

*My parents brought me the wolf, but when I was looking at it, it made me think of you, so I wanted to give it to you. I don't know. I hope you feel better soon.*

*Erin*

He clutches the wolf close, staring into its yellow thread eyes.

*"Are you right all the time?* I'm *not."*

But he *is* right. He knows it. And this proves it. Someone else can see.

Someone institutionalized for schizophrenia, his logical mind points out. That doesn't exactly make her the best witness.

It doesn't matter, he argues with himself. She saw me. It doesn't matter if the doctors believe.

You're talking to yourself, a third part of his mind points out, causing him to first giggle and then laugh so hard his sides hurt and his eyes tear. Drugs, maybe, or stress, or relief, or *something*.

No one ever believed him before.

"Sassy? Are you all right?" asks the day nurse as she peers nervously into the room.

He manages to nod, and as she comes closer, concerned that he might be choking, he waves her back and manages to gasp out, "I'm fine. Really. Just. Something funny."

He gets to group and is disappointed to find that Erin isn't there. Discreet inquiries to other patients reveal that she had an episode the day before, probably around the time that he was busy screaming at Doctor Madison.

It doesn't take long for him to convince some of the other patients to create a distraction for him so he can slip past Erin's guards and into her room. He can be very persuasive when he chooses to be.

She is still asleep and would look peaceful if not for the way that she occasionally tugs at her restraints, without quite waking. In spots, her brown hair sticks up in frayed bunches, where something not quite sharp enough sheared through the waist-length locks and cut them to only a few inches long.

He touches one of those ragged tufts, wondering what happened, and then sighs.

"How do you accept it, when you see something, and everyone around you tells you that it isn't there?" he asks. Her eyelashes flicker, but she doesn't wake. "How do you know they're right, when your senses tell you different?" His voice is nearly a whisper, and cracks as he says, "How do I know I'm not just crazy?"

Her eyes flutter open. It takes a while for them to focus on him, and when they finally mostly do, she frowns a little. "Sassy? What are you doing here?" Except the words are slurred: *Sas's . . . Whattayoodo'ghere?*

He smooths hair back from her face. "Just came to say hi. Thank you for the gift."

She squeezes her eyes shut with a wince.

"Erin?" He asks because he realizes he doesn't even know if she's herself. He hasn't met her alter.

"It's me," she says. "They messed with my meds. New ones aren't working."

"What do you see?" he asks.

She shakes her head and says something too softly for him to hear.

"What?"

"I wish I was as sure as you," she says, struggling a little to form the sentence. "Even if I was wrong and no one believed me, I think I would be happy, if only I was *sure.*"

"You're something of a philosopher, Erin," he says, smoothing her hair. On a whim, he leans down and kisses her. "And you might be my prince charming," he adds as he stands up straight again.

Despite the drugs, she manages to look startled. "I—what?"

"Never mind. I'll talk to you later, when you're more awake."

* * *

He walks toward his daily appointment with Doctor Madison with his thoughts alternating between contemplation and dread. Erin is right. Whether or not the doctors believe, *he* knows what the truth is. Right?

But even so, tonight will be another bad night. Tomorrow he will again wake in bandages and restraints. Even if he stops trying to get the doctors to believe him, he can't help what will happen when the moon rises, and the doctors will never let him go free until he *can*.

The thought makes him run a hand down the wolf's fur.

"Sassy?"

He turns as Nurse Sanford calls his name. "Yes?"

"I heard the end of your fight with Doctor Madison."

"I imagine most of the building did."

She nods. "Obviously, I can't help you much with a day trip. I just don't have the authority," she says, which makes him *huff* and start to walk past her, "but I wondered if it might make you feel better if you moved into a room on the other side of the building? Another patient checked out of here a few hours ago, and the free room has a very nice view of the grounds, instead of looking straight at a brick wall like your current room. Would that—"

She doesn't have a chance to finish her question before he throws his arms around her neck in a hug.

As he pushes open the door to Doctor Madison's office a minute later, he cannot help the spring in his step. A view of the grounds would mean a view of the sky. Of the moon. Please, God, a view of the moon.

"Are we feeling better today?" the doctor asks.

"I don't know about 'we,'" he replies, "but *I* am."

"Where did the dog come from?" she asks.

He is still holding the wolf, and now he clutches it against his chest. "Gift from God. Came through my window on a rainbow. God talks to me in my sleep, you know."

He is perhaps the only person in the ward who can claim to hear God speak to him and receive only a "Mm-hmm." The doctor doesn't even bother to write down a note.

"Erin gave it to you, right?"

"Isn't it boring to constantly ask questions you know the answers to?" He picks up the book that is once again on the coffee table and idly flips through the pages. He is in a good mood, but that doesn't mean he is in a mood to play Freud.

"So, the lies are meant to spice up my life, are they?" Doctor Madison asks.

He shrugs. "What can I say? I'm a giver."

She laughs and shakes her head. "It's nice to see you and Erin getting along."

He pets the wolf again. "Erin's okay. Garbled in the brain, but maybe we all are. Ain't nothing till you call it, right?" He drops the book suddenly enough that Doctor Madison jumps at the *thump* it makes as it hits the table.

"The table is empty," he declares.

"Are we back to this?"

"It *always* comes back to this," he says. "Reality. Fantasy. And the fact that you don't care what's *true*. You just care about what's *easy*."

"Sassy." At his sharp look, she realizes she has just sighed his name again, so she continues quickly. "I've been working with you for two months now. What can I possibly do to earn your trust?"

"*Believe me*. But you won't. I get it. I wouldn't want to, either."

Tonight. A view of the moon, and then he would show her, and she would *have* to believe him.

Dusk falls slowly. The light drains from the sky like molasses dripping, as he waits impatiently, one hand against the shatterproof glass windowpane.

He has started to feel the itch all along the surface of his skin, not intolerable yet, but growing rapidly.

The moon, when it rises, seems to make an audible *ring*, like a bell inside his head. He was right; it is full, and it is beautiful in the clear night sky. He watches it rise, feeling the pressure inside grow, grow. . . .

He rubs his hands along his arms. He closes his eyes, but he can still see the moon. Feel it. Hear it. Almost *smell* the moonlight.

"Checks!" Nurse Sanford peers inside. "Enjoying the view, Sassy?"

"Yes. Thank you." His voice is tight, but the gratitude is real.

"Do try to get some sleep."

"In just a little while."

The door has barely closed behind her when his knees give out. The moonlight seems to sear his skin, but it isn't fire that crosses his flesh but fur. Muscles expand, twist, contort—ecstasy.

The hyena stretches, shaking its coarse coat. He rolls onto his back, kicking his legs, his *real* legs. He would like to run, but he is content for now to stretch. He can be patient, now that he has the proof: This is *real*, and he will show them, and they will believe.

Suddenly, the memory of walking into school that last day washes over him so vividly he thinks he can taste the pills and smell the blood. Fear, desperation, despair; he hadn't known any other way to get anyone to listen to him, to do anything but laugh and say, "Sassy's such a wit."

*. . . if only I were sure.*

The hyena bounds onto the bed, muzzle down to lift the blankets so he can wriggle under them. He stretches out, which makes him just as long as a man, and rests one paw on the plush wolf Erin gave him.

The door opens, with a quiet, "Checks?"

Nurse Sanford is a good woman. She can keep her easy understanding of reality.

"Good night, Sassy," she whispers upon seeing the shape, apparently fast asleep, bundled up under the covers.

The final diagnosis was generalized anxiety disorder, compounded by severe claustrophobia, and treatable in the eyes of psychopharmacology through simple antianxiety medication.

The diagnosis was a lie that everyone was comfortable with. It didn't matter that they believed him. He not only didn't need to try to change their reality, maybe he didn't have a *right* to.

All that mattered was, the next month, he could run.

# INCIDENT REPORT

**Joshua Gee**

**Infraction #1 of 3: Failure to Execute Primary Directive**

"Sylvia, my dear, how many times do I have to tell you not to leave your manual lying on the patient?"

"Three," I muttered. "Probably. I don't know."

That was only a guess, of course. I didn't even remember taking the Diagnostic Manual out of my pocket. As soon as I began working on the ward three days ago, I'd quickly made a habit of forgetting most if not all of the things Rosalita told me. Forgetting was something I knew how to do. Forgetting was my talent—my only talent, said Rosalita—and it got me through the day.

She withdrew the E.V. needle from the patient's wrist-lock, carefully wiping a stray drop of blood from the device's access point. "I think we're going to need something a little bigger," she said, disguising a demand as an opinion.

"Are you sure I'm ready to be doing this?" I asked.

Without looking at me, she squinted at a blurry red splotch on the wrist-lock's magnifier lens.

"Hurry up," she said. "It's not going to dilate forever."

"Here," I said, unsure if "it" referred to the vein or the patient—and handing Rosalita what looked to me like a seven-millimeter. Shaking her head in disapproval, she got up from her stool, dropped the used Number Six down the biohazard chute, and took a fresh Number Seven from the utility tray.

"Of course, you're *supposed* to be doing this," she finally said, not quite answering my question, her voice resembling the inexplicably happy chirping of a canary being swallowed by a snake. "They wouldn't have sent you up here if you were insufficiently trained. And besides—the Administration doesn't make mistakes. Especially not mistakes like that. Where were you before this?"

"Breakfast."

"Are you really this dumb, or did they send you to test me?"

"Oh, you mean, like, where was I assigned? I carried canisters. I don't know what was in them. I only carried them."

"A canister carrier?" she bellowed in disgust. "They sent me a canister carrier? You mean like these?"

I nodded as she stood up and placed a calloused, bloated hand on the one-gallon barrel dangling from a hook in the ceiling, then pressed a glowing switch on the apparatus tower attached to the bottom of the canister. "Well, okay, *canister carrier*"—she kept repeating the word as if it were a synonym for *cavegirl*—"I have a different job for you now that I've gotten the needle in."

She placed the E.V. tubing in my right hand. It pulsated, rubbery and leechlike, between my thumb and my index finger.

"You're about to find out what's inside the canisters."

This was my first day on E.V. duty. I didn't know what might happen next because, like so many aspects of my life inside the Facility, I deliberately hadn't thought about the details. I didn't want to know the meaning of the word *extravenous*. Nonetheless, as I sat beside the patient's bed, I guess my curiosity did compel me to stare up at the canister and await something, anything, that might explain what exactly happens in these patients' rooms and in their bodies, day after day after day.

I was staring in the wrong direction. The canister—or the apparatus attached to the bottom of it—began to jostle. The pastel green tubing turned dark. Fluid was traveling *from* the patient. "It's a vacuum pump," I murmured.

"What a gifted young lady," said Rosalita. "The Administration told me you have potential, if only you'd apply yourself. And, silly me, I didn't believe it."

"What happens now?"

"Set it and forget it," she chirped, her smile as fake as the vitamin-enhanced, biogenetic salad bar in the cafeteria. "You monitor the flow. I'll be in the break room."

She tossed me her clipboard and finished tidying up the utility tray.

"No, wait," I said, but my hollow voice disappeared amid the hum of the E.V. apparatus. Seconds later, a quick glance at the clipboard changed everything. I was startled to discover the patient had a name, and even more startled by something else.

"Rosalita! Wait! I'm not supposed to be doing this. . . ."

"Doing what? I don't know what you mean." The uncharacteristic lack of arrogance in her voice told me otherwise. She obviously knew the clipboard was not on her side. It clearly stated who was to do what to whom in Room 219 that morning.

"It was *my* job to attach the E.V. apparatus and press the switch."

"The switch is to be pulled, not pressed," she said, her eyes peering fiercely in my direction without really looking at me, as if she were planning her next move. Then she tugged at the hem of her blouse and straightened her posture. "Front Desk?"

"Yeah . . . they'll need . . . wait—what?"

"Not you, Sylvia. Front Desk? This is room two nineteen."

Rosalita was now facing a mirror on the tile wall opposite the bed. I assumed the intercom in this room was somewhere underneath the mirror or the tiles . . . or maybe everywhere. *Maybe the tiles are the intercom!* I theorized, making sense not even to myself. I had never noticed the tiling before, though—not in this room or in any other. Each tile was only two-by-two inches at the most. Each cell in the endless grid so dry and green and dull, like synthetic mucus hardened into squares.

Four walls, a ceiling, and a floor. One window and a door. No tiles on the window, of course, and no tiles on the door. How many tiles were inside this room if *x* equaled tiles and *y* equaled inches? Was the same tiling in the hallway? In my dormitory? I couldn't remember.

This is why my bedside manner needs improvement. A nurse's life requires no theories. The Administration performs the algebra. My only goals should be efficiency and versatility and the unflagging will to perform one task—*any* task—every day. Otherwise, I'm of no use to anybody.

I looked at Rosalita as she tightened the bun in her graying hair, and I silently resolved to be more like her.

Finally, a staticky, hissing sound, and then . . .

~*This is Front Desk. Query?*~

"Could you please confirm Sylvia's Primary Directive for today?"

~*Of course. One minute, please.*~

Only it didn't take anywhere near that long.

~*She's to attach two nineteen's E.V. tube and flip the switch.*~

Rosalita began to say, "*Press* the—" but bit her bottom lip instead. "If that's her Primary Directive, then what's mine?" she finally asked in a hushed whisper, as though it was possible for me not to hear the remainder of the conversation.

~*Your role is to assist.*~

"I'm sorry, Front Desk," she said. "I must have an outdated call sheet on my clipboard."

~*Will that be all, Rosalita?*~

"Yes, Front Desk. Thank you." She didn't seem to notice that the crackle and the hiss had stopped a moment before. The wall had finished listening.

"Well, the needle's already in, so you can do that tomorrow—if your directive remains the same."

We stared awkwardly at the patient. "Doesn't it scar?" I finally asked.

"What? The needle?"

"Yes."

"No. On the forearm, nothing smaller than a sixer leaves a scar. The same is true of the vertebrae and the temporal lobes. Discretion is of utmost importance to the Administration."

It seemed rude to point out the fact that we had inserted

something larger than a "sixer" in 219's arm, so I exercised restraint.

"You are dismissed," she said. "Go study your manual—from the beginning."

She hadn't looked me in the eye since conversing with the wall. Why did she humiliate herself like that when she must have known we'd been given the correct orders? It didn't seem like Rosalita, and all it did was make me angry.

**Infraction #2 of 3: Failure to Accommodate Patient's Needs Quickly and Courteously**

The next day was a tetrodotoxin day. Rosalita was anxiously tapping the FLUSH button on the tetrodotoxin-saline drip, eager for the ancient-looking apparatus to unclog itself and reverse suction.

"Did you hear me?" she asked.

"Yes, you said the interval has almost lapsed. He's in danger of waking up unless—"

"Don't think I'll hesitate to notify the Front Desk of your little hearing problem."

Really, it was more of a staring problem. The day before, it had been the tiles. Now, it was the patient.

I'd heard rumors about the patients on the ward: The blood goes out; the medicine goes in. During previous assignments, I had never really looked at what—or rather, *who*—was actually attached to the apparatus. It's like the way some people can't look at needles, except I'm that way about patients. *An arm and a vein*, I reminded myself. *That's all he is*.

It didn't work. A few things that I had noticed about 219: He was male; he was around my age; and even beneath two bedsheets, he appeared to be the thinnest person I had ever seen.

I wanted to go back to being just another human utility designed to carry unidentifiable objects—except I knew it didn't work that way. At the Facility, there's nowhere to go but up.

Rosalita, obviously more of a "people person" than I am, was presiding over the patient's bedside like a chef waiting for a pot of sauce to boil, when she whispered the first of many odd statements. "First we kill them," she said. "Then we make them mad."

"What?"

"It's an old saying. It's not entirely accurate, I suppose. The process doesn't always happen in that order, of course. Whatever the donor wants, the donor gets, right?"

"The donor?"

"Whoever submitted him for treatment."

"What does the donor want for him?"

"In this case . . . nothing," she murmured, glancing at her clipboard. She seemed to disappear inside herself for a moment. "They just wanted to get rid of him. I'm guessing they sold him to the highest bidder."

"Meaning, us."

"Correct. He still has a lot of years left in him, though, if he learns to do what he's told. His resale value will be enormous." She was busily unsealing a fresh canister of chemicals, and I was surprised to discover the liquid looked exactly like blood. "You know, Sylvia, a lot of the girls, they arrive on the ward and they discover what we do and they think we take the patient's vital fluids. You probably thought that, didn't you?"

"But . . . don't we?"

"Don't we what?"

"Take their blood."

Rosalita looked at the canister as if she had never actually thought about any of this before. "Well, yes, I *suppose*, but we always give it back right after we process it. Most of it, at least." She hoisted the canister up onto the hook. "Anyway, there's no money in processing blood. We process people."

I couldn't understand why she was revealing all of this to me. It didn't seem like information an Assistant Nurse needed to know. "Why do you keep whispering? He can't hear you, can he?"

She seemed frustrated with me, but I couldn't figure out why. "The problem with all the new girls is that they're either slow or they're stupid," she said, much louder now. "Which one are you?"

I didn't know if that was a rhetorical question, or what.

"At any rate, Sylvia, everything is in your Diagnostic Manual, but you wouldn't know that, would you?"

I casually brushed my hand against my hip pocket to make sure I'd even remembered to bring the manual on the ward.

"It's right here," she said, handing it to me. "Did you read Chapter One last night, like I told you?"

"Yes," I lied. "Of course."

"Well, it's not enough to read it. You must commit it to memory. Internalize it. Make it your own."

"That's not the chapter I'm worried about," I said as I gazed up at the tetrodotoxin-saline canister, and she knew exactly what I was getting at. "It's just, I don't know if I can put this stuff in him."

"I don't care," she replied instantly, as if she'd been expecting this act of treachery the whole time. "If you don't fulfill your Primary Directive for today, somebody else will. And then somebody else will do it tomorrow, and the day after. Somebody will also resuscitate him in three weeks; somebody else will deprogram him, educate him, and train him. He will perform whatever vile duty his next owners prescribe for him. The integrity of the Administration depends on it. Therefore, *your* integrity depends on it. Now, Sylvia, need I remind you how much the Administration values your integrity?"

She was fixing her hair in the mirror, addressing my reflection, and smiling devilishly. I didn't know how to respond, so I only listened.

"You want my advice? My advice would be to not trouble yourself with any of life's tough little questions. All you need to do is obey your Primary Directive. The Administration never burdens us with any task we're incapable of performing. Our jobs couldn't be more simple, Sylvia, and girls like you make my life considerably more complicated than necessary."

"Girls like me?" I shouted, astonished by my own words. "You don't even know me!"

My outburst was short-lived. Somebody else responded to Rosalita's tirade, but with only a word. No, a syllable . . .

*"—ah—?"*

I thought maybe it was the word *stop*. The intercom? Obviously incorrect because Rosalita appeared panic-stricken, too. She sprang to action, swooping around me and expertly clicking the patient's wrist-lock into the metal rail on the side of the bed.

"Attach the wrist," she said. "Now! I've got the other one."

The patient had spoken. Could patients do that? I didn't know until then.

"Do you see what you did, Sylvia? I mean, *really*! This is what happens when you distract me and fail to execute orders as promptly and courteously as possible. There's no way in hell that I'm going to take one iota of responsibility for this little mishap. I'll file a full report about this if that's what it takes."

Throughout Rosalita's entire diatribe, the patient continued murmuring, although anything he had to say was clearly irrelevant to her. As I secured 219's arm, I leaned down and turned my ear toward him as closely and inconspicuously as possible. I was unspeakably curious to know how it felt to be so close to one of them. May the Administration forgive me.

Suddenly, his breath kissed the back of my neck, and I recoiled in disgust.

*"Mom?"*

"What?" asked Rosalita. "What did he just say?"

"No!" I shouted. "No!" Even now, I'm uncertain if I was addressing 219 or Rosalita. All I can remember is the way his eyelids popped open so violently and then fluttered shut, slowly, as Rosalita pressed—no, *pulled*, this time—the switch. The tetrodotoxin-saline drip entered his body, and with that he quickly drifted away to a different place.

"These things don't happen when we obey orders, Sylvia. Shut the door tightly behind you, and I'll see that he doesn't wake up again."

I desperately resented the patient—whoever he was—for subjecting me to that one intolerable act of intimacy. Or did I resent him for leaving me just as fast?

"Go study your manual, Sylvia! You'll be thankful you did!"

No, I didn't resent the patient at all. The enemy, I realized, was Rosalita.

**Infraction #3 of 3: Inability to Maintain Effective Rapport with Coworkers**

*I'm just not going to look this time*, I said to myself, and obviously, that was my first mistake. Tell yourself not to look at a boy and you'll look at him all day long.

No, I should have told myself nothing and then I would have thought of nothing, and only then would I have done nothing.

"You're late," said Rosalita as she handed me a pair of powdery, black latex gloves. "So I've taken the liberty of withdrawing the drip without you. Today, of course, we reinsert the E.V. I hope you hit the books last night because I won't be picking up the slack. If the Administration wants you to insert the E.V., then it's your Primary Directive, not mine. And it will be *your* worthless little butt, not mine, that—"

The tirade continued—although, because I've been denied access to some surveillance transcripts, I can't convey all of her words exactly.

Here is how I experienced what happened next: I was transfixed by 219's contorted body, and I was more dubious than ever about the Diagnostic Manual's claims that treatment is painless. His wrists were locked into the bed, and his chest was arched higher than his head and abdomen. He looked something like the letter *W* written in desiccated flesh and bone.

And his face—so frozen, so hideously pale. As recently as six months ago, he might have been living in a college dorm. What could he—or anybody—possibly do to deserve such absolute erasure?

For some reason, he looked like a soccer player to me. I momentarily pictured him on the field, the hero of his parents and his friends and maybe his entire school. I could see it—vividly—if only he had a little more meat on his body and a less-than-grotesque look on his face.

Or maybe I knew a soccer player once. A boy who looked just like him . . .

And then it was gone. I couldn't remember soccer, or boys, or anything that came before this place, but I wanted it back. All of it. Even if I had to take it.

So, on this isolated occasion, thought triggered action; stimulus led to response. And that's how I found myself gripping the clipboard securely with both latex-protected hands; rotating it so the clip faced the side of Rosalita's head; and pummeling her, forcefully and promptly and not at all painlessly.

And then—perhaps, in hindsight, to insulate myself from the severity of my actions—I found myself swinging my right arm in a big circle and giggling, only a little. *A soccer player?* I remember thinking. *No, maybe softball was my sport. . . .*

I describe these profane thoughts at length to explain exactly how and why I cracked Rosalita's clipboard this morning. Beyond all of that, the degree to which my actions were premeditated will be for the Administration to decide.

My mentor—my tormentor—was bruised but not yet unconscious until I offered one more blow. The muscles in my arms—the biceps, I believe the manual calls them—stretched in ways that felt eerily unfamiliar, like I was borrowing somebody else's body. Regardless of its owner, my body thanked me with an unexpected jolt of adrenaline, and along with the surge of energy came an even greater tsunami inside me that I can only describe as a sense of purpose, dangerous and addictive.

I took Rosalita's place on the bedside stool, mindful of the fact that the E.V. tube was detached, but the tetrodotoxin-saline needle hadn't yet been inserted.

"Two nineteen, can you hear me?" I said. "The Primary Directive for today has changed."

The interval had been a few minutes already.

"Please wake up, two nineteen. I am obligated to notify you of a reversal in protocol. Rosalita, whom you've already met, will be on break while you assist me in my efforts to . . . ugh!"

I couldn't listen to the sound of my own voice. Probably because it *wasn't* my own voice. All I could hear were the Administration's words, carefully prescribed by the Diagnostic Manual for any eventuality. Seemingly even this.

It was time for a different approach.

"Mr. Ackley . . . Clayton? Is that your name? I want you to tell me if you think you can go for a walk."

His eyelids were quivering. I looked around the room and made sure the door was shut. Of course there wasn't much to see. Just the medical apparatus and a chair and those awful green tiles, some of which were now speckled with the former contents of Rosalita's lower jaw area.

It was a day of new thoughts. (Or were they very old thoughts?) But I quickly identified one emotion that was not at all foreign to me.

"Trapped," I said.

*"Mom?"*

"Mr. Ackley! No, no . . . not your mom."

"But . . . where? I heard . . ."

Looking at Rosalita—the tone of her voice so soothing unless you listened to the meaning of her words—I suddenly realized the mistake 219 had made. "Yes, that was your mother. She wants you to wake up. She had to go, but she'll be back soon. And you'll get to see her again. I promise."

By now, I had taken off one glove and placed my right hand against the side of 219's face. His hand clutched mine. He was so cold!

"Please," I begged, somehow whispering and shouting at the same time. "Please, I need you to wake up. We have to move you before—"

*Before a lot of things*, I thought. What was I doing? I had no plan. Just my anger, which was rapidly turning inward toward myself.

I looked around the room one more time. There were three options:

1. The door: This led to the hallway, and the hallway led to the Front Desk.

2. The window: Even if it wasn't cemented shut behind two layers of Plexiglas and a steel grate, it led to a ten-story drop, if the rumors about the Facility's exterior were to be believed.

3. The biohazard chute.

"There's no way," gurgled 219. Apparently, he had been watching me. For how long was I opening and closing the chute? Sizing it up? Sizing *us* up?

"Well, we have to try!" I said. "If we can just get the door off, I think we can both fit. You're even skinnier than I am, Clayton."

"What are you talking—"

Before he could finish the sentence, he was silenced by the sight of his own frail body. For some reason, he seemed particularly disturbed by his fingernails, which were extremely long, until he noticed the wrist-lock on his left arm, which was extremely leaky. He gazed up at the E.V. apparatus, and judging by the look of horror on his face, he summed it up pretty fast—much faster than it took me to figure it all out.

"Clayton. Wherever you think you are, you are probably someplace much, much worse. I'm going to get you out of here, though. We're going to get each other out."

"No," he said, leaning back in the bed again.

"What?"

"I don't deserve it."

"What are you talking about? Do you know what they're trying to do to you? They're replacing your blood with chemicals!"

"I was sent here for a reason."

"Clayton—"

"Why do you keep calling me that?"

"Because that's your name, Clayton." I assumed it was the "medicine" talking, not him.

"My name is Brian. Brian . . ."

I looked at his data sheet again while he struggled to recall his last name. "No, it's not Brian. The clipboard says . . ."

But it didn't matter what the clipboard said. It was a lie. The Administration had already taken his name, just like they'd taken everything else.

"Your name still belongs to you. Try to remember."

"No, I don't want to. I hurt somebody."

"Hurt somebody how . . . ?" I asked, nauseous, my voice growing quieter and quieter.

"I did things," he said. "To somebody." The muscles in his face undulated and tightened. "No, I did . . . a lot of things."

"Well," I said, without looking at him, "I don't care. Just let me find my . . . and I'll . . . I don't know. The manual has an answer for . . ."

Unable to focus, I groped around the bed for the Diagnostic Manual, the only thing that felt familiar. I got up and looked beneath the bed. It wasn't there.

*But Rosalita's two feet suddenly were.*

Standing now, fully conscious, looking me in the eye, Rosalita was creeping forward and slowly raising her hand. I readied myself for a blow to the side of the head. None came. Instead, she put her index finger to her mouth, both caked with blood, as if to say, "Shhh."

She wasn't looking at me. She was looking at 219. He was now holding the Diagnostic Manual at an odd angle and trying to make sense of something he was reading in Chapter One—or on those same pages, at least.

*"Sylvia, don't,"* he whispered in a strangely monotone voice. *"It's a test."*

"What? How do you know my name?"

He turned the page and read, "*'You are being trained to kill.'*" And there was more:

"*'Statistical profiles predict you'll assault soon.'*"

"*'Take a life and graduate to permanent staff.'*"

"*'Kill no one and escape.'*"

He handed me my manual. There was one handwritten message for each day I had worked alongside Rosalita, hidden in tiny print in the margins along the binding.

"His mother sold him to us," she said with much effort—and too few teeth by half. "This boy was practically born to kill. It's all on the clipboard. But you never were good at preparing, were you?"

Staring my own violence in the face, I tried to comprehend her agony but knew I never would.

Turning back to the first page of the manual, I saw my name—*"Sylvia"*—written in quotation marks. "And me?" I asked urgently. "How do I figure out my . . . donor?"

"If you don't remember, you've lost it forever."

Those were Rosalita's final words. She smiled—perhaps vengefully, perhaps not. I'll never know.

All I could hear now was the crackle and the hiss of the intercom. I didn't need the Front Desk to inform me that they had been listening all along, but the Front Desk informed me, regardless.

Rosalita had been right. They never make mistakes.

# SCAPEGOAT

**Robin Wasserman**

After I mopped up most of the blood, I buried her in the backyard. There were still a few spatters on the wall and some gunk lodged in the corner where a mop wouldn't do much good, but there'd be plenty of time later to scrub it by hand. I wanted to get the shoveling out of the way before nightfall—they were calling for rain.

Does it make me a murderer, what I've done? I don't know. I prefer the term mercy killer.

Though there wasn't much room for mercy, not at the end.

I guess it doesn't matter what you call me—sticks and stones, and all that. I can bear any label. Except for "hero," that is. Much as it may seem to apply, it just doesn't feel right. This isn't false modesty. I know what I've done. I know how many lives I've saved. And don't get me wrong—sometimes I wish I didn't have to keep the secret. It would be nice to be thanked, just once.

But mostly I'm okay with staying undercover. I don't need gratitude, I don't need a parade, a comic book, a catchy theme song. Like I say, I'm no hero. I just did what needed to be done. Anyone would have done it, if they'd seen what I saw.

It's just that I was the only one who knew to look.

She was good, I'll give her that. The day Parker Kent first appeared, I had no idea I'd soon be burning towels stained with her blood or planting a new row of seedlings along the fresh mound so that, come spring, her body would disappear beneath the rosebushes.

Parker was annoying on that first day, sure, her pink hair band matching her pink shirt matching her pink shoes, her face all wide-eyed and smiley, her voice so sweet and perky as she pleased and thank-you'd everyone from the cafeteria ladies to the freshmen. But plenty of people are annoying.

Not all of them are evil.

You might think that the other girls detected it before I did, from the way they shielded their faces from her in the halls and erected a quarantine space around her in the cafeteria, like they could sense what lay behind the curtain of blond hair and the dimpled smile. But I knew better. After all, there was a quarantine space around me, too.

So I knew that when they avoided Parker Kent, it wasn't because they sensed what she was capable of. They weren't picking up some invisible vibrations of impending doom. Their radars weren't tuned for the music of the soul; they were calibrated to measure hemlines, brand names, purse size, eyeliner color, whether a heel was chunky or stiletto, an earring stud or hoop, a nail properly manicured or bitten down until the cuticle bled. They'd needed only thirty seconds to appraise Parker.

It was obvious she'd set the alarm bells ringing.

Danger.

Loser alert.

Stay away.

I used to think those girls were evil, especially when they did things like hide my clothes during gym so I had to wear my gym uniform all day, or leave a dab of red paint on my chair the day I was stupid enough to wear white pants. (Now I wear only black; problem solved.) I threw the word "evil" around a lot, back in those days. Back before I knew what it really meant.

Don't get me wrong, I still hate them. But that doesn't mean they deserve to die.

Parker sat down across from me in the cafeteria, even though the table was empty from end to end and I shot her the look that screamed, *Go away*. Now I know that even then, the thing was inside of her—that she *chose* me. But at the time, I just thought she was an imbecile.

So I hunched over my tray, stuffing my face like always—fast and messy, without pause, because the sooner I finished, the sooner I could escape—and waited for her to get a clue.

"My name's Parker," she chirped. "We just moved here—my dad got some big job at a law firm in town."

I grunted.

A piece of popcorn landed on the table, then rolled off. Another one sailed over and lodged in Parker's hair. I waited for her to start crying.

"So you just sit here every day and let these bitches throw crap at you?" she asked instead.

I looked up. "You got a better suggestion?"

"We get out of here." Parker didn't wait for me to agree. She just sauntered out of the cafeteria while the hall monitors weren't looking and, by the time I caught up with her, was already busting through the back doors and heading for the parking lot. Strictly out of bounds and against the rules.

We ate at Burger King, then decided that seeing the new Jacques Millard movie would be more beneficial than calculus. It was in French, which, as Parker pointed out, technically made it educational.

And when Parker sneaked us in for free, I got a decent lesson in economics, too.

The movie sucked. But I didn't care. And after a while, I didn't care that Parker dressed like a Tupperware lady. She had a pack of clove cigarettes hidden in her flowery pink purse and wasn't stingy about sharing. She liked Ayn Rand and Vonnegut and had the correct opinion on Salinger (yes to *Nine Stories*, a resounding no to *Catcher in the Rye)*. She snagged us a couple bottles of soda from the back of the drugstore, smiling brightly at the rent-a-cop by the door as we strolled out without paying, then, also from the pink purse, produced a miniature bottle of rum to go with our Coke.

She was, in short, what my mother used to call a bad girl. Just the way I like them.

Which is maybe why, even though it's in my nature to be suspicious, I didn't think anything of the dark red stain smeared across the front seat of her car. She said it was nail polish.

I believed her.

Bloodstains.

There's a reason Lady Macbeth had so much trouble washing it off her hands. And she's not the only one.

But the real trouble, I've found, is getting it out of the carpet.

I like to treat it with liquid soap crystals and then saturate it with a borax solution. Hydrogen peroxide works well, too, if you let it soak. But Parker's blood has proved especially stubborn, and I suspect it will leave a brownish smear no matter what I do.

I can always buy a throw rug.

"Get your cat away from me," Parker complained. She was stretched out on the couch while Mr. Magoo paced along the edge. He crouched by her head, his hind legs quivering as they always did when he prepared to pounce. To him, her face probably looked like a giant pink rat.

He couldn't see very well—at least, that's what we figured from the way he was always running into walls. It's why my father named him Mr. Magoo. But usually I just called him Maggie.

Maggie hissed at Parker. Parker hissed back. "I'm allergic," she said apologetically as I picked up Maggie and tossed him into the den. He was just a skinny stray when we took him in, but by that day he must have weighed at least twenty pounds. He slept in my bed, curled up between my feet.

Except that night, he didn't. That night, after we'd finished experimenting with different pizza toppings, stuffed ourselves with coffee ice cream, and dozed off in the middle of *Saturday Night Live,* Parker padded upstairs to my room and stretched out on the sleeping bag I'd laid next to my bed. Maggie got dumped in the hallway, mewing and scratching at the closed door. Parker said she wouldn't be able to sleep, lying there in the dark imagining the cat about to pounce. And also that he made her sneeze.

I turned out the lights.

"Josh Porter asked me out," Parker said suddenly, like she'd been waiting for dark.

I didn't say anything.

"He wants to go to the movies Friday night." She giggled softly. I'd never heard her giggle before. "He's hot, but I could never fall in love with him. Imagine if we got married. Parker Porter? Gross."

"So you're not going?"

It seemed like a stupid reason not to go out with someone. I could think of plenty of better ones. Like the fact that he was an asshole. Or the fact that he was a moronic meathead who didn't know how to talk about anything but sports. Or maybe the fact that he only dated the kind of girl who plucked her eyebrows and had tinkly hip-hop ring tones on her cell phone.

"Of course I'm going!" she said. "It's *Josh Porter.*"

"I thought we were going to the *Rocky Horror Picture Show* on Friday."

"Oh . . . yeah." She paused. "Can't we do it on Saturday or something?"

"It's not playing on Saturday," I pointed out. "Only Friday." But she already knew that.

Parker sighed. "Look, I didn't want to say anything before, because you were so into it, but the whole *Rocky Horror* thing, dressing up in costumes, and those freaks who've got all the lines memorized—"

"Freaks like me?" I asked quietly.

"Of course not."

I didn't like talking to her in the dark. I couldn't see her face.

"Can't you just go to the movies with someone else on Friday?" she asked, her voice tight and thin. "We can hang out sometime next week."

"What happened to Saturday?"

"Well . . . Josh said something about a party on Saturday, some guys from the soccer team, and I thought I might check it out. You know, if the date goes okay? You could come, too . . . I just know you hate that kind of thing."

"Yeah," I muttered. "And you're *so* going to love it."

Parker sat up in her sleeping bag and turned her face to me, but all I could see was her silhouette outlined against the dark. "What's your problem?"

"Nothing. Do whatever you want."

"Oh, don't worry." Her voice was cold. "I always do."

Josh Porter would never go out with someone like Parker, I thought, unless it was the setup for some kind of elaborate joke. And the Parker *I* knew would never go out with Josh Porter. It was unnatural, out of place, which made it a clue, some glimpse of what she really was—and maybe if I'd seen it then, a lot of things would be different. Maybe I could have stopped her in time.

But I wasn't looking for clues. I'd convinced myself there was no need for vigilance; I'd convinced myself the worst was over. So I just turned over on my side and waited to fall asleep. I couldn't. I stared into the dark, my knees curled up toward my chest, listening to her breathe. I pressed my hand against the wall, grazed my fingers against the pitted paint. It was comforting to touch something concrete, something *real*—like a weapon against the shadows.

I clung to the concrete, the talismans of normal life, the wall, the bed, the steady breathing in and out of a friend drifting into sleep. They helped me forget what I knew to be true, that there was plenty more to fear than fear itself. But it's dangerous to forget too much, and remembering tended to keep me awake. So I heard her unzip the sleeping bag, stand up, and tiptoe out of the room. And I was still awake when she finally came back.

The next morning, I found Mr. Magoo dead on the porch. A rusty stain of blood crusted the fur around his mouth.

That's when I knew what she was.

Because I'd been there before. The last time, it had started with our dog, his head bashed in with a hammer. That had been the beginning.

I'd told myself it had ended, that the evil was vanquished, that I was safe. But now it was starting all over again.

Parker found me on the porch, cradling Maggie, his body cold and stiff in my arms.

She gasped, her eyes wide with fake horror. "What happened?"

"I think you know," I said, and behind her eyes, I saw something flicker. It wasn't like they flashed red or started spinning in circles; real evil isn't so cartoonish. It's subtle, and it's quiet, and it's something you can only see if you know how to look. "I heard you get up in the middle of the night. I know what you were doing. I just don't get why."

"Are you crazy?" she said, playing defense. "Why would I do something to your cat?"

She was right, of course. It sounded crazy. But it was also true, and we both knew it. I could see it in her tense smile, in the tiny muscle that twitched at the corner of her eye. I could *smell* it on her. Not the cat—the hunger.

An appetite for destruction.

And she planned to use me to get the job done.

It took a couple hours and left my knees red and tender from kneeling on the linoleum for so long, but I finally got the blood cleaned away. I burned the rags in the fireplace, along with Parker's clothes and the clothes I wore when I had to kill her. It's too bad about my black turtleneck—it'll be hard to find another wool sweater that doesn't itch around the collar.

I don't know how many of them are still out there.

I know now that more will come—and, like the thing that called itself Parker, they will choose me. They always choose me.

I don't know why.

I know a lot—I know too much—and yet there are still questions. Endless questions, and no one to ask. No rulebook. No mystical adviser appearing out of the fog to reveal my destiny. If this were a movie, I'd have one, and he'd probably be hot. Maybe British. But it's become clear that no one's showing up—I'm on my own. My only weapon is my ability to recognize them for what they are. The things I don't know may keep me awake at night, but the things I *do* know have kept me alive.

What I know.

I know it starts with animals. The innocent ones, the ones close to me, are the first to die. This is their warm-up, their appetizer, their kindling. They lay the groundwork, prepare themselves—prepare *me*. Then, when the hunger grows unbearable, the real killing begins.

I know they depend on trust. They need me to believe in them, while doubting myself. Doubt makes them strong.

I know they're parasites. Invisible invaders. One of them chose Parker Kent—and I know there was, once, a real Parker Kent, a normal, good, *human* Parker Kent—and stole her away from herself. Then it, the thing that used to be Parker Kent, chose me. Not to inhabit.

To destroy.

But I ruined its plans: I refused to trust it. I refused to doubt myself. And so I destroyed it first.

In the movies, when a monster dies, the body vanishes or turns into green sludge or a pile of dust. Proof that the killer is a hero, a dragon slayer. But when a monster dies in real life, the body only bleeds and turns stiff and starts to rot. Just like any other dead body. And that makes things trickier. Because people don't like to believe in monsters. Not without proof.

The next to die was the neighbor's dog. They found him in the front yard, bloated with poison. Someone had tossed him a mound of raw meat soaked in turpentine.

That afternoon I found the bottle of turpentine sitting on the dashboard of my car. I didn't know how Parker broke in, but I knew it was her. She was getting obvious, which meant she was getting hungry, which meant time was running out.

She didn't return my calls or my text messages, and at lunch she sat with Josh Porter and his idiot friends. I went back to sitting alone. But I watched her. She still looked the same, pretty and pink and perfectly harmless. I hated myself for not seeing through the act sooner, before the bodies began piling up. I didn't know what she would do next—I just knew she would find a way to pin it on me.

That's how they operate.

So I followed her when I could, waiting for her to make a move.

I was at the mall, hiding behind a mannequin as she tried on clothes with her new friends, the girls who'd decided that a perfect size two with glossy blond hair and a platinum card couldn't be all bad, not if Josh Porter had decided to date her.

I lurked outside her window as they painted their nails and smoked her clove cigarettes, ducking away every time they leaned toward the screen to blow out the smoke.

I sat a few rows back in the movie theater while she let Josh Porter slide his meaty hand up her shirt, and I saw her jam her tongue down his throat and then toss aside the popcorn so she could grab for his lap.

Days passed; nothing happened.

And then came the night she took Josh into the woods, lay down on his blanket, and let him inside of her.

I pressed my cheek against the bark and squeezed my eyes until they were nearly shut, not wanting to watch but knowing I couldn't afford to look away. It didn't last very long. Afterward, she cried fake tears, and he drove her home.

By morning, he was dead.

They found him in the woods the next day, thanks to an anonymous tip. I didn't have to see the spot to know it would be the same one, the cramped clearing between the crooked oak trees where they lay down together, where he had stripped off her clothes while she marked him for death.

There were drugs in his system, but the police had no reason to suspect an overdose, voluntary or otherwise.

They were more concerned with the fact that his throat was slit.

I woke up at six that morning, just after the sun rose, knowing something was wrong. And when I went downstairs to get the paper, I found the front door swinging open in the wind. Just inside, sitting on the welcome mat for anyone to see, was a pair of sneakers. *My* sneakers, though I hadn't worn them in months. Their treads were gunky with mud and twigs; the toe of the left shoe was scraped with blood.

Something, some tide of dread rising within me, told me to look underneath the mat.

And that's where she had hidden the knife.

Ancient history is clogged with sacrifice. Animals of all kinds massacred, mangled, gutted, burnt in offering, all as a bargaining tactic, a plea for trade. One death in exchange for rain, for harvest, for peace. For penance. Nothing special. Just another day at the altar, just another dead goat.

But once a year, one goat was spared; one goat was special. Selected by lot, the goat would tremble before the high priest, awaiting its fate. The priest would lay his hands on the head of the goat and confess all the sins of his people. A few words, a brief ceremony, a year's worth of evil deeds dumped into the goat, and the people's souls were cleansed. To redeem the community—to purify the sinners—the goat was then driven away, into the wilderness. According to some sources, it was driven over a cliff.

The Hebrew name for this goat was *Azazel*. In the 1500s, the word was misread as *ez ozel*. In English, "the goat that departs."

The goat that escapes.

The scapegoat.

The one held to blame for the sins of the world.

I knew Parker—or the thing that called itself Parker—would want me to believe that I had killed Josh. That this was *my* sin. Parker would prefer I voluntarily take the burden upon myself.

But that wasn't necessary to its plan. It was only necessary that everyone else believe it. That when someone took the blame, it would be me.

I was to be the scapegoat. Driven mad by guilt, I would throw myself off the cliff—or Parker would give me a push.

And she—it—would escape to kill again.

I knew this because I'd been through it before. And because the first time around, I'd almost fallen for it. I was the one who discovered our dog, broken and bleeding. Dead. And I was the one who discovered the hammer buried beneath a heap of clothes at the bottom of my closet, Mr. Peeper's brains still coating its head. A stray cat was next, the orange tabby that used to mew at our door begging for milk. I found its blood streaking my gray fleece gloves.

It was my secret. It was my shame.

The last time, there was no body—only tufts of fur lodged in the tread of my old boots. And still, I had no memory of it, of any of it. But I believed. And I confessed.

My parents put on such an elaborate performance—so shocked, so horrified, so many whispered conversations that were oh-so-conveniently loud enough for me to overhear—conspiring to send me away, into the wilderness, shouldering the blame for their sins. They almost had me, right up until the end. Up until they went too far.

I was crying when they stepped into the room, my head

against her body, even though it was sticky and already cold. I didn't want to remember her that way, the way I'd found her, all cut open and gushing. She hadn't just been some woman who cleaned our house once a week. She'd been like a part of the family, telling me stories of her childhood while she vacuumed the carpet or washed the windows. Sometimes I would help her mop the floor and she would tell me I reminded her of someone.

I never found out who.

They pulled me off her, their grips purpling my arms with bruises as they dragged me away. They screamed and yelled and shook me, and for a moment, I let myself believe their lies. I let myself imagine how it would have felt to wrap my hand around a kitchen knife and sneak up behind her while she scrubbed the tile. It was possible, I told myself, that I had done it—for whatever insane reason, I had actually done it—and then pushed it away, forced myself to forget, just like they said. I dug deep, trying to pry the secret out of my brain. I lost myself in that moment. I lost everything, drowning in a dark well that went down and down forever.

And then I hit bottom. It was a rock-solid barrier between what I was capable of and what they said I had done. It was impenetrable. I could never have spilled that blood; I could never have picked up the knife. But I knew who had.

I looked up at them, and for the first time in my life, I saw it. Evil. I saw past their eyes, into their souls, and knew that both of them had been somehow, irrevocably, changed. It was as if I had a new sense, as if I'd been blind from birth and then suddenly, miraculously, given the power to see.

I saw them for who they were.

For what they'd become.

Monsters.

Evil.

And so I did what needed to be done.

It's been nineteen hours since Parker showed up at my door. I called her, blubbering that something horrible had happened. I begged her not to tell anyone and swore that when she arrived I would do whatever she thought was best. She probably thought she'd defeated me, that I'd found the little gifts she'd left and decided I was losing my mind. She arrived cocky, just as I'd planned, probably expecting me to cry on her shoulder and then turn myself in. I'm sure if that had taken too long, she would have turned me in herself. She knew what the evidence was, and where—after all, she'd planted it herself. So she showed up on my doorstep dripping fake tears and fake snot for her fake boyfriend. I cried, too. We both knew that tears made people relax; it made them think they'd won.

It's been nineteen hours since I slit her throat.

She kept up the act right until the very end, whimpering and begging. Pathetic.

It was only when the knife dug in that I saw her eyes grow cold, and knew that she—it—had lost the strength to lie. The facade fell away, and her glare was cruel, calculating. Evil. And then it was just dead.

When it's not a movie, when it's real life, and the body is just a body, no matter what kind of cancer has taken up residence on its soul, it's easy to suffer a moment of doubt. A crisis of faith, even, staring down at the familiar face, so still and peaceful, so innocent, now that the eyes are closed and the vileness faded away—it's easy to begin to wonder.

I learned that the first time, when I had to drag their bodies into the kitchen and light the fire, when I had to wash their blood off my hands and walk away. Doubt creeps in. And I let it.

Maybe that makes me weak, I don't know. I don't care, really. Like I said, I don't claim to be a hero. I don't need to be invincible. I just need to survive.

Which is why I don't allow myself doubt until the deed is done.

I let myself mourn Parker as I wrapped her in the sheet and dragged her into the yard. I tried to remember the good things about her, hoping they weren't all part of the game, that there was, once, a girl named Parker Kent who chain-smoked clove cigarettes and could curse in four languages. I even let myself wonder, as the dirt spattered down on her body, whether there had been anything left of that girl once the creature took over. Whether there had been anything left of the real Parker, the innocent Parker, when the knife skidded across her throat. For her sake, I hope not. But if there was, I'm glad I got to be the one to end her suffering.

It's been nineteen hours since I became a killer for the third time.

Someone will come looking for her, but I'm not too worried. I've become a good liar these last few months—playing the victim has honed my acting skills. The pathetic sole survivor, the orphan, her whole life consumed in the tragic fire, everyone she knew, everyone she loved, burned beyond recognition.

Lucky for me I escaped the flames.

Lucky for me the fire burned hot and slow, destroying the bodies, destroying the evidence, sparing the house.

Lucky for me the repairs were finished just before my eighteenth birthday, so I could move back in, live on my own. I could take care of myself. As I always have.

I try to believe that my luck will hold. Because I know that even if I clean away every spot of blood, even if I burn everything that will burn and bury the rest, there's still a chance I'll be caught—caught by someone who can't understand what I've done. But there's no point in worrying about that now. Whatever will be, will be.

Just like the song says.

I hum it while I'm scrubbing the floor. It helps me pass the time.

I finished early enough to get a few hours of sleep. And I slept well, for the first time in weeks.

But when I woke up this morning, I found the dead dog on my porch. It was the yappy dachshund from down the block that used to bark all night, keeping the whole neighborhood awake. And now it's dead. My back still aching from the night before, I wrapped it in another sheet and dragged it into the backyard, burying it next to Parker.

It's beginning again, I know that. There's another one of them out there, warming up, preparing for the big kill. I was planning to stay home today; after yesterday, after Parker, I could use some downtime. But instead I'll throw on some clothes and drag myself to school, so I can start the search all over again. It's out there somewhere, eager and hungry—which means today I begin my hunt.

I understand that they need a scapegoat. I just don't understand why they always choose me. It's as if they can't resist. They're like cockroaches skittering into one of those cardboard boxes, chowing down on a tasty treat until the only exit snaps shut and the trap becomes their coffin.

Except that's not quite right, because I'm not just the trap—I'm also the bait.

They sense something weak in me, something they can use. And maybe they're right. I used to be weak. But they've made me strong. I know what I'm capable of now. I know what I'm willing to do to protect the innocent—and to protect myself.

Because I refuse to be punished for someone else's sins.

I refuse to be sent into the wilderness.

I refuse to be their scapegoat.

I will always escape—no matter how many of them have to die.

# IMAGINING THINGS

**T.E.D. Klein**

I once saw a scary movie on TV. Maybe you've seen it, too. It was about a babysitter who, one night, gets a series of threatening telephone calls from someone unknown. She's in this big spooky house with a couple of little kids asleep upstairs. At first she thinks the calls are just a prank, but as they continue she becomes more and more frightened. Somewhere out there, she realizes, lurks a dangerous psycho. She phones the police and has them put a trace on the line. After she gets still another call from the psycho, the police phone her back. Quick, they tell her, get out! We've just discovered where the calls are coming from—right inside the house with you.

My little brother and I were watching that movie in our basement, sprawled on the broken-down old couch, and we were so stunned we almost fell onto the floor. We had no idea, at the time, that the movie was based on a popular campfire tale that had been told to generations of Boy Scouts and summer campers; it caught us completely by surprise. The notion that the thing you feared most might be hiding inside your own house, practically *beside you*—well, neither one of us ever forgot it.

Weezy—that's my brother—was always more affected by things like that than I was. Mom once said he was more "sensitive." I still remember that; I remember looking up the word in the dictionary and trying to figure out whether it meant she liked him more. His real name is Eugene, but when I was little I couldn't pronounce that—it came out "Weezy"—and the name stuck. I guess that sort of thing happens in a lot of families.

Sensitive or not, we both watched the same type of movies—the type where, if half the cast isn't either dead or bloody by the end, you haven't gotten your money's worth. Probably the main reason Weezy watched those movies was because I did. He liked them well enough when I was sitting there on the couch next to him, but afterward, at bedtime, he'd regret it, like someone addicted to the very thing he was allergic to. In fact, Weezy had to sleep with a pink seashell night-light. I didn't need one—night-lights were for babies—and I slept with my door closed, because the light spilling out from Weezy's bedroom would have kept me awake. Mom and Dad's room was around the bend in the hall, so the light must not have bothered them.

I was thirteen when they split up, which meant that Weezy was eleven. Dad moved to the city and hardly ever came to see us, and when he did he looked sheepish and uncomfortable. There's no getting around it, it was a rotten thing he did, and all the explanations in the world don't make it better. Mom had to pull Weezy and me out of school at the end of the term. We ended up in a different school district on the other side of town, in an apartment upstairs from a family called the Mundlers—Weezy and I immediately dubbed them the Mumblers. He and I had to share a room now, or as Mom put it, making it sound jolly, "bunk together." At least we were spared the indignity of bunk beds; there's only so much togetherness a guy can stand. Also, since he regarded me now as his protector, Weezy agreed to give up his night-light; I wouldn't have put up with it.

Mom had to go back to work. She hadn't held a job since before I was born, and she was relieved to find one at a bank less than half an hour's drive from where we lived. I've heard people joke about "banker's hours," meaning a short workday of nine to three, the time banks used to close; but that wasn't true of our mother. She'd be out before eight in the morning and wouldn't be home till after six—or later, if she'd been shopping for groceries. She was tired all the time, and out of patience.

There's a word for a change like the one we'd just gone through: "traumatic." A father leaves, a family gets uprooted, and the kids are supposed to go wrong. The funny thing is, Weezy began going wrong before any of this happened. Even when all four of us were living in the old house and life seemed relatively secure, he had begun to have what my mother called "episodes."

For example, there was the episode at the zoo, when he wouldn't go near a cage of monkeys and instead dashed behind my father and hid. He was young then, but not so young that this behavior didn't draw puzzled stares from the people around us. He said the monkeys were whispering things to him—"bad things" was all he would tell us—and then, more mysterious still: "They say they've been expecting me."

And there was the time he broke the tall mirror in the downstairs clothes closet—smashed it with his fist. Mom had to drive him to the doctor, and I think he got nine stitches in his hand.

He claimed he'd seen someone in the mirror that wasn't him.

I knew my brother was odd. "He's certainly an *odd* duck, isn't he?" my father once said, and when I was with Weezy, I often found myself repeating that expression to myself: "an odd duck." But some things didn't become apparent till I actually began living in the same room with him. Like how little he seemed to sleep. We usually went to bed around the same time, but I would almost always drop off before he did, and if I'd wake in the middle of the night, he'd often be lying there with his eyes open. Once, or maybe more than once, I woke to hear him talking softly in his sleep. I couldn't make out the words. "Weezy!" I said. "You're having a nightmare. Wake up!"

"I *am* awake," he said.

Mostly, he was fine. In school he got better grades than I did. His teachers described him as "impulsive," "erratic," "prone to fantasizing," but they also found him "a delight" and "a real asset to the class," which is more than they ever said about me.

That's why it was so shocking when he went after one of them with a microphone stand.

It was in the new school district, our third year there. I didn't hear about it till I got home, because I was in high school by then, and Weezy was still in middle school.

Weezy had shown up for Tuesday afternoon chorus practice as usual, only to find a substitute for Mrs. Morton—some man from outside the district. No sooner had Weezy laid eyes on him than, in front of everyone, he ran to the heavy steel microphone stand, picked it up base and all, and swung it at the man's head.

He'd missed; it was way too heavy for him to control. I came home just in time to see Mom driving up with Weezy in the car, both of them looking stunned, neither looking at the other. He'd been expelled, would probably be sent to a special school, and would have to be monitored by youth counselors. We never found out what had set him off, and he never chose to explain it. There'd been nothing special about the new chorus master, certainly nothing threatening that any of us could see; he was just an ordinary man, a bit on the tall side, with glasses, dark hair, and a dark, fuzzy beard.

I confess that, when I heard Mom talk about a "special school," my heart leapt—just for a moment—at the thought that Weezy would be going away and I'd have our room to myself. That's not how it worked out; he was transferred to a different school but got to live at home. In fact, for all his trouble with the authorities, his weekly appointments with a therapist at the county clinic, his prescription medications, and his official new status as a youthful offender, Weezy's day-to-day existence didn't seem to change much. He just seemed to have less homework. Thanks to the pills, he slept better at night, which meant I slept better as well.

When, a year later, I found a minimum-wage weekend job checking inventory at Allied Industries, an easy couple of bus rides from where we lived, Weezy soon managed to get one, too, in the company mailroom; Mom had forced me to recommend him. It was, if anything, a cushier job than mine. I had to spend my Saturdays pushing a wagon through the aisles of a warehouse full of lawn-care products, insect spray, and fertilizer; Weezy worked in the adjoining building, sorting mail-in cards from potential customers. He didn't even have to get his hands dirty.

He held that job at Allied until the weekend before he was due to start high school—the local branch where I was about to be a senior. Maybe he was stressed out by the prospect of entering the normal world again, of returning to an ordinary school, not the one for "special needs" kids that he'd been attending. All I know is that Phil, one of the guys I worked with, hurried up to me in the warehouse that afternoon and told me there'd been some trouble with my brother and that I was to take him home. "He went after Mr. Lowell with some bug spray," Phil told me. "They're not gonna press charges—no one was hurt."

Mr. Lowell was Weezy's boss. He wasn't a bad guy, either, just a mild, inoffensive old man who, because of a breathing problem, barely raised his voice above a whisper. Later that day, I heard my mother on the phone with him, apologizing over and over. It was still light, but Weezy had already gone to bed.

"Do you think it has anything to do with Dad?" I asked her when she'd hung up. I'd been reading a family psychology Web site on the computer. "I mean, dealing with a male authority figure?"

"I wish it did." She looked grim. "More likely Eugene's problem is organic—the chemistry of the brain. That's what Dr. Perelmutter thinks."

I wondered uneasily, just for a moment, if the same chemicals that flowed through my brother's brain might be seeping into my own.

Sometime after midnight, I woke to find Weezy crouched at our bedroom window. It was late August, with a sliver of moon, and in its light I could see that he was staring intently at something outside. As a rule, he now slept soundly, but maybe he hadn't taken his meds, or maybe he'd just gone to bed too early. And of course, it had been a pretty upsetting day.

"Weezy," I said, "what are you doing?"

"C'mere." His voice was hushed, frightened. I got out of bed and crossed the room. "Can you see it?" he said, not turning his head.

I peered into the night. There isn't much of a view—mainly the neighbors' house and, between it and ours, a twisted old maple.

"I don't see anything."

"Something's out there, clinging to the tree," he said. "You don't see it? You don't *hear* it?"

"No. What is it?"

"I'm not sure," he said, squinting as if to see better. "It's big—like some kind of big, dark, furry caterpillar, covered all over with . . . you know, like our brushes."

I knew what he meant—the two matching hairbrushes Dad had given us one Christmas. They were labeled GENUINE BOAR'S BRISTLE, and I remember asking Dad what that meant. "Pig hair," he'd said, grinning.

"Well," I said gently, "there are definitely caterpillars in that tree. *Little* ones. It's gypsy moth season."

He took no notice. "It's whispering things."

"What's it saying?"

He paused, caught his breath. "It's—it's promising to come for me." He turned. "You can't hear it?"

To humor him, I listened. I could hear the crickets, a soft breeze, nothing more. Or so it seemed; it's never hard to hear word sounds in the breeze. The tree was just a dark, shifting mass with an occasional flicker of moonlight on leaves. Who knows what might have been hiding in it? Was that a dark face I saw? Who knows?

The last time I'd been taken to the eye doctor, he had measured my vision for glasses. As I stared at the chart on the opposite wall, he would slip a lens into the mechanical device I was looking through and he would say, "Now, is it better this way—" He would slip in another lens."Or this way—" He would remove the second lens. "Or hard to tell?" He would do it again. "Is it better this way? Or this way? Or hard to tell?"

Tonight was a case of hard to tell.

"Weezy, there's nothing out there. It's all in your mind."

"Honest?"

"Believe me, you're imagining things."

He gulped, seemed to relax a little. "So it's just in my head?"

"Trust me."

"Well . . . all right, then." He stood up. "Don't tell Mom, okay?"

"Of course not."

The next morning, as she was driving me to the mall to buy school clothes, with Weezy at home blinking sleepily in front of the TV, I told Mom.

The hospital where they sent him was on the other side of the county, but it could just as easily have been in another country, because for at least the first three weeks, he was supposed to have no visitors and no communication with family members. It sounds harsh, but I guess it was for his own good.

With Weezy gone, I set up my computer at his desk and used mine for homework and books. I piled my extra clothes on his bed. I missed Weezy in some ways, I really did, but it was good to have my own room again.

Only two weeks had passed when I heard, from Mom, that he was going to come home. She got off the phone with a smile. "They say he's been making great progress."

"Great," I said.

The next day, when I came back from school, I saw a letter addressed to me in Weezy's handwriting. He wasn't supposed to communicate with us, and I wondered how he'd managed to get it in the mail. Mom wouldn't be home for an hour or two. I took the letter into my room and read it at my desk. It was written in pencil on a piece of lined paper yanked from a notebook, leaving the three holes torn.

*"Hey, bro,"* he wrote, *"I've been thinking about what you told me. There's not much else to DO here. I mean, except think. And make nice for the doctors. Which I'm getting very good at. I know just what to tell them. And what NOT to tell them. Because they're jerks. They're blind. They know nothing, and less than nothing.*

*"I'm imagining things—that's what you said. It's all INSIDE MY HEAD, right? And maybe that's supposed to be comforting. Right, bro? But remember that movie? The one about the babysitter? Remember what it showed? That you want to keep the things OUT. You want them OUT THERE. In the night. You don't want to let them in the house. You don't want to turn around and find them inside with you. They're MUCH WORSE when they're inside, in here with me. In here where they're REAL. Real because I IMAGINE them. To imagine means to INVENT—and what you invent becomes real.*

*"I'll be home soon, and I'll show you what I mean."*

He had drawn a sort of picture at the bottom of the letter—a kind of stick figure seeming to reach out, maybe in friendship, maybe not—only the figure had jagged lines scribbled all over, giving it a certain bulkiness.

There's an expression I've heard in the old crime movies: "dropping a dime" on someone. It means, basically, tattling on someone—ratting on him. It comes from the days when a call at a pay phone cost ten cents. You want to turn someone in, you drop in your dime and call the authorities.

Well, you might say I dropped Weezy's letter on him. I folded it up and put it back in the envelope, took the bottle of Elmer's from the kitchen drawer, and carefully resealed the flap. I left the letter lying with the rest of the mail and went out for a bike ride.

Mom was holding the envelope when I got home, but she hadn't opened it. She watched me as I pretended to read the letter for the first time.

"What does he say?"

"I really shouldn't tell you."

"*Tell* me."

"I really shouldn't."

She was as upset when she read it as I'd known she'd be. Before the week was out, it was decided that Weezy wasn't coming home after all, and once again communication ceased.

"They're planning to run some tests on him," she announced one October evening over dinner. "To see if they can find out what's wrong."

"I thought they agreed it was schizophrenia," I said, proud of my ease with the term. I'd been spending more time on the Web.

"No one's sure," she said. "Apparently a Swiss doctor has been doing some experiments. . . ."

"They're flying Weezy to Switzerland?" Awful as it sounds, I had instantly felt a twinge of jealousy.

"Hardly!" she said. "They're just hoping to use a similar method here. Something very up-to-date."

That night, I Googled around a bit and found a lot of stuff about the latest psychiatric research in Europe. One series of experiments in particular kept coming up, going on somewhere outside Geneva. They involved electrical stimulation of certain regions of the brain. I saw lots of references to how "surprising" and "controversial" the results were, but I couldn't get through the technical language— "vestibular" and "proprioceptive" and references to things like a "dysembryoblastic neuroepithelial tumor." Why do they have to use such big words? I soon gave up; even homework seemed more fun.

Weezy had always been better at science than I was. Maybe he could have figured it all out if he hadn't, at this very moment, been on the receiving end of it.

I got a glimpse of what those tests he was undergoing might be like when, less than two weeks later, I received some unexpected news. It was a chilly gray Saturday morning, and I had just arrived at my job at the Allied warehouse. Grinning as he ambled up to me, Phil, my coworker, handed me a pale blue printed card. "Hey, pal," he said, "this showed up in the mailroom yesterday. It's addressed to you."

I saw immediately what it was—one of those free postpaid cards that the company stuck in magazines alongside their ads. If you wanted further product information, you filled out the card with your name and address and dropped it in the mailbox. On the address side, above the words "Allied Industries," someone had penciled in my name. I recognized the handwriting.

"I think it's from that crazy brother of yours," said Phil. He stood regarding me curiously as I turned the card over. The printed words—"Please rush me FREE information about . . ."—were not what caught my eye. Rather, it was the message scrawled in the spaces for name and address:

> "They've got me wired up here—in more ways than one. It doesn't hurt, though. It's like a game. They tell me I'm producing good results."

There was no signature, but I didn't need one.

The card probably dated back to Weezy's days in the mailroom, or else he'd ripped it from a magazine at the hospital. It was a clever way of reaching me without a stamp—and without Mom knowing. I decided not to tell her, at least not yet.

At night, after dinner, I made myself a cup of instant cocoa and sat down at the computer, ready to give that European research another try. I skipped the technical details this time and tried to figure out what made those experiments so special. From what I could understand, the subjects had been epileptics and people with histories of everything from migraine headaches to hallucinations. A hospital staff had implanted dozens of electrodes in the surfaces of these patients' brains and, on others, had experimented with something called "low-intensity magnetic stimulation." While the patients were awake and fully conscious, the current was turned on for a couple of seconds, during which they were asked to report what they felt.

That much didn't seem especially new. But the researchers had discovered that when they stimulated an area called the angular gyrus, in a part of the brain an inch behind and above each ear called the temporoparietal junction, they got some rather startling reactions.

Most of the patients said they felt themselves floating; sometimes right there in the hospital room—the classic "out-of-body experience"—but, in one woman's case, floating outdoors, over hills and meadows. That sounded nice. Another saw and felt her legs moving when they weren't. Still another, identified only as Patient 3, had a strange feeling that something—a shadowy figure—was behind her, and she kept turning her head to try to see it. When the left side of her brain was stimulated, she kept looking behind her to her right; when the right side was stimulated, she sensed the figure to her left.

It's this mysterious presence that seems to have caused the biggest sensation. Though the experiments had been going on for several years, they weren't well known till the British journal *Nature* published an article on them in 2006: "Brain Electrodes Conjure Up Ghostly Visions." I couldn't find that article on the Web, but I found plenty of others, some with headlines out of a horror movie: "Creepy Experiment Exposes Paranoia and Sense of Alien Control," "Inducing the Shadow-Self by Stimulating the Brain," "Brain Stimulation Creates Shadow Person." The *Chicago Tribune* spoke of "Brain Zaps" and "Eerie Feelings," and the *London Daily Telegraph* reported "'Shadow' Sheds Light on Schizophrenia." I felt rather proud when I saw that; I'd been right about Weezy after all.

I was glad I'd taken the time to read up on this stuff, because at work the following Saturday, Phil walked over and, with a sympathetic little nod, gave me a second card from my brother. I suppose it should have occurred to me that if Weezy could get his hands on one blank card, he could obtain more; maybe he'd stolen a pile of them before he'd been fired and had smuggled them into the hospital. Still, his message came as a surprise:

"I was right. The thing exists."

That's all it said. Once again there was no signature, and this time, I noticed, Weezy hadn't even bothered to write my name on the address side. "Good thing that guy in the mailroom recognized it," said Phil. "Otherwise it would've been tossed in the trash."

I almost wished it had been. I thought about the message all day—the simple certainty in those words.

Of course, how could Weezy be expected to understand? Surely, from what I'd read, he was prey to a delusion, a phantom conjured up in his brain by a two-second jolt of electricity.

I found more about that phantom—or at least about one that might as well be its brother—in the library the next day; in fact, I spent my whole Sunday afternoon there. *The New York Times* had run an article on the subject: "Out-of-Body Experience?" the headline read. "Your Brain Is to Blame." It confirmed my suspicion that what Weezy was going through was nothing new. Patient 3, the one in the experiments, had reported that the thing behind her—described by the newspaper as a "strange presence," a "shadow figure"—had attempted to exert its will on her.

Another news report provided more details about what this "presence" was capable of. A patient who'd sat up on the operating table and clasped her knees had felt someone she described as "a man" put his arms around her from behind; the feeling, she said, was "unpleasant." When she'd been given a card and asked to read it, she could feel the figure try to snatch it from her hand. "He wants to take the card," she had explained. "He doesn't want me to read it."

The hospital staff had concluded that this shadow figure was simply the patient's illusion of her own body. There were only two things this theory failed to explain: why a woman had described the figure as being of the opposite sex—and why, if it was merely a projection of herself, it seemed to treat her with such hostility.

Weezy's next message, the following weekend, suggested, against all reason, that the figure might be more than just a product of his mind:

> "I couldn't see it—it was standing behind me.
> But I think the doctors saw it."

There was no card waiting for me the weekend after that, and I was relieved. Maybe the experiments were at an end.

But the next weekend brought a new message:

> "Felt it today. It was behind me, and I felt it on the back of my neck. I heard a doctor say, 'What the hell is that?' "

A week later:

> "Felt it again. It's the thing from the tree."

And the next:

"It tried to put its arms around me. I could feel it even after the current was turned off. Not pleasant. I'm getting out of here."

No word came from Weezy for the next two weeks. I wondered if maybe he had actually gotten out—if anyone was clever enough to find a way, he was—and night after night I wrestled with the thought of warning Mom about it, or of contacting the hospital. But I didn't. Maybe I was reluctant to betray him a third time. Or maybe I just figured that this time I'd get caught.

December had arrived. Midterms occupied me, and when I got home from school, I'd pull down the shades in my bedroom to shut out the early darkness and would try to study. When I'd ask Mom about how Weezy was doing, she'd say, "They tell me he's doing fine," but she'd look worried.

"Do you think he's getting out soon?" I asked her once, careful to keep all emotion from my voice.

She shook her head. "Not for a while."

Yet each day, when I entered the house, I almost expected that I'd walk upstairs and find him standing there to greet me. I imagined him asking me to hide him, or to give him some money so that he could escape, and I wondered what I'd do.

Eventually, I put him from my mind. The holidays were coming, and I looked forward to a week of vacation. Weezy was safe where he was, with the best of modern medical science to vanquish his demons.

And then, that Saturday, came another pale blue card with another message from him, the shortest one of all, yet the one that most haunts me. The card's heavily printed commercial text seemed to fade into insignificance, framing the area of blank white space, in the middle of which, scrawled in pencil, were four simple words:

"It has a friend."

Since then, the cards have stopped. Their absence—the resumed silence, you might call it—has been welcome. Mom has been making preparations to visit Weezy for the holidays, and I can see that the thought makes her happy.

But today after school I came upstairs, my last day of classes now behind me, vacation ahead, and she wasn't yet home; and I pulled down the shades and was sitting at Weezy's desk in our room, alone in the apartment, though I could hear, below me, the Mumblers going about their evening business and the sound of carols from their TV; and as I sat listening, I could swear I felt something brush the back of my neck. I turned, but no one was there. The room was empty. But for a moment, I had felt a touch, tentative but oddly familiar. And bristly.

BEASTS

6

# GRANDMA KELLY

**David Moody**

I must be stupid. I knew it was going to happen. All I needed to do was make that one catch and the game would have been safe. The ball seemed to hang in the sky over my head forever, and I think I'd already decided I was going to drop it. I kept staring up and I could feel everyone else watching me. I blew it. I made a mistake. I stretched up for the ball instead of waiting for it to come down. I felt it hit the tips of my fingers and bounce away. That was at eleven o'clock this morning. No one's talked to me since. Plenty of people have been talking about me, though. I overheard Connie Franks moaning about "that idiot, Amy" outside the upper school toilets between classes. I'm not an idiot, I just get it wrong sometimes.

I guess everyone has days like this, long, difficult days where everything seems to go wrong and you can't do anything right. At lunchtime I upset Carrie—the last person who was still talking to me—and this afternoon I found out I'd made a huge mistake with my Literature assignment. I copied the question down wrong last week, and I've answered it all wrong. It has to be in tomorrow. I'll be up all night rewriting it.

It's been raining hard like this for hours now and the streets are flooded. It was dry and bright this morning. I didn't even bring a coat. I've had to tuck my notes inside my jacket to try and keep them dry. I'm really going to need them tonight. If I don't start work on my assignment as soon as I get back, I've had it.

That's just perfect—some stupid car driver has just gone racing past me, straight through a huge puddle of rainwater which stretches from the gutter to the white line in the middle of the road. It sent a wave of dirty, cold water crashing down over me. Now I'm soaked through, and I can feel the water dripping and dribbling down my neck. My notes are soaked, too. By the time I get home all I'll have left is a soggy, inky mess. I'll never be able to make any sense of it.

It's almost five o'clock already. The bus is late tonight. What should I do? Do I wait here or start walking? Maybe Mom, Dad, or Pete will come and pick me up. Who am I kidding? They'll probably all be at home now, warm and dry, sitting with their feet up in front of the TV and their cars parked on the driveway. I bet they haven't even noticed I'm not back yet.

I really don't like this stretch of road. Moseley Street, I think it's called. It's long, straight, and steep, and it's very dark tonight. The houses are all along one side of the road and there are just a few street lamps dotted along the way. I always seem to be on my own when I'm walking up here. Most of the other kids who go to Rothery College live closer to the centre of town, and they go the opposite way home. I'd phone Dad and ask him to come and pick me up but I don't have any calltime left on my phone.

I should have stopped at the store this morning and topped it up, but I was running late, and . . .

What was that?!

Someone just crashed into me and knocked me flying. I'm on my knees in a puddle before I know what's happened, and I've dropped my notes. My papers are blowing all over the place. Quick, I have to make sure I don't lose them. . . . Wait, someone's helping me. I can't make out who it is. I scramble back to my feet, and the light from the nearest lamppost is just strong enough for me to see that it's a lady, older than me but about my height. She's got a handful of my notes. She thrusts them at me and I take them from her.

"Sorry," she mumbles. "I'm sorry."

Something's not right. She looks about as old as my mum and she's only wearing a dress and a cardigan. It's freezing cold and pouring down with rain and she's not even wearing a coat! Her face is ghostly white and behind her glasses her eyes are wide, dark, and frightened.

"Are you okay?" I start to ask. Before I can finish my question she's gone. She pushes past me and disappears into the darkness.

I keep walking. If I wasn't so tired I'd try and run up the hill, but I'm cold and I'm wet and I don't think I could manage.

"Where did you come from?" I shout suddenly. Another woman has just appeared in front of me and my heart's in my mouth. She really scared me, just appearing like that. What is it with the people on this street? At least this one didn't knock me over. There must be something wrong with her. She's really old, and like the other woman I just saw, she's not dressed to be outside. All she's wearing is a thin white nightdress, and she's drenched. She doesn't even have anything on her feet.

"Are you lost?" I ask because I don't know what else to say. "Do you live here? Were you with that other lady?"

She doesn't answer. In fact, she doesn't do anything. She just stands there right in front of me, perfectly still. I wave my hand in front of her face but she doesn't react. I don't even know if she can see me. Her eyes aren't moving.

What am I supposed to do now? I can't just leave her out here to freeze, can I? I look up and down Moseley Street but all I can see is darkness in every direction. Wait a second, the front door of the nearest house is open. It's blowing open and closed in the wind and I can see a light on inside. I'll take this woman back indoors. Even if it's not her house, someone in there might know who she is.

"I'm going to get you inside," I tell her. "We'll get you into the warm and out of this rain."

Still no response. I look around again, hoping I'll see someone who can help. There's no-one there. I don't seem to have any choice so I take hold of the old lady's limp hand. She feels icy cold. She should be shivering and shaking (I am), but she isn't moving at all. I pull her gently toward me, and her feet slowly begin to shuffle in my direction. Walking backward so that I can watch her, I carefully lead her through the garden gate toward the front door of the house.

"Hello," I shout as we reach the door. "Hello, is anyone here?"

Nothing.

"Is this your place?" I ask her, even though I know I won't get an answer. "Do you live here?"

The rain is still clattering down all around us. Even if this isn't her house I'm going to get her inside. I pull her through the door. It's not much warmer in here, but it's dry and quiet and we're finally out of the howling wind. I push the door closed behind me and just listen. The house is silent.

"Hello," I shout again. My voice echoes around the walls. "Hello!"

The old lady stands behind me in the middle of the hallway, still not moving. Rainwater is dripping off her body and splashing down onto the bare wooden floorboards. I take a couple of steps further into the house, leaving her where she is for now. On a little round table next to an old-fashioned telephone is a pile of unopened letters. I pick them up and look at the name and address.

"Mrs. Kelly?" I ask. "Are you Mrs. Kelly?"

She lifts up her head and looks at me. My heart starts to beat faster again. At the mention of her name she's finally starting to react. Now she's staring right at me, and the expression on her face is changing. She looks confused . . . now she looks hurt . . . now she looks angry. I'm getting scared.

"Look," I start to say, backing away from her, "I'll just leave, okay? I'll get out of your way and let you get on with . . ."

I don't get to finish my sentence. She starts to run at me, and I'm so surprised, it takes me a couple of seconds to react. Considering the fact that she must be numb with cold and about eighty years old, Mrs. Kelly moves with frightening speed. I want to get to the front door, but she's blocking my way and I can only go deeper into the house. Suddenly, she leaps at me—flying through the air like an attacking animal—and I put my hands up to defend myself. I shove her to the left and manage to bundle her through an open door into a pitch-black room. I quickly reach into the darkness and grab hold of the door handle and pull it shut. There's no lock. She's got hold of the other side of the handle and she's trying to yank it open. There's a high-backed chair across the hall. I stretch and just about manage to reach it with my fingertips. I drag it over and wedge it under the handle before taking a couple of nervous steps away.

This is crazy. I have to get out of here. I have to get out right now and get back home and tell Mom and Dad about . . . Wait, what was that? A heavy *thump* comes from inside the room. The door clatters and rattles in its frame. After another couple of seconds it happens again. Then again and then again. The old lady must be throwing herself against it! She's trying to break out! What's wrong with her?

None of this is making any sense. I try the phone but it's dead. I should just walk out of here right now, but my conscience is stopping me. What would happen to Mrs. Kelly if I did? I can't just leave her, much as I want to. Who knows what damage she'll do to herself? Feeling scared and uneasy, I walk past the room where Mrs. Kelly is trapped (she's still hammering against the door) and then go into the next room and switch on the light. It's a cold and empty living room. There's hardly anything in here other than a few sticks of old furniture. It looks like it's been cleared out. There's a space where a TV used to be, and the bookcase and shelves are empty. The kitchen at the end of the hallway is the same, although the light's already on in there. There's no food in the cupboards. Everything looks really old-fashioned and outdated.

There's a bad smell at this end of the house. It's so bad that I get distracted by it, and it's only the banging from the old lady in the room down the hall that makes me remember what's happening. The stench is like stale vomit, and it seems to be coming from a glass that's been left on the draining board. It's a long, tall glass which is filled with something dark, black, and sticky, like that horrible strong beer that Dad drinks but a thousand times worse. I pick it up and I can't help sniffing it. I think I'm going to be sick. . . . Before I throw up I tip the stuff down the sink and watch it slowly seep down the plughole like thick molasses.

The noise has stopped.

She's finally gone quiet. Has she worn herself out, or has she realised that she can't escape? Maybe she's hurt herself. I don't want to, but I make myself go back to the door and listen. It sounds awfully quiet in there. Perhaps I should have a look inside?

"Mrs. Kelly," I whisper. "Mrs. Kelly, are you all right?"

She throws herself at the other side of the door again, and the sudden noise makes me trip back with surprise. I end up on the floor on my backside, and I look up as she starts banging and thumping again, a hundred times harder than before.

"Stop it!" I shout. "Just stop!"

There's a moment's pause before the loudest *thump* of all. Mrs. Kelly hits the door with such force that one of the wooden panels near the top begins to crack. I hear the muffled *pad, pad, pad* of her quick footsteps inside the room and then another massive, clattering, splintering *bang*. I crawl away from the door as I hear her footsteps again. This time her head smashes right through the top of the door, sending sharp bits of wood flying across the hall. She reaches her arm down through the hole and starts yanking at the chair that's keeping her trapped. What's going on? A few minutes ago she could hardly walk, now she's smashing down wooden doors?!

Mrs. Kelly is hanging out of what's left of the door now, swinging and slashing her arms through the air furiously, stopping me getting to the front of the house. Maybe there's another way out? As I start to move back towards the living room she manages to move the chair and free herself. Now she's running down the hallway towards me. She's moving faster than I am! I dive into the living room and slam the door shut. Almost immediately I can feel her hammering on the other side. I drag a dusty old sofa across the room and manage to push it hard against the door. Then I shove a table and a chair behind it and drag the empty bookcase into the gap so that there's a line of furniture running right across the room. She won't get in here now. Problem is, how do I get out?

*Bang, bang, bang!*

What was that? Jumping with fright and surprise, I spin around to see another ghostly white face pressed against the window just behind me. I scream so loud it hurts my throat. The figure at the window bangs its hand against the glass, and I suddenly feel like I'm trapped in some bad horror film surrounded by zombies. But I can't be, can I?

It's the other woman I saw out on the street. I didn't recognise her at first. Her wet, windswept hair is plastered across her face, and she's shouting at me to let her in. She hammers on the window again. What do I do? Will she be like Mrs. Kelly or will she be worse? I don't have any choice. At least if the window's open I can try and get out.

I reach out and flick up the latch. I push the window open, then move back across the room. It's hard to keep calm with Mrs. Kelly smashing against the door on one side of me and this lady climbing in on the other. She drags herself headfirst through the window and ends up in a heap on the threadbare carpet. She stands up and reaches back outside. She heaves a heavy shopping bag into the room and pulls the window closed.

"I'm Sheila Hogarth," she says, breathing heavily and dripping with rain, "and I'm sorry."

"Sorry?" I mumble, surprised. "Why are you sorry?"

"Because all of this is my fault. I didn't think it would happen so soon. I thought I'd be able to stop it before it got this bad."

Mrs. Kelly slams against the door again and startles us both. I feel more scared and confused than ever, and jumping through the open window seems like my best option. I start to shuffle slowly along the wall, trying to keep as far away from Mrs. Hogarth as I can.

"Why is it your fault?" I ask her. "And who is that outside?"

"That used to be Grandma Kelly," she answers, sniffing back tears. "It used to be my grandma. I don't know what it is now."

"What do you mean, *'it'?* Why's she trying to kill me?"

Mrs. Hogarth sighs and leans against the nearest wall.

"I got it wrong. I made a mistake and I'm sorry."

I can't get my head around any of this. I'm next to the window now but I stop before going outside.

"Would you please tell me what's going on? I'm cold and I'm wet and I need to get home. I've got an assignment to write tonight and . . . and I'm scared."

Mrs. Hogarth takes another step towards me and I take another step away. The door at the other end of the room rattles and clatters again, distracting us both. She looks back at me, then clears her throat and finally starts to explain.

"Grandma died on Monday," she says quietly.

"So why is she still here? It's Thursday. Shouldn't someone have taken her away by now? And anyway, how can she be dead? She's out there banging on the door!"

It sounds even more crazy when I say it out loud. This can't be happening. Mrs. Hogarth starts to walk toward the door. It's beginning to give way under the pressure of Mrs. Kelly's constant battering.

"Have you ever lost anyone close?" she asks me. She's crying.

"My uncle died last September," I answer.

"When he'd gone, did you start to think about all the things you wish you'd said to him but never did?"

"Dad did. He still says he should have made more of an effort to see him. Why?"

"If your dad had a chance to see your uncle one last time, would he take it?"

"Of course he would."

"That's what I did. I knew how to get that chance. Well, I thought I did. . . ."

"What do you mean?"

"Grandma's sister, Aunt Peggy, she told me what to do. She lives just round the corner. I saw her after Grandma died and she told me."

"Told you what?" I ask her. Mrs. Kelly's hand smashes through the door and I start to move toward the window again.

"She showed me how to make up a solution. . . ."

"A solution?" I interrupt. "What do you mean? A medicine or something like that?" I stop and think for a second. "Are you talking about a potion?"

She turns round and frowns at me.

"Don't say potion." She scowls. "That sounds ridiculous."

"Nothing sounds ridiculous when there's a dead old lady banging at the door," I mumble.

"Call it what you like." She sighs. "Whatever it is, you administer it to the body, and it sort of calls the spirit back for a while."

Sounds crazy.

"So what went wrong?" I ask.

Now she looks almost embarrassed.

"Bit silly, really," she says, looking down at the floor and shuffling her feet like a little kid who's getting told off in class. "I mixed it up wrong. I've never been that good with numbers. I put too much of one thing in and not enough of another. I got confused with grams and ounces."

"What happened?"

"I called Aunt Peggy," she begins, stopping for a moment as Mrs. Kelly's second bony fist smashes through the door. "She told me that the solution attracts the spirit back to the body. . . ."

"And if the solution's not right?"

"She said a spirit would still find its way to the body. . . ."

"But?"

"But it wouldn't necessarily be the right one. I realised what I'd done as soon as I'd given it to her. I'm so sorry, it's bad enough that I have to clear this mess up. I didn't mean for anyone else to get involved. . . ."

I'm having trouble believing this.

"So who's inside your grandma's body now?"

"Don't know. Could be anyone. Thing is, Aunt Peggy says it doesn't matter. She says the wrong spirit in the wrong body is bad news, whatever. Doesn't matter who or what it is."

Can any of this be true? The fact is, there's a crazy old woman pounding on the door who just a few minutes ago could hardly move. A few more minutes and she'll be inside. We have to do something.

"Aunt Peggy told me how to fix it," Mrs. Hogarth says suddenly. She bends down and starts looking through her shopping bag. "She said if I don't act quickly, Grandma will get stronger and stronger. The longer we leave it, the worse it will get."

She stands and holds a small thermos up in front of her.

"What's that?"

"Another solution," she answers. "It'll put a stop to this."

"How?"

She shrugs her shoulders and starts to open the thermos. The room is suddenly filled with a horrible stench, worse than the one in the kitchen. My stomach starts to turn somersaults, and I have to concentrate to stop myself from being sick. I look up and see that Mrs. Kelly has smashed her head and shoulders right through the top of the door now. She's reaching down, trying to move the sofa.

"We have to get her to drink it," Mrs. Hogarth says.

"How are we supposed to do that?"

She shrugs her shoulders again.

"We'll just have to let her in and hold her down."

"She's your grandma," I tell her, thinking about how strong and unpredictable the dead old woman has quickly become. "You can hold her."

"We can't do it yet," she whispers secretively. "We have to finish the solution first. Aunt Peggy says it needs to be tuned to the person who died."

"Tuned? How?"

"You have to add a bit of body to it."

That's it. I can't take any more of this. I run to the window again and start to climb out.

"Please," Mrs. Hogarth wails. "Please don't go . . . I need your help."

"And I need to get out of here," I mumble, one leg already outside.

"Please!" she cries. I stop and look back at her. She looks helpless and terrified. What happens if I don't help? How strong will Mrs. Kelly become? "I'm not talking about cutting off a finger or an arm or a leg," she sobs. "Just a little bit of her. Some hair or skin . . ."

I know I can't leave her.

"So how are we going to do this?" I ask as I climb back inside.

"Cut her nails," Mrs. Hogarth says suddenly, grabbing a pair of scissors from her bag. It's like she had this all planned. "You hold her arm still and I'll cut her nails."

I can't believe I'm doing this. I run across the room and grab hold of one of Mrs. Kelly's bare, spindly arms. She's so strong! She almost picks me off my feet, and it's all I can do to keep my balance and hold on to her. Mrs. Hogarth manages to prise her vicious fingers apart and then makes a few nervous snips with the scissors. Mrs. Kelly smashes me back against the wall, knocking all the wind out of my body. Still I keep hold of her as Mrs. Hogarth drops down and combs the carpet for the tiny, boomerang-shaped nail clippings.

"Have you got enough?" I scream as Mrs. Kelly throws me forward and gets ready to hurl me back again.

"Think so," she replies, dropping the nails into the thermos and fastening the lid and shaking it. "Hope so," she adds under her breath.

Mrs. Kelly is starting to get really, really mad. I let go of her arm and manage to duck out of the way as her hands swipe at me. I watch as she steps back and gets ready to throw herself forward again. I run for cover as she smashes through the door with more strength than ever. Splinters of wood fly around the room in every direction as she breaks through and crashes down onto the sofa. She turns toward me and I'm terrified. I can't move. Her face is twisted with anger and hate, and thick strings of sticky dribble are dripping from her yellow teeth and running down her chin.

"Grab her!" Mrs Hogarth screams as Mrs. Kelly lunges for me, springing up from the sofa and flying through the air. She wraps her arms around me and I fall backward, cracking my head on the floor. I look up into her cold, black eyes. I try to free myself but I can't. She's too strong.

"Roll over," Mrs. Hogarth shouts. "When I tell you, try and roll over onto your front."

"I can't," I wail, trying not to cry. Mrs. Kelly's face is close to mine now. I can feel her spit dripping onto me.

"Yes, you can," she hisses. "Do it now!"

Last chance. I can't get this wrong. For a split second I think about my dropped catch this morning. I have to concentrate this time. I can't let myself mess this up; everything depends on what I do now. Grunting with effort, I bring my knees up to my chest and lift the frail frame of the old lady up into the air. She might be strong but she's still light. I push her up as high as I can and then roll over to my right. I can feel Mrs. Hogarth helping, shoving Mrs. Kelly's shoulder down. A sudden rush of movement and we've done it. Now Mrs. Kelly's lying on the carpet and I'm the one who's on top looking down.

"Move your head!"

I do as I'm told and I tilt my head away as Mrs. Hogarth pours the horrific, sticky, foul-smelling liquid into Mrs. Kelly's open mouth. She keeps pouring—far more than she needs to—until the old lady's mouth is full and the gross stuff is trickling down the sides of her wrinkled face. She grips me even tighter, and I can feel her fingers digging into my skin. I scream as she grips tighter and tighter and tighter until . . . she lets go. Her bony hands loosen and I quickly push myself away. I roll away and crawl into the furthest corner of the room. Mrs. Kelly lies still.

"Is that it?" I whisper.

"Think so," Mrs. Hogarth replies, standing over the body of her grandma.

But it isn't. The fingers on the body's right hand start to twitch. Now its whole hand is moving, and now it's spread to both of its arms and its legs. Now the whole of what used to be Mrs. Kelly is shaking and twitching so badly that it's almost lifting itself off the ground. Is she going to attack us again? It gets worse and worse and worse and then . . . it stops. Mrs. Kelly's remains finally lie still. I'm too scared to move. Mrs. Hogarth waits for a second and then slowly shuffles forward and prods her dead grandmother's shoulder. She doesn't react. She shoves her, this time a little harder. Still nothing. Now she's shaking her and shaking her. Nothing.

"Sorry, Grandma," she says quietly as she lifts up the body and holds her tight.

* * *

I didn't say anything to anyone else about what had happened once I got home last night. In fact, by the time I got home, got changed, had eaten, and started work on my assignment, I was having trouble believing any of it had happened myself. The assignment took almost all night to finish, and by the time it was finally done everything that had happened with Mrs. Kelly and Mrs. Hogarth had faded away to little more than a bad dream.

This morning I'm more concerned with school than dead grandmothers. I'm dreading class today. Another day of being called a loser by my so-called friends. I might have lost the game yesterday, but they didn't see what I did last night, did they? If I hadn't helped Mrs. Hogarth, who knows what might have happened? They'll never know how I . . .

"Get up!" a voice screams.

Mom's just burst into my room.

"What's the matter?" I ask.

"Just get up," she yells. She sounds scared. "Get dressed and pack a bag. We're leaving."

"Why?" I shout after her but she's already gone. I get up and run to the door. "Mom? Mom, what's wrong?"

She's halfway down the stairs. She stops and looks back at me. She looks terrified.

"Crazy people," she explains, wiping frightened tears from her eyes. "Town's full of crazy people. Your dad's gone to work. I can't get hold of him. . . ."

I go downstairs and stand in front of the TV. I can't believe what I'm seeing. The middle of town is like a war zone. There are massive crowds of people running around, fighting with each other and tearing the place apart. They're all acting like Mrs. Kelly was last night. But how could that be? They'd have needed to drink the solution, wouldn't they? How could they have . . . ?

I sit down on the edge of the sofa and hold my head in my hands. It was me, wasn't it? I feel like I did when I lost the game yesterday, but a hundred times worse and a thousand times more frightened. I did this. How could I have been so stupid? I wasn't thinking. Three-quarters of a glass of solution poured down the sink and the end of the world has begun.

I have to find Mrs. Hogarth. . . .

# SHELTER ISLAND

**Melissa de la Cruz**

It was the light that started it. Hannah woke up at three o'clock in the morning one cold February day and noticed that one of the old copper sconces on the wall was turned on, emitting a dim, barely perceptible halo. It flickered at first, then died, then abruptly came back to life again. At first she chalked it up to a faulty wire, or carelessness on her part—had she turned off the lights before bed? But when it happened again the next evening, and again two days later, she began to pay attention.

The fourth time, she was already awake when it happened. She felt around the nightstand for her glasses, put them on, then stared at the glowing bulb and frowned. She definitely remembered turning off the switch before going to bed. She watched as it slowly burned out, leaving the room dark once more. Then she went back to sleep.

Another girl would have been scared, maybe a bit frightened, but this was Hannah's third winter on Shelter Island and she was used to its "house noises" and assorted eccentricities. In the summer, the back screen door would never stay closed; it would bang over and over with the wind, or when someone walked in and out of the house—her mother's boyfriend, a neighbor, Hannah's friends whose parents had houses on the island and spent their summers there. No one ever locked their doors on Shelter Island. There was no crime (unless bike stealing was considered a crime, and if your bike was gone, most likely someone had just borrowed it to pedal down to the local market and you would find it on your front doorstep the next day), and the last murder was recorded sometime in the 1700s.

Hannah was fifteen years old, and her mother was a bartender at the Good Shop, a crunchy, all-organic café, restaurant, and bar that was only open three months out of the year, during the high season, when the island was *infested* (her mother's word) with city folk on vacation. The *summer people* (also her mother's words) and their money made living on the island possible for year-rounders like them. During the off-season, in the winter, there were so few people on the island it was akin to living in a ghost town.

But Hannah liked the winters. Liked watching the ferry cross the icy channel, how the quiet snow covered everything like a fairy blanket. She would walk alone on the windswept beach where the slushy sound of her boots scuffing the damp sand was the only sound for miles. People always threatened to quit the island during the winter. They had enough of the brutal snowstorms that raged in the night, the wind howling like a crazed banshee against the windows. They complained of the loneliness, the isolation. Some people didn't like the sound of quiet, but Hannah reveled in it. Only then could she hear herself think.

Hannah and her mother had started out as summer people. Once upon a time, when her parents were still together, the family would vacation in one of the big colonial mansions by the bay, near where the yachts docked by the Sunset Beach Hotel. But things were different after the divorce. Hannah understood that their lives had been lessened by the split, that she and her mother were lesser people now in some way. Objects of pity ever since her dad ran off with his art dealer.

Not that Hannah cared very much what other people thought. She liked the house they lived in, a comfortable, ramshackle Cape Cod with a wraparound porch and six bedrooms tucked away in its corners—one up in the attic, three on the ground floor, and two in the basement. There were framed antique nautical prints of the island and its surrounding waters in the wood-paneled living room. The house belonged to a family who never used it, and the caretaker didn't mind renting it to a single mother.

At first they moved around the vast spaces like two marbles lost in a pinball machine. But over time they adjusted and the house felt cozy and warm. Hannah never felt lonely or scared in the house. She always felt safe.

Still, the next night, at three o'clock in the morning, when the lights blinked on and the door whooshed open with a bang, it startled Hannah and she sat up immediately, looking around. Where had the wind come from? The windows were all stormproofed and she hadn't felt a draft. With a start, she noticed a shadow lingering by the doorway.

"Who's there?" she called out in a firm, no-nonsense voice. The kind of voice she used when she worked as a cashier at the marked-up grocery during the summers when the city folk would complain about the price of arugula.

She wasn't scared. Just curious. What would cause the lights to blink on and off and the door to bang open like that?

"Nobody," someone answered.

Hannah turned around.

There was a boy sitting in the chair in the corner.

Hannah almost screamed. That she was not prepared for. A cat. Maybe a lost squirrel of some sort, she had been expecting. But a boy . . . Hannah was shy around boys. She was fast approaching her sweet-sixteen-and-never-been-kissed milestone. It was awful how some girls made such a big deal out of it, but even more awful that Hannah agreed with them.

"Who are you? What are you doing here?" Hannah said, trying to sound braver than she felt.

"This is my home," the boy said calmly. He was her age, she could tell, maybe a bit older. He had dark shaggy hair that fell in his eyes, and he was wearing torn jeans and a dirty T-shirt. He was very handsome, but he looked pensive and pained. There was an ugly cut on his neck.

Hannah pulled up the covers to her chin, if only to hide her pajamas, which were flannel and printed with pictures of sushi. He must be a neighbor, one of the O'Malley boys who lived next door. How did he get into her room without her noticing? What did he want with her? Should she cry out? Let her mother know? Call for help? That wound on his neck—it looked ravaged. Something awful had happened to him, and Hannah felt her skin prickle with goose bumps.

"Who are *you*?" the boy asked, suddenly turning the tables.

"I'm Hannah," she said in a small voice. Why did she tell him her real name? Did it matter?

"Do you live here?"

"Yes."

"How strange," the boy said thoughtfully. "Well," he said. "Nice meeting you, Hannah." Then he walked out of her room and closed the door. Soon after, the light blinked off.

Hannah lay in her bed, wide awake, for a very long time, her heart galloping in her chest. The next morning, she didn't tell her mom about the boy in her room. She convinced herself it was just a dream. That was it. She had just made him up. Especially the part about him looking like a younger Johnny Depp. She'd been wanting a boyfriend so much, she'd made one appear. Not that he would be her boyfriend. But if she was ever going to have a boyfriend, she would like him to look like that. Not that boys who looked like that ever looked at girls like her. Hannah knew what she looked like. Small. Average. Quiet. Her nicest features were her eyes, sea-glass green, framed with lush dark lashes. But they were hidden behind her glasses most of the time.

Her mother always accused her of having an overactive imagination, and maybe that was all it was. She had finally let the winter crazies get to her. It was all in her mind.

But then he returned the next evening, wandering into her room as if he belonged there. She gaped at him, too frightened to say a word, and he gave her a courtly bow before disappearing. The next night, she didn't fall asleep. Instead, she waited.

Three in the morning.

Lights blazed on. Was it just Hannah's imagination or was the light actually growing stronger? The door banged. This time,

Hannah was awake and had expected it. She saw the boy appear in front of her closet, materializing out of nowhere. She blinked her eyes, her blood roaring in her ears, trying to fight the panic welling up inside. Whatever he was . . . he wasn't *human*.

"You again," she called, trying to feel brave.

He turned around. He was wearing the same clothes as the two nights prior. He gave her a sad, wistful smile. "Yes."

"Who are you? What are you?" she demanded.

"Me?" He looked puzzled for a moment, and then stretched his neck. She could see the wound just underneath his chin more clearly this time. Two punctures. Scabby and . . . blue. It was a deep indigo color, not the brownish-red she had been expecting. "I think I'm what you call a vampire."

"A vampire?" Hannah recoiled. If he was a ghost, it would be a different story. Hannah's aunt had told her all about ghosts—her aunt had gone through a Wiccan phase, as well as a spirit-guide phase. Hannah wasn't afraid of ghosts. A ghost couldn't harm you, unless it was a poltergeist. Ghosts were vapors, spectral images, maybe even just a trick of the light.

But vampires . . . there was a Shelter Island legend about a family of vampires who had terrorized the island a long time ago. Blood sucking monsters, pale and undead, cold and clammy to the touch, creatures of the night that could turn into bats or rats or worse. She shivered and looked around the room, wondering how fast she could dash out of bed and out the door. If there *was* even time to escape. Could you outrun a vampire?

"Don't worry, I'm not that kind of vampire," the boy said soothingly, as if he'd read her mind.

"What kind would that be?"

"Oh, you know, chomping on people without warning. All

that Dracula nonsense. Growing horns out of my head." He shrugged. "For one thing, we're not ugly."

Hannah wanted to laugh but felt it would be rude. Her fright was slowly abating.

"Why are you here?"

"We live here," he said simply.

"No one's lived here in years," Hannah said. "John Carter—the caretaker—he said it's been empty forever."

"Huh." The boy shrugged again. He took the corner seat across from her bed.

Hannah glanced at him warily, wondering if she should let him get that close. If he was a vampire, he didn't look cold and clammy. He looked tired. Exhausted. There were dark circles underneath his eyes. He didn't look like a cold-blooded killer. But what did she know? Could she trust him? But he had visited her twice already, after all. If he wanted her dead, he could have killed her at any time. And there was something else about him—he was almost too cute to be scared of.

"Why'd you keep doing that?" she asked when she found her voice.

"Oh, you mean the thing with the lights?"

She nodded.

"Dunno. For a long time, I couldn't do anything. I was sleeping in your closet but you didn't see me. Then I realized I could turn the lights on and off, on and off. But it was only when you started noticing that I began to feel more like myself."

"Why are you here?"

The boy closed his eyes. "I'm hiding from someone."

"Who?"

He closed his eyes harder, so that his face was a painful

grimace. "Somebody bad. Somebody who wants me dead—no, worse than dead." He shuddered.

"If you're a vampire, aren't you already dead?" she asked in a practical tone. She felt herself relaxing. Why should she be scared of him when it was so obvious it was he who was frightened?

"No, not really. It's more like I've lived a long time. A long time," he murmured. "This is our house. I remember the fireplace downstairs. I put the plaque up myself."

He must be talking about that dusty old plaque next to the fireplace, Hannah supposed, but it was so old and dirty she had never thought to notice it before.

"Who's chasing you?" Hannah asked.

"It's compli—" But before the boy could finish his sentence, there was a rattle near the window. A *thump, thump, thump* as if someone—or something—was throwing itself against the window with all its might.

The boy jumped and vanished for a moment. He reappeared by the doorway, breathing fast and hard.

"What is that?" Hannah asked, her voice trembling.

"It's here. It's found me," he said sharply, standing edgy and wired as if about to flee. And yet he remained where he was, his eyes fixed on the vibrating glass.

"Who?"

"The bad . . . thing . . ."

Hannah stood up and peered out the window. Outside was dark and peaceful. The trees, skeletal and bare of branches, stood still in the snowy field and against the frozen water. Moonlight cast the view in a cold, blue glow.

"I don't see any—oh!" She stepped back, as if stabbed. She

had seen something. A presence. Crimson eyes and silver pupils. Staring at her from the dark. Outside the window, it was hovering. A dark mass. She could feel its rage, its violent desire. It wanted in, to consume, to feed.

*Hannah . . . Hannah . . .*

It knew her name.

*Let me in. . . . Let me in. . . .*

The words had a hypnotic effect. She walked back toward the window and began to lift the latch.

"STOP!"

She turned. The boy stood at the doorway, a tense, frantic look on his face.

"Don't," he said. "That's what it wants you to do. Invite it inside. As long as you keep that window closed, it can't come in. And I'm safe."

"What *is* it?" Hannah asked, her heart pounding in her chest. She took her hand away from the window but kept her eyes on the view outside. There was nothing there anymore, but she could sense its presence. It was near.

"A vampire, too. Like me, but different. It's . . . insane," he said. "It feeds on its own kind."

"A vampire that hunts vampires?"

The boy nodded. "I know it sounds ridiculous."

"Did it . . . do that to you?" she said, brushing her fingers against the scabs on his neck. They felt rough to touch. She felt sorry for him.

"Yes."

"But you're all right?"

"I think so." He hung his head. "I hope so."

"How were you able to come inside? No one invited you," she asked.

"You're right. But I didn't need an invitation. The door was open when I came. Doors were open at all the houses, but this is the only one of them I could enter. Which made me think that I'd found it. My family's house."

Hannah nodded. That made sense. Of course he would be welcome in his own home.

The rattling stopped. The boy sighed. "It's gone for now. But it will be back."

He looked so relieved that her heart went out to him.

"What do you need me to do?" she asked. She wasn't scared anymore. Her mother always said Hannah had a head for emergencies. She was a stoic, dependable girl. More likely to plant a stake in the heart of a monster than scream for rescue from the railroad tracks. "How can I help?"

He raised his eyebrow and looked at her with respect. "I need to get away. I can't stay here forever. I need to go. I need to warn the others. Tell them what happened to me. That the danger is growing." He sagged against the wall. "What I ask you to do might hurt a bit, and I don't want to ask unless it's freely given."

"Blood, isn't it? You need blood. You're weak," Hannah said. "You need my blood."

"Yes." The shadows cast his face in sharp angles, and she could see the deep hollows in his cheeks. His sallow complexion. So perhaps some of the vampire legends were true.

"But won't I turn into . . . ?"

"No." He shook his head. "It doesn't work that way. No one

can make a vampire. We were born like this. Cursed. You will be fine—tired and a little sleepy, maybe, but fine."

Hannah gulped. "Is it the only way?" She didn't much like how that sounded. He would have to bite her. Suck her blood. She felt nauseous just thinking about it, but strangely excited as well.

The boy nodded slowly. "I understand if you don't want to. It's not something that most people would like to do."

"Can I think about it?" she asked.

"Of course," he said.

Then he disappeared.

The next night, he told her a little more about the thing that was after him. It had almost gotten him once before, but he had been able to get away. Now it was back to finish the job. It had tracked him down. Hannah listened to the boy's story. The more he talked, the closer she felt to him. He was running out of time, he said. He was growing weaker and weaker, and one day he wouldn't be able to resist its call. He would walk out to meet his doom, helpless against the creature's will.

Something thumped on the window, breaking the spell of his speech. They both jumped. The glass vibrated, but it held and didn't shatter. Hannah could sense the thing was back. It was out there. It was close. It wanted to feed.

She turned to him, reached out for his hand. Her eyes were wide and frightened. "I'm sorry, but I can't."

"It's all right," he said mournfully. "I didn't expect you to. It's a lot to ask."

The light blinked off, and he was gone.

* * *

Hannah thought about him all the next day, remembering his words, his desperation to get away from the creature in the night that was hunting him. How alone he had looked. How scared. He looked like how she had felt when her father had told her he was moving out, and she and her mother were left with no one to turn to. That evening, before going to bed, she put on her nicest nightgown, one her aunt had brought back from Paris. It was black and silk and trimmed with lace. Her aunt was her father's sister and something of a *bad influence* (again her mom's words).

She had made a decision.

When the boy appeared at three in the morning, she told him she had changed her mind.

"Are you sure?" he asked.

"Yes. But do it quickly before I chicken out," she ordered.

"You don't have to help me," he said.

"I know." She swallowed. "But I want to."

"I won't hurt you," he said.

She put a hand to her neck as if to protect it. "Promise?" How could she trust this strange boy? How could she risk her life to save him? But there was something about him—his sleepy dark eyes, his haunted expression—that drew her to him. Hannah was the type of girl who took in stray dogs and fixed birds' broken wings. Plus, there was that thing out there in the dark. She had to help him get away from it.

"Do it."

"Are you sure?" he repeated.

She nodded briskly, as if she were at the doctor's office

and asked to give consent to a particularly troublesome but much-needed operation. She took off her glasses, pulled the right strap of her nightgown to the side, and arched her neck. She closed her eyes and prepared herself for the worst.

He walked over to her. He was so tall, and when he rested his hands on her bare skin, they were surprisingly warm to the touch. He pulled her closer to him and bent down.

"Wait," he said. "Open your eyes. Look at me."

She did. She stared into his dark eyes, wondering what he was doing.

"They're beautiful—your eyes, I mean. You're beautiful," he whispered. "I thought you should know."

She sighed and closed her eyes as his hand stroked her cheek.

"Thank you," he whispered.

She could feel his hot breath on her cheek, and then his lips brushed hers for a moment. He kissed her, pressing his lips firmly upon hers. She closed her eyes and kissed him back. His lips were hot and wet.

Her first kiss, and from a vampire.

She felt his lips start to kiss the side of her mouth, and then the bottom of her chin, and then the base of her neck. This was it. She steeled herself for pain.

But he was right, there was very little. Just two tiny pinpricks, then a deep feeling of sleep. She could hear him sucking and swallowing, feel herself begin to get dizzy, woozy. Just like giving blood at the donor drive. Except she probably wouldn't get a doughnut after this.

She slumped in his arms and he caught her. She could feel

him walk her to the bed and lay her down on top of the sheets, then cover her with the duvet.

"Will I ever see you again?" she asked. It was hard to keep her eyes open. She was so tired. But she could see him very vividly now. He seemed to glow. He looked more substantial.

"Maybe," he whispered. "But you'd be safer if you didn't."

She nodded dreamily, sinking into the pillows.

In the morning, she felt spent and logy and told her mother she felt she was coming down with the flu and didn't feel like going to school. When she looked in the mirror, she saw nothing on her neck—there was no wound, no scar. Did nothing happen last night? Was she indeed going crazy? She felt around her skin with her fingertips and finally found it, a hardening of the skin, just two little bumps. Almost imperceptible, but there.

She'd made him tell her his name before she had agreed to help him.

*Dylan,* he'd said. *My name is Dylan Ward.*

Later that day, she dusted the plaque near the fireplace and looked at it closely. It was inscribed with a family crest. Underneath were the words WARD HOUSE. Wards were foster children. This was a home for the lost. A safe house on Shelter Island.

She thought of the beast out there in the night, rattling the windows, and hoped Dylan had made it to wherever he was going.

# LA FLEUR DE NUIT

**P. D. Cacek**

NEW HOPE, PENNSYLVANIA –1794

He was caught as sure as a rabbit on open ground and he knew it . . . but knowing it only made it worse.

Pushing back a lock of thick, straw-colored hair, he felt his fingers slide across the thin layer of sweat that suddenly covered his forehead. He'd stayed too long at the Johnsons' pretending to listen as Resolve, his closest friend, retold his epic battle with a giant shad on the banks of the Delaware River—"with naught but string 'n' bent nail"—while he made faces and otherwise teased Resolve's younger sister, Hannah.

Benjamin wiped his fingers off against the leg of his serge trousers and tugged at the banded collar of the calico shirt that suddenly, and without reason, felt too tight. Neither the teasing nor his inattentiveness were unusual, as he was more often at the Johnson cabin than at his grandfather's hearth fire . . . but somehow he simply lost track of time.

Generally, on the five or six evenings that found him roosting before Mrs. Johnson's cooking fire, Benjamin kept a steady, and he hoped inconspicuous, watch on the piece of greased parchment that had been set into the cabin's west-facing wall and served as a window. When the light coming through the paper faded to dull gray, he generally said his farewells and departed.

Night-fear was his secret shame and had been since he could remember.

Yet somehow this night had crept up on him while the scent of baking apples and venison stew filled the warm cabin and Mrs. Johnson made clear that she would be hurt twelve ways to Sunday if he would not stay and sup with them.

If that had not been incentive enough, Hannah had made a grand point of telling him how "completely terrible" he was for badgering her about the blacksmith's son . . . who "was *not* her beau" despite what he, Resolve, or the entire township might think. It was an opportunity that Benjamin, without siblings of his own to harass, could not pass up.

Thus not once throughout the meal, which included, along with pestering Hannah, his humble consent to a second helping of apple crumble, did he cast so much as a glance toward the parchment window.

When he finally did, it was the color of coal.

Nights came early now that the frost was in the air, and he had near a full mile of woods to walk through before he even came within sight of the canal towpath.

He should have paid more attention.

And now he was going to pay the price for his carelessness.

"Did I ever tell you boys about the Night Flower?"

Benjamin saw the eager anticipation in his friend's face but felt his innards tighten up so fast they squeezed the last bite of apple crumble back toward his throat. If it hadn't stopped him he might have been able to say something before Resolve answered, whip-quick, "No, Paw, don't think you ever did."

It was all the incentive Mr. Johnson needed. Nodding, green eyes sparkling, he pulled a split-log stool closer to the fire and made himself comfortable.

It was a known fact among mule-bargemen, locktenders, and every tavern-keeper along the canal route from Bristol to Easton that when it came to tales of haints and haunts none could beat Mr. Johnson as storyteller. Benjamin's own grandfather, who'd been the New Hope locktender before the position was given to a younger man, said Mr. Johnson collected them . . . although Benjamin was not sure, or ever had the nerve to ask, if his grandfather meant stories or ghosts.

However, what Benjamin was sure of—horribly sure—was that he and Resolve were about to be treated to one or the other.

And he wasn't looking forward to either.

Benjamin swallowed and felt the lump of spiced apples hit his belly like a stone.

"Hmm, surprised I never mentioned La Fleur de Nuit . . . that's what her Frenchy paw called her. Means 'Night Flower,' and that's what she was. Hair and eyes black as pitch, just like her Lenape maw, and them that saw her say she was a beauty beyond compare. You *sure* I never told you about her?"

Mr. Johnson, it was also said, liked to make sure he had his audience's undivided attention.

"Well, that is honestly strange . . . considering she's said to haunt the old New Hope cemetery up on Kitchen Hill. That's right close to your grandpappy's place, isn't it, Benjamin?"

Benjamin hardly had time to think before Resolve nudged his shoulder. "Hear that?"

How could he not?

"I hear," he said, and returned the nudge before meeting Mr. Johnson's eyes. "Yes, sir, it is. But my grandfather's never mentioned . . . her."

Mr. Johnson sighed deeply and pulled a briar pipe from his vest pocket. When he spoke again it was to the pipe.

"Ah, now. Well, he wouldn't, would he? Not many who'd talk about her . . . considering what she is."

Silence as thick and heavy as flue smoke filled the cabin. Benjamin took a deep breath to begin his farewells, but it was Resolve's voice that stole his chance of escape.

"What *is* she, Paw? A ghost?"

Mr. Johnson began filling his pipe while Resolve drew his knees up to his chest . . . and Benjamin turned his back to the greased-parchment window and tried to get comfortable. There was no use his measuring time now. If it wasn't full night already, it would be by the time the story ended.

"I don't think anyone knows exactly what she is," Mr. Johnson began, "but she's more than just a ghost. Although she was a dark beauty, like I said, her nature was as fair and sweet as honey. There wasn't a man who didn't fall in love with her at first glance, and she could have had any of them. But her paw wanted to find her a man who would take care of her as he had. So one day he comes back from his traplines toting more than fox pelts.

"The man was a stranger, come from someplace up north, the story goes. Tall as a young sapling and strong as a bull, they say, with golden hair and eyes like ice . . . and a temper like fire.

He fell in love with her, of course, this bright man, same as all men did . . . but she didn't feel the same. Unbeknownst to the bright man or her paw, Night Flower had given her heart to a river man with barely two coppers to rub together."

Mr. Johnson paused to light his pipe with the glowing end of a willow twig and contented himself with a few long puffs before continuing. "Of course, her paw wasn't happy when he found out, but he loved her enough to give his blessings . . . and to warn her that the bright man wouldn't take it well. He told her to leave New Hope with her river man as quickly as she could.

"But they weren't quick enough. The bright man caught them up on Kitchen Hill near the cemetery . . . and they say he broke the river man in half like he was no more'n a piece of kindling."

Mr. Johnson snapped the willow twig between his fingers, and both Benjamin and Resolve jumped at the unexpected sound.

"What happened . . . to her?" Benjamin heard himself ask.

Mr. Johnson tossed the broken twigs into the fire and nodded. "Story goes that she got clean away . . . then, about a year later, folks began seeing her up on Kitchen Hill where the river man died. She wouldn't let anyone near her, they say, not even her paw. No one knows how she survived out there, but for years folks'd see her . . . dressed in the tattered rags of what would have been her wedding dress . . . weeping on the spot where the river man died. She grew old up on that hill, they say, mourning for her lost love.

"A woodsman found her body one winter's day . . . blue as a robin's egg, frozen solid. They buried her up there, but" — Mr. Johnson looked up, ruddy face glowing, firelight dancing in his eyes—"it didn't seem to matter. There're stories of folks still seeing her up there . . . gliding pale and tattered and haggard among the headstones on moonlit nights. Like tonight."

Resolve whooped and thumped his boot-heels against the cabin's slate-stone floor until his mother scolded him quiet. Benjamin took a deep breath and shrugged with as much indifference as he could muster.

"Then maybe I'll see her tonight," he said, and wondered why in all God's glory he had done such a thing . . . until he saw the look of awe and admiration on his friend's face.

Mr. Johnson's face, however, had an entirely different look.

"You best pray you don't, boy."

Benjamin's mouth felt strangely parched. "Why not? Everyone knows ghosts can't hurt the living."

He said that with some measure of certainty. It was 1794, after all, not the Dark Ages. Mr. Johnson exhaled a long plume of smoke.

"You're right, boy, and that's true—for ghosts. But La Fleur de Nuit isn't like most ghosts. She's what's called a *mangeur d'esprit*—a spirit eater—and that's a whole different kind of haunt. A spirit eater's a hunter, boy . . . and what they hunt is the living. Know what'll happen if a man meets up with Night Flower . . . as she is now?"

"Th-the man dies?" Benjamin guessed, but Mr. Johnson shook his head.

"Worse than that. She feeds on him until she walks away with solid bone and firm flesh, leaving the man in her place—a spirit eater . . . doomed to haunt and *hunt* until he can become whole again."

The story ended with a puff of smoke and a deep chuckle. "There, and now you know the story. 'Course, I never heard of anyone actually meeting up with her, but . . . far as I know, she's still waiting." Mr. Johnson stretched his arms above his head. "Ah, me, I do like to prattle on sometimes, don't I?"

"*Sometimes?*" Mrs. Johnson asked. She was standing by the cabin door, holding Benjamin's coat open before her—a clear signal it was time for him to go. "It will be black as pitch before he gets home. I'm sorry we kept you so late, Benjamin. Give our regards to your grandfather."

"I will, ma'am." He slipped his arms into the heavy boiled wool and followed Mrs. Johnson to the front door. Mr. Johnson followed, but Resolve kept his place by the fire, and poor little Hannah was already asleep in front of the spinning wheel. "And thank you again for supper. Good night, Mr. Johnson. Resolve."

His friend nodded a yawn as Benjamin stepped out into the cold. There were still traces of twilight above the western hills, but he'd be traveling almost due east, directly into the approaching night.

Mr. Johnson waited until Benjamin was well past the split-rail fence that bordered the property before shouting his farewell.

"Good night, Benjamin, and take care that you walk quick past Kitchen Hill . . . La Fleur de Nuit's been waiting up there almost a hundred years now, so I suspect she's powerful hungry."

Benjamin looked back just in time to see Mrs. Johnson slap her husband's arm. He hoped it stung good and proper.

Shoulders hunched, eyes downcast, and feet keeping a steady cadence against the frost-sheathed path, Benjamin tried very hard to concentrate on absolutely *nothing*. Not the cold, or the feel of the ground beneath his boots, or the dark, or Mr. Johnson's story. Especially not Mr. Johnson's story.

La Fleur de Nuit.

Stuff and nonsense. It was only a story to frighten children, and *he* wasn't a child. He'd been apprenticed a year now to the miller and could, if he chose, marry once his apprenticeship was over. He'd be seventeen, a bit old perhaps, but he might even decide to marry Hannah Johnson if she outgrew her silliness. Two years to go, but even so, he was still near enough a man to know the way of things. Stories were naught but words, and ghosts were . . .

Before Benjamin could finish the thought, an owl hooted from the darkness above him and he stumbled to a halt.

For a moment he stood silent, frozen to the spot as if he'd suddenly been turned to stone . . . the very image of a scarecrow with straw hair and hollow gray eyes, its hand-me-down coat fluttering softly in the wind. *Stop. It was only an owl.* Very slowly his eyes moved upward toward the night-hidden branches.

With the moon still behind the eastern hills, he could see nothing but the occasional glint of stars through the leafless branches. The owl refused to show itself, but as he continued to look, Benjamin thought he saw something move at the far edge of his vision.

His head turned of its own accord, and Benjamin found himself gazing at the tomb-dotted slope of Kitchen Hill . . . and the *thing* that moved along the weathered stones.

It seemed no more than a pale patch of floating mist, but Benjamin felt the hair slowly rise across the back of his neck.

A name came unbidden to his lips, but he couldn't stop himself from saying it.

"La Fleur de Nuit . . ."

For a moment the pale shape seemed to stop, hovering motionless above the ground; then it shifted direction and slowly began drifting down the slope of the hill.

*Fog . . . just a patch of ground fog carried by the wind . . .*

But the wind was at his back. Benjamin could feel it blowing toward Kitchen Hill and the old cemetery. Whatever the pale shape was, it moved against the wind.

Toward him.

*No . . . it's only fog, and it was only a story. It's not real.* La Fleur de Nuit. *Mr. Johnson only told that story because he knew I had to walk home this way. She's not real . . . she can't be real . . . she's not . . . .*

*"M'aidez."*

The words hovered in the darkness between them, and there was no mistaking or denying it. He *heard* it, heard it plain—a woman's voice—but it wasn't until it . . . the pale shape . . . *she* reached for him that Benjamin turned and ran.

And kept running until his boot-heels left fresh scars on the towpath leading to his grandfather's cabin.

"HAH! You'll have to come up with a *new* story, Benjamin," Resolve said around a growing smile. "I heard that one, same as you."

"You don't believe me?"

"Believe that you saw a ghost and it talked to you?" For answer, Resolve dropped the sack of field corn he'd carried in for grinding and brayed like an overworked mule. The noise scattered a flock of pigeons off the roof beams.

Benjamin folded his arms across the front of his leather apron to keep from boxing his friend's ear, and idly flicked a piece of chaff from his shirtsleeve. The only reason he'd said anything—save for mention of running scared—was his confidence that Resolve, of anyone in the village, would understand.

And believe him.

Resolve wiped his eyes and took a deep breath. "What was it she said again?"

"Sounded like 'mayader.'"

"Mayader? Hmm. Couldn't have been some ol' she-fox calling to her kits, could it? They sound like folks sometimes."

Benjamin felt the blood rise steadily to his cheeks. "I know the difference between a fox and a person . . . and this was a—it was a woman's voice."

"A ghost's voice, you mean."

The anger that had been building inside Benjamin suddenly cooled, and he shivered in its absence. "Yes."

"What's this? Two strapping young men standing around gossiping? I somehow don't think it was about grinding corn. Benjamin, a man can't better himself if he's idle."

A different sort of heat rose into Benjamin's cheeks as he unfolded his arms and reached for one of the waiting sacks. Mr. Parry, the miller, winked his approval and nodded to the tall man in a dark suit at his side. Dr. Todd smiled back.

"Oh, I don't think there was any idleness here, Mr. Parry," the doctor said. "Was there, boys?"

They both solemnly shook their heads in agreement; but

Resolve, never one to let a subject drop without cause, hooked both thumbs into his suspender straps and met the doctor's eyes.

"We were talking about words, sir," he said. "Benjamin heard a new one."

"Oh?"

The sack of field corn over one shoulder, Benjamin closed his eyes and desperately wished Resolve would disappear. When he opened them a moment later, Resolve was still there, and now both Dr. Todd and Mr. Parry were looking at him with a new and, given the circumstance, somewhat misplaced admiration.

"Yes, sir. I was . . . wondering what 'mayader' meant."

"Mayader?" Mr. Parry shook his head. "Not familiar with it. Unless it's a name, May Ader."

Benjamin hadn't thought of that.

"No, no, I don't think so," Dr. Todd said. "You don't mean *'m'aidez,'* do you?"

A chill caressed his spine. "It—it sounded just like that. Yes, sir."

"Ah, then it's not a name, Parry." The doctor seemed pleased that he'd solved the problem. "It's French for 'help me.' Where did you hear it?"

Benjamin tightened his grip on the sack and watched the color fade from Resolve's face until it was almost as white as . . . a patch of moving ground fog.

"In a story, sir."

*"I don't believe it . . . but even if I did I'd not be party to it. If she's real, and I'm not saying she is, you know what she can do. You go back there and you'll only prove yourself a fool."*

*"Better a fool than a coward."*

With the memory of their conversation still ringing in his ears, Benjamin gently touched the spot on his cheek where Resolve's fist struck. He hadn't intended on calling his friend a coward any more than he actually thought he'd find himself standing at the entrance of the old cemetery as the sun fell behind Kitchen Hill.

Yet both happened.

After a deep breath and silent prayer, Benjamin walked up the gentle slope until he reached the Coryell family's granite marker. As clear as he could recall, the patch of fog had been near this spot when he heard the voice.

*Asking for help.*

Benjamin took a deep breath and squared his shoulders. Though daylight was quickly fading, the sky was still bright enough for at least a moment's counterfeit courage.

"Hullo?"

He didn't shout, but his voice was loud enough to frighten a groundhog into lumbering retreat. Benjamin watched it disappear beneath the roots of a lightning-struck buttonwood as the wind shifted.

"You've come back."

He turned, fists clenched, muscles bunched in preparation for flight, breath coming too quick for his lungs to catch . . . and stumbled over his own feet when he saw her. Not old or haggard or ragged, but fresh and young and alive; the girl pulled a pale gray shawl tighter across the shoulders of her bleached muslin dress and giggled. She was pale, but not extraordinarily so, and her dark eyes sparkled with life.

In the fading light her ebony hair shone like a raven's wing.

"I'm sorry. I didn't mean to frighten you again."

"A-again?" Benjamin got to his feet and tried not to make too much of a show of brushing dried leaves and dirt from the seat of his trousers. The girl looked away shyly.

"Yes, last night." She trailed a long-fingered hand across the top of a weathered headstone. "I . . . lost something and hoped you could help me find it. But it's no matter"—she looked up, her eyes meeting his—"now. I am glad you came back so I could apologize."

"I—I've never seen you in these parts before. Who are you?"

Her smile brought a faint touch of roses to her cheeks. "My name's Fleur."

La Fleur de Nuit. A tremor started in his legs and quickly worked its way into his belly. "Are you a . . . ghost?"

She cocked her head to one side, the smile growing dimples as her black hair tumbled over one shoulder. "Do I *look* like a ghost?"

"No—but your name . . ."

"It means 'flower' in French. My papa named me that."

"La Fleur de Nuit?"

"Night Flower." Her smile grew wistful. "That's lovely. Do you speak French?"

Benjamin slowly began backing down the hill. "No, I—there's a story about a girl named Night Flower."

"Oh."

He stopped next to the grave of a long-forgotten child. "And you have the same name."

"It's a common enough name." Suddenly shy, she dipped her chin and looked at him from beneath lowered lashes. "What's your name?"

"Benjamin Thomas."

Smiling as evening deepened into night, she closed the distance between them. The hem of her shawl fluttered and her long, pale skirt trailed over the ground—*like fog*—as she offered him her hand.

Her skin was cool against his work-hardened palm, but firm and solid and very real.

"*Comment allez-vous*, Benjamin Thomas?" She curtsied. "I'm very happy to meet you."

He nodded back but didn't pull his hand away. "Likewise. But last night . . ."

"Yes?"

Benjamin swayed as he tried to remember exactly what he'd heard, and felt her grip tighten to steady him. "Did you . . . find what you lost?"

"Yes." She sighed, and the night seemed to grow warmer around him. "I think I did."

They sat among the graves and talked while daylight faded into dusk and dusk deepened to evening without his notice—just like the night before. He told her about his apprenticeship and Resolve—briefly—and how his parents had died of sickness while he was still a baby. When he pointed out their graves, she gathered bouquets of leaves to place on each one. She was so sweet, so kind . . . he'd never met anyone like her before.

And it wasn't only her beauty or compassion that captured him; he found interest in everything she said. Moreover, he ached with pity for her. She had no friends, and her father kept her a virtual prisoner, never allowing her out of the house until the evening shadows appeared.

"Poor Papa. He thinks someone is going to steal me away," she told him, and then laughed. Benjamin laughed with her, although he didn't understand the reason for it.

When they finally said good night, the moon was high in the sky and the shadows were like ink. Any other night would have found him looking back over his shoulder every few minutes, but she had changed him. He no longer feared the dark.

Smiling to himself, Benjamin strolled with slow, easy strides back to his grandfather's cabin and fell into blissful sleep the moment he lay down.

He met her the next night after supper, and the next.

And so it went.

It was late on the afternoon of the sixth day when he found Resolve Johnson waiting for him on the road leading from town.

"Mother Maybelle . . . What's *wrong* with you?"

It took Benjamin longer than it should to shake free of his friend's grip. "What are you talking about? I'm fine."

"Fine? You haven't been at the mill in two days. I just came from there, and now I know why. Have you seen yourself? You look like death!"

When Resolve reached for him again, Benjamin stepped back. "I caught a chill."

"A chill? Looks more like you caught a blizzard. If you're ill, why aren't you tucked under blankets in front of the fire? Your grandpappy's half crazed with worry."

Benjamin dug his hands deeper into the pockets of his coat and felt the sleeves of his shirt ride up his arms. A shiver overtook him and, for a moment, held him in its unrelenting grasp. Lately, no matter how hard he tried, he couldn't seem to get warm. But that was of little consequence. Fleur was waiting.

"You've been troubling my grandfather, as well?" he shouted. "Don't you have anything better to do than spy on people?"

Resolve stared at him. "Spy? I'm your friend. I was worried about—"

"I said I'm fine." The air suddenly rattled in Benjamin's lungs, but he managed to stop the cough before it had a chance to start. "I have to go."

"Where? Back to Kitchen Hill?"

Benjamin felt the muscles in his neck creak as he slowly turned to face his onetime friend. "You have been spying on me."

"Gol' amighty, Benjamin, you are. How can you, knowing what it is, what *she* is? Please, you can't go back. . . ."

"It's none of your business where I go, Resolve Johnson. And you don't know what you're talking about. None of you do . . . not even your father!"

"Benjamin, listen to me."

Benjamin knocked against his friend's shoulder as he passed in minor payback for the bruise on his cheek. "I'm done listening to you. Do you have so little to do that you feel it's my obligation to keep you entertained?"

Pain and hurt had flashed across Resolve's face when he looked back.

"I only wanted . . ."

"To bother me," Benjamin added. "That's the only thing you ever want. Leave me be."

It took a moment, but the concern in his friend's eyes slowly hardened to something else.

"Fine. So be it."

This time it was Resolve who turned and stomped off without another word in the direction of his family's cabin. Benjamin watched him until his outline blended with the evening's shadows and disappeared. Then he turned toward the path leading to Kitchen Hill and thought no more about his friend or the cold or the growing weakness in his arms and legs. There wasn't room in Benjamin for more than one thought. And that was of her.

She was waiting for him, arms open wide, eyes shining, bright roses in her cheeks. Her name suited her. She *was* a Night Flower.

La Fleur de Nuit.

"You're late." She giggled as they hugged. Benjamin felt the vibrations against his ribs and sighed. He couldn't remember ever being so content. Her arms tightened around him. "I almost gave up hope."

"I said . . . I'd be here."

"I know."

"You're just . . . being . . . sil—"

The words suddenly faltered on Benjamin's tongue as dizziness engulfed him, misting his vision. Gasping for breath, he would have pitched forward had she not caught and held him. When his legs finally buckled under him she lowered him gently to the ground and touched his face.

The last thing he saw was her sweet smile.

He must have fallen asleep, because when he woke up he was stretched out on the ground staring up at the clear, star-dotted night sky, his head resting on a shallow grave mound. Fleur stood over him, and he could see her shivering beneath her shawl.

Had the night grown colder? It didn't seem cold at all.

Benjamin stood up and ran a hand through his hair. There wasn't a trace of dizziness or weakness. He felt . . . nothing. Frowning, he took a step but couldn't feel the ground under his feet. His body had lost its shape, the once familiar outline of feet and legs melting as he gazed into something that looked like—

A patch of ground fog.

Benjamin reached for her with a hand as pale and insubstantial as moonlight.

"What's happening to me?"

Fleur lifted the shawl to cover the top of her head, the way he'd seen women do at funerals, and backed away.

"*Merci,* Benjamin. *Je suis désolée,* but I've been waiting so long for someone to come . . . and take my place. Please try to understand."

"Wait. Help me!"

Shaking her head, La Fleur de Nuit fled the place that had been her prison for so long. She stopped when she reached the path and turned, looking for him among the shadows. Benjamin watched her dark eyes and knew she couldn't see him

"I am sorry, Benjamin, but this needn't be forever. *Bonne chance."*

She left without another word or look, the echo of her steps—light, eager—fading as the night settled around him.

Benjamin hunched shoulders he could no longer feel and glided toward an ornately carved granite marker. He wasn't worried, not in the least.

After a day or two, when the anger had passed, Resolve would come looking for him.

Until then, he would wait.

# EVER AFTER

**Isobel Bird**

"Hey, wake up. It's your move."

Julia, who had been staring at the fire, looked across the table at her sister. Elizabeth was watching her, waiting for a response. "It's your turn," she said, nodding at the Monopoly board.

Julia picked up the dice and halfheartedly let them fall from her fingers. She moved the little metal shoe ahead five squares.

"Marvin Gardens," Elizabeth said cheerfully. "And I have a hotel on it, so you owe me twelve hundred bucks."

"I only have seven hundred," Julia informed her. "I guess you win. How sad for me."

She tossed her remaining bills at Elizabeth, who scooped them up and added them to her already thick pile. Julia stood up and stretched. Her legs ached from sitting on the floor for so long.

"It's never going to stop raining," she predicted, looking out the window at the downpour. It had begun moments after their arrival at the cabin on Wooden Island and hadn't let up for three days. "This vacation officially sucks."

"At least we have a lot of board games," Elizabeth said. "Come on, let's play Sorry!"

"I'm already sorry," said Julia. "I'm going to go read."

"I don't know how you can read so much," her sister remarked. "Especially those fantasy books you like. They're so boring."

"It's real life that's boring," Julia snapped.

"Maybe *your* life," countered Elizabeth.

Julia ignored her. Despite their bickering, she and Elizabeth really did like each other. *It's the rain,* Julia thought. *It's making us go crazy a little bit more every day. Pretty soon we'll start planning ways to kill each other.* She imagined hiding in a closet, waiting for Elizabeth to walk by so that she could hit her over the head with the heavy cast-iron skillet that sat on the kitchen stove. Thinking about it made her laugh.

"What's so funny?" Elizabeth demanded.

Before Julia could answer, the cabin door banged open and her father came in, his arms full of brown paper grocery bags. Her mother was right behind him, carrying another bag. She quickly shut the door, locking the wind and rain outside. Water dripped from their raincoats and pooled on the cabin's floorboards.

"What'd you get?" Elizabeth asked.

"Help us put this stuff away and you'll find out," her father answered as he disappeared into the kitchen. "I might even share the big gossip we picked up in town."

"Gossip?" said Elizabeth, suddenly interested. "What gossip?"

Julia rolled her eyes. *Typical,* she thought as her sister bounced into the kitchen.

"Julia, this might interest you, too," her mother called out, poking her head through the kitchen doorway.

"I'm sure," said Julia. "What is it, someone's cat got knocked up? Oh, I know, they caught a bored tourist trying to swim for shore."

"Fine," her mother called back. "If you don't want to hear about Serena Locke living next door, that's all right."

"Serena Locke?" Julia said, certain she'd heard incorrectly. "Here? On Wooden Island?"

"Who's Serena Locke?" asked Elizabeth, clearly disappointed by the quality of the gossip. "Should I know her? Oh, is she that Dutch supermodel, the one with the drug problem?"

"She's Julia's favorite author," her mother informed her.

"Serena Locke?" Julia repeated. "You're sure?"

"One of the local fishermen told us," said her father. "Apparently, she's the local celebrity."

"Authors aren't celebrities," Elizabeth complained. "I thought you were going to tell us something good."

"Why would Serena Locke live here?" Julia wondered aloud, ignoring Elizabeth's comment.

"Why not?" answered her father as he took cans from the grocery bags and stacked them in the cupboard. "It's beautiful. It's private. There's no one to bother her. Sounds to me like the perfect place to write."

"Where's her house?" asked Julia.

"Down the road a little," said her mother. "The other side of the hill."

Julia couldn't believe it. Serena Locke. Her neighbor. Well, sort of her neighbor. After all, her family was only there for two weeks. Still, suddenly Wooden Island didn't seem quite so dull.

Elizabeth, noticing her sister's expression, began teasing her. "Maybe she'll invite you to tea," she said. "Then she'll write a story all about you. 'For my very *dearest* friend in the whole world, Julia Faderman,'" she added in a singsong voice.

"Shut up," Julia said, the wheels of her mind turning rapidly. She hoped Elizabeth couldn't see her cheeks turning red.

*What a great idea this was,* Julia thought blackly as she trudged through the forest fifteen minutes later. She'd wrapped herself in an old green raincoat she'd found in the cabin's closet. It was way too big for her. The hood surrounded her head, and it smelled faintly of dead fish.

Although the branches of the redwood trees, interlaced like fingers above her, kept out the worst of the rain, cold drops dripped down. And here and there, where the trees were farther apart, the rain fell freely. The raincoat helped, but Julia had been unable to find any waterproof boots, and her sneakers were now soaked through.

*You'll be stricken with the ague,* she scolded herself. *Or consumption. That would be tragic.* She practiced coughing, and imagined her family gathered around her bed as she grew weaker and weaker before dying. She knew the reality was that she'd probably only catch a cold—at worst the flu—but it was more fun to imagine something grimmer.

She was walking uphill now, her feet slipping a little on the dead needles that carpeted the ground. She felt herself begin to breathe harder, and for a moment she was tempted to turn around and find an easier path. But the top of the little hill wasn't that far off, and soon she reached it.

Below her sat a small house. It was larger than the cabin she and her family were renting, but not by a lot. It was nicer, though. Unlike their rental, you could tell that someone lived there. A car was parked out front. Plants and flowers grew around the sides, and Julia saw what looked like a large garden in the back. Puffs of smoke floated from the chimney. It reminded Julia of a cottage in a fairy tale.

As she watched, a woman stepped outside. Tall and thin, she had long dark hair and pale skin.

"It really is her," Julia whispered. She recognized Serena Locke from the pictures on her book covers.

As if hearing Julia's words, Serena Locke turned toward the hill and looked right at the spot where Julia was standing. Julia quickly ducked behind the trunk of a big tree. Her heart was pounding, and suddenly she was afraid. But why? *She's just a writer,* she told herself. *She's nothing to be afraid of.*

Still, she couldn't bring herself to look around the edge of the trunk again. She shivered. Her feet were freezing, and the wind had started to blow the rain sideways. Her hair was wet, and she wanted to change into some dry clothes. She couldn't meet Serena Locke looking like a drowned rat. She would, she thought, just go home and get warm and dry. Then, tomorrow, she would come back and introduce herself like a normal person.

*Don't be stupid,* she reproached herself. *You came all this way; another few yards won't kill you.*

She hesitated another minute. Then, taking a deep breath, she turned and started down the hill toward the house, practicing what she would say when Serena Locke opened the door.

"I love your books," she said out loud, testing the sound of it. *No, that's too dorky.* She mulled over other possibilities as she navigated the slope of the hill.

She was near the bottom when she saw the lights. At first she thought someone had set off fireworks. But there were no pops or explosions, and besides, it was too wet for fireworks. Then she saw them again, bright flickers that broke through the dim at the rear of the cottage. They shot upward, then went out, smothered by the rain and fog.

Intrigued, Julia made her way toward the lights. She forgot all about Serena Locke, her mind occupied by the strange flashes that kept coming like shooting stars in reverse. When she reached the back of the house, she stopped and peered around the corner.

Serena Locke was standing in the middle of the garden Julia had glimpsed from the hill. Wild and overgrown, it was made up mostly of rosebushes. The roses—bloodred and white—formed a large circle. Their branches were knotted, the roses hanging heavily from them, their heads wet with rain.

But Julia wasn't interested in the roses. Her gaze was fixed on Serena Locke. She was facing away from Julia, wearing a cloak made of a purplish-gray material. The hood was thrown back, and Serena Locke's long hair cascaded down her back. Her hands were raised, and around her head a swarm of bright lights swirled like stars.

Julia watched as Serena Locke's hand shot out and grabbed one of the stars. Just as quickly, she plunged the hand down, out of Julia's view. As she did, the other stars became agitated. The swarming grew more frantic, and Julia heard a thin, high sound, like wind whistling through the trees. A few of the stars shot up and away, disappearing into the mist.

Several times Serena Locke reached out and snatched another star. Each time, the keening sound came again. Hearing it, Julia felt herself shiver. There was something both sad and frightening about the sound, but she couldn't say exactly what it was.

When she saw Serena Locke start to turn around, Julia once again found herself wanting to hide. Before she could stop herself, she had backed around the corner of the cottage. She kept going, walking quickly toward the front of the house. *I'll wait for her there,* she told herself. *I don't want her to think I've been spying.*

But when she reached the front of the cottage, her resolve failed her. She dashed over to the car parked in the driveway and ducked down behind it. *What's the matter with you?* she reprimanded herself. *She's not going to eat you.*

Raising her head, she saw Serena Locke turn the corner and approach the front door. In her hands she held a large glass jar. Inside, perhaps a dozen stars swirled frantically. *Fireflies,* Julia realized. *She was catching fireflies. That's all.*

Again she felt ridiculous. She and Elizabeth had done that very thing dozens of times when they were little. They'd punched holes in the top of the jar and set it in their bedroom like a lantern. When they were asleep, their father had let the fireflies go.

If explaining herself wouldn't have made her feel even worse, she would have stood up. But she remained frozen in place, her body refusing to move. She could only watch as Serena Locke opened the front door and entered the cottage.

Only after Serena Locke had gone inside and shut the door behind her did Julia breathe freely. Leaning her head against the tire, she scolded herself for being so stupid.

*She was just catching fireflies,* she thought. *Fireflies! What were you afraid of?*

She'd overreacted. But despite knowing this to be true, she also had to acknowledge that she really had been afraid. Something about the scene in the back garden had frightened her. She couldn't say what. All she knew was that there was something peculiar about the twinkling lights, something that made her think they weren't just ordinary fireflies.

An angry rumbling jarred her out of her thoughts. She looked up and saw thick, dark clouds rolling overhead. They swept across the sky like enormous bats, growling angrily. Heavy drops of rain spat from their mouths, chilling Julia even more as they spattered against her face.

She raised her head, peering over the edge of the car's trunk. If she hurried, she could make it across the short patch of grass to the trees, then home. With a little luck, Serena Locke wouldn't be looking out a window and would never know that Julia had been there. She gathered herself together and prepared to sprint to safety.

But she couldn't get her feet to move. As much as she wanted to get back to the cabin, where she couldn't embarrass herself any further, she wanted even more to get a closer look at Serena Locke. So instead of heading for the forest and the cover of the trees, Julia found herself once more skirting the edge of the cottage.

This time she went around the left-hand side. Foxgloves were planted all along the cottage's wall, and the pink-and-cream-colored flowers nodded their dark-spotted heads at her as she crept silently through them. When she came to the first set of windows, she paused momentarily before chancing a look through the glass.

It was a bathroom, and not a very interesting one. A plain white towel hung on a hook beside the shower. A toothbrush stood in a glass beside the sink. Looking at the room, Julia was slightly disappointed. She would have thought that someone like Serena Locke would have a bathroom filled with candles, maybe even rose petals scattered in the tub or something.

She continued on, feeling a little braver. *She's just a normal person after all,* she told herself. *She uses Ivory soap and flosses.* The idea of Serena Locke flossing struck her as funny, and she let out a muffled laugh. How stupid she'd been. She had nothing to fear from Serena Locke. In fact, she thought, she should just turn around and go knock on the front door instead of creeping around like some kind of Peeping Tom.

She came to the next set of windows. This time she brazenly looked inside, expecting to find yet another boring room. But after a quick look, she turned away, her heart pounding. Serena Locke was standing not a dozen feet from the window. The room was some kind of a library. Bookshelves lined the walls. There was a fireplace in which a fire crackled brightly. Across the room from it, facing the window, was a large desk.

*That's where she writes her books,* Julia thought excitedly, despite the panic filling her head. *If she'd been sitting there, she would have been looking right at me.*

But Serena Locke was not sitting at her desk. She was standing near the fireplace. Her back was to the window, and to Julia. Unable to stop herself, Julia took another look. Serena Locke was now kneeling by the fire. The big glass jar was sitting on the floor beside her. It was filled with a swirling tornado of gold and red, which then turned silver and blue. The lights inside changed colors rapidly, reminding Julia of tiny wings beating frantically, as if the jar were filled with butterflies.

As she watched, Serena Locke unscrewed the lid of the jar. Very carefully, she lifted one side of the lid. Her hand darted into the jar and returned holding something that writhed and twisted in her fingers. She tightened the lid once more and pushed the jar aside, concentrating on the thing in her hand.

With one quick movement, she plucked at the flashing lights. Julia saw a spark leap from the thrashing thing, and the lights went suddenly dead. The thing in Serena Locke's hand was revealed to be some kind of small bird. It was terribly thin, and it hung limply. It twitched twice, then was still.

Julia recoiled at the sight. Why would Serena Locke want to kill a little bird, especially a bird as beautiful as the ones in the jar? And what kind of birds were they, anyway? Julia had never seen anything like them.

*They must be hummingbirds,* she thought. *That's why the wings beat so quickly.*

She wondered why Serena Locke would want to kill hummingbirds. They were beautiful creatures and did nothing but good. It didn't make sense that someone would want to harm them.

Serena Locke was doing something else now. She had picked up what looked like a long, thin needle. It glinted in the light of the fire, the metal cold and deadly. Julia watched, horrified, as the woman pushed one end of the skewer into the body of the little hummingbird. Julia saw it spasm, and realized with a wrenching sickness that the poor thing was still alive.

*She only pulled its wings off,* she thought. *So it couldn't fly away.*

Once she had it skewered on the needle, Serena Locke thrust the tiny bird into the flames. The heat licked hungrily at the body, and again the creature writhed. It was being burned alive.

Julia felt herself getting sick. She bent over and vomited into the grass. She'd never seen such a display of cruelty in her life. How could Serena Locke, the woman who wrote such beautiful books, be so mean? Julia's stomach wrenched again, and the foul taste of sickness filled her mouth.

*I have to stop her,* she thought. She had to save the rest of the beautiful little birds. She couldn't stand to think of them dying, their wings pulled off, their bodies roasting in the fire. What kind of monster could do such a thing to innocent creatures?

Wiping her mouth, she looked through the window again. Serena Locke had removed the hummingbird from the fire and was pulling the body from the skewer. It was blackened and smoking. Holding it between her fingers, Serena Locke lifted it up and peered at it.

*She's going to eat it,* Julia thought, sickened by the notion.

But Serena Locke didn't eat it. Instead, she held the bird over a small silver bowl. Then she squeezed it. Dark liquid dripped from her fingers and into the bowl. It glimmered wetly as it fell in thick strings. She continued to squeeze until the flow of blood—for Julia was certain it must be blood—slowed and finally stopped. Then Serena Locke tossed the small drained body back into the flames, where it was consumed in a ball of fire.

Once more she picked up the glass jar. The birds trapped inside began to batter the glass with their wings. Julia, watching, wanted to scream out for Serena Locke to stop torturing them. But she knew that she had to do something more. She had to free the birds.

Her thoughts racing, she turned and ran back to the front of the house. She looked at the front door. Maybe, she thought, if she knocked on the door Serena Locke would come to see who it was. If she could get inside—maybe by telling Serena Locke what a fan she was—she could distract her long enough to save the birds.

*She won't let you in,* she told herself. *She'll make some excuse and send you away.*

No, she needed a better plan. Something that would distract Serena Locke for more than a minute. But what?

She looked at the car. *Maybe it has an alarm,* she thought suddenly. She could break one of the windows and set it off. That is, if it was even turned on. *It's not like there's anyone around to steal it,* Julia thought darkly. *Why would she even lock it?*

Still, it was the best she could come up with. But breaking a window? The idea of doing something so extreme frightened her. She'd never done anything like that. And if Serena Locke ever found out who she was, her parents would kill her for sure, little birds or no little birds.

*She pulled its wings off,* her inner voice said. *She roasted it alive.*

There were several good-size rocks sitting in the grass along the edge of the driveway. Before she could stop herself, Julia picked one up. Standing next to the car, she hesitated only a moment before raising her hand and bringing the rock down on the driver's-side window. It shattered, sending tiny pieces of glass raining down.

Immediately, a screeching sound filled the air as the car's alarm went off. Startled, Julia recoiled from the noise. Then, regaining her senses, she ran to the side of the house and hid herself. She watched the door, her heart beating wildly.

*Come on,* she thought anxiously. *Come on.*

The door opened, and Serena Locke came outside. She looked at her car, as if she couldn't believe it was making so much racket. Then she began to walk toward it.

Julia turned and scuttled along the side of the house. She knew she had only a minute or two to do what had to be done. She tried not to think about everything that could go wrong; she thought only of the little birds in the jar.

Reaching the rear of the house, she was relieved to find that there was a back door. *Now if it's only unlocked,* she thought as she reached for the handle.

She pulled, and the door opened. Julia stepped into a small room. It was what her mother called a mud room, a small space for leaving wet shoes and odds and ends that didn't have a place anywhere else. Julia dashed through it and into a hallway. She looked to her right and saw the doorway to Serena Locke's library.

The jar was sitting on the desk. The birds inside had stopped moving around. Julia prayed they weren't dead. She went to the desk and took up the jar, peering inside. When she saw what was contained within the jar, she almost dropped it.

They weren't birds, although she saw how she had made the mistake of thinking they were. They did have wings. But those wings were attached to bodies. Human bodies. At least, they resembled humans. They had arms and legs, heads and faces. But the skin of the creatures in the jar was blue and green, silver and purple, red and gold, each of them a different color.

One of the things opened its eyes and looked straight at Julia. The eyes were amber, and they glinted with fire. Julia brought the jar closer to her face and looked into the creature's face.

*Help us.*

The voice was like rain, cold and wild. Although Julia could hear it clearly, she was fairly certain that the words had not been spoken aloud. They seemed to exist only inside her head.

*Free us.*

The creature raised one blue hand and pressed it against the glass. It tried to sit up but slumped to the bottom of the jar again. Its thin legs were tangled in the arms, legs, and wings of the other creatures. Julia counted quickly. There were ten of them. She wondered if the blue one was the only one still alive.

"What are you?" Julia whispered.

The creature cocked its head and blinked its wild eyes. *We are the Children of the Other World,* it thought-spoke.

Julia recognized the description. Then it came to her—it was from one of Serena Locke's own books. Realizing what the creature was saying, she shook her head. "But you aren't real," she said, unable to believe.

"And yet, they are."

Julia whirled around. Serena Locke stood in the doorway of the library, blocking the only exit. She looked at Julia, and the expression on her face was unreadable.

*She sounds just like I thought she would,* Julia thought despite her terror.

"I assume you're to thank for my broken window," said Serena Locke.

Julia swallowed. How had she not heard the alarm go off? The past minutes seemed to have passed in the blink of an eye. She felt disoriented, and for a moment forgot why she was even there.

"I, um, I . . ." she said stupidly.

"You were spying on me," Serena Locke suggested.

Julia nodded. "I saw you catch the . . ." She hesitated again, not knowing how to finish the sentence. She looked down at the jar in her hands. The creatures were all still.

"The Faeries aren't dead, if that's what you're thinking," Serena Locke said.

Julia raised her eyes and looked at Serena Locke. The woman was staring intently at the jar. An expression of fierce hatred had come over her, as if she gazed upon a jar of poisonous spiders. Suddenly, Julia remembered the spit, the squirming body, the blood.

"You kill them," she said, her voice shaky. "I saw you." Her eyes went to the fireplace.

Serena Locke nodded. "Yes," she said. "I kill them."

"You stab them and then burn them," Julia accused.

"Silver and fire," said Serena Locke. "It's the only way."

Julia shook her head, not believing what she was hearing. "Are they really . . . Faeries?" she asked. Despite her fear, she was fascinated by the possibility.

Serena Locke said nothing. She advanced into the room, walking toward Julia. "Why don't you just give me the jar?" she said softly. "This is all a big mistake. Give me the jar. Then you and I can sit and talk. Would you like that?"

*I'd like that very much,* Julia thought. She was face-to-face with her favorite author. She thought about her favorite of Serena Locke's books, *A Bustle in the Hedgerow*. She had so many questions about it. Now she could ask them. Maybe, she thought, she and Serena Locke *could* be friends.

*Don't listen to the witch!*

The voice slashed through her dreamy thoughts, and Julia

remembered the jar in her hands and the Faeries inside of it.

*She lies! The witch lies!*

Suddenly, Julia realized that Serena Locke had almost reached her. The woman was stretching out her hands, ready to rip the jar from Julia's grasp.

Julia lunged to the side, away from Serena Locke. She ran behind the big desk, putting it between herself and the now angry woman.

"You're a witch," said Julia. It made sense, she supposed. But she knew enough about witches—real witches—to know that they weren't like the ones in fairy tales. *Then again,* she told herself, *you never really believed in Faeries, either.*

Serena Locke laughed. "Yes," she said. "I'm a witch, and this is my gingerbread cottage. I lured you here to fatten you up and bake you into a pie. Is that what you really think?"

"But you kill them," Julia protested.

Serena Locke's face hardened. "Enough of this," she said. "I don't need to explain myself to you."

*Look at her desk.* The voice was pleading, weak, as if the Faerie was using its last breath to communicate with Julia.

She looked down. The little bowl Julia had seen in Serena Locke's hands earlier was still there. It was filled with the dark liquid. Up close, it was the color of rubies. She knew that it was blood. Unlike human blood, however, it glinted with flecks of gold. It pulsed with a strange energy, almost as if it were alive.

Then Julia noticed the pen lying beside the bowl. It was an old-fashioned fountain pen, with a silver nib. Next to the pen was a notebook. It was open, and one page was half filled with writing. Writing the color of the Faerie blood. The words shimmered on the page, as if they'd been written in fire.

"You use their blood for ink," said Julia as she realized what she was looking at. Then, another realization. "You write your books in their blood."

"You don't understand," Serena Locke answered. "You have no idea what you're dealing with."

Julia looked at her, shaking her head. "Maybe not," she said. "But I understand that you're killing them. You're using them."

"No more than they've used me," Serena Locke said angrily. "It's no more than they deserve."

Julia didn't understand. "What are you talking about?"

Serena Locke's face softened. She hesitated before speaking. "They stole my child," she said. "My daughter. When she was a baby. They came and they took her in the night."

*Lies!* hissed the Faerie voice. *She gave the child to us. In exchange for our help. In exchange for our stories.*

Julia wondered if Serena Locke could hear what the Faerie said to her. She didn't think so, as the woman continued to look at the floor. Her eyes were sad, and Julia thought she might be crying.

"They took my child," she repeated. Then she looked up at Julia. "And for that, they must pay."

"Why do you write in their blood?" Julia asked.

Serena Locke gave a little laugh. "Because it contains magic," she answered. She paused before continuing. "But mostly because it gives me satisfaction, however small."

*Murderer!* cried the Faerie. Its shrill voice, filled with terror, sliced through Julia's mind. She could feel it physically, a piercing pain in her head.

"No," she said, shaking her head to ease the pain. "It's not right. You shouldn't kill them."

She began to unscrew the top of the jar. Inside, a buzzing commenced, and she saw that the Faeries were stirring, lifting their heads and stretching their crumpled wings as they gazed at the slowly turning roof of their prison.

*Yes,* came a chorus of sibilant voices. *Free us. Help us avenge this wrong.*

"Stop!" Serena Locke said. "You don't know what they are. You don't know what they will do."

Julia's hand hesitated. She felt a wave of jumbled thoughts reach out to her from the jar, a cacophony of voices. *Open it. Save us. She's a murderer. She gave us her child willingly.*

"Is it true?" Julia asked Serena Locke. "Did you give them your child?"

Serena Locke began to protest, then stopped. She wrung her hands. "Yes," she said finally.

A rush of joyous voices filled Julia's mind. *See, she admits it. She asked us to take her child. In exchange for our stories.*

"How could you do that?" Julia asked.

Serena Locke's eyes were damp when she looked at Julia. "I didn't know," she said. "I was confused. They bewitched me and made me think it was right."

*More lies. More untruths. The witch knew. She knew!*

Julia's mind whirled in confusion. Serena Locke had given her baby to the Faeries in exchange for something she wanted. She'd read about that before. In fact, she realized, one of Serena Locke's best books was about that very thing.

*"The Stolen One,"* Julia said. "It's about your baby."

Serena Locke nodded.

"You gave her away so that you could write a book about it," Julia said, horrified by the realization.

"No," said Serena Locke, shaking her head.

*Yes,* said the Faeries. They were on their knees now, their eyes twinkling like jewels. Julia could sense their excitement, their longing for freedom.

"You gave her away," Julia said. "And then you felt guilty, so you started killing them. When you realized you couldn't get her back."

She gave the top of the jar another twist. One of the Faeries, its skin as green as a dragonfly, rose up and pressed its tiny hands against the metal lid. Below it, the others looked up expectantly.

Distracted, Julia didn't see Serena Locke fly at her. Only when the woman's hands gripped Julia's wrists did she know what was happening. And then the world spun. Serena Locke shrieked in rage. Her hands scrabbled at Julia, trying to wrest the jar from her hands. Julia twisted her body, trying to turn away. She tripped, and felt herself falling toward the floor.

The jar flew from her hands. As Serena Locke came down on top of her, Julia watched helplessly as the jar arced through the air and landed on the fireplace hearth, where it shattered.

The Faeries exploded into the room in a shower of green and gold. Their tiny bodies zipped in intricate patterns, leaving trails of fire in the air. Their voices rang joyously as they laughed. Hearing them, Julia felt herself filled with happiness. Even though it had been an accident, she'd done the right thing.

The Faeries swarmed around Julia and Serena Locke, who had fallen on the floor beside Julia and was groaning in pain. They hovered in midair, looking at the two humans. Their eyes blazed. The blue one came close to Julia's face.

*You saved us from the witch,* it said. *We must reward you.*

Julia wondered what her reward would be. In the fairy tales it was usually something like a lump of coal that turned into a pile of gold coins if the recipient was smart enough not to throw it away. Well, she wouldn't be so stupid. She would take whatever they gave her, even if it seemed like something useless.

*Give her the gift.* The voices of the Faeries poured out. Julia felt herself growing sleepy.

Then she felt a hand on her arm. Her eyes heavy, she turned her head and saw that Serena Locke was attempting to press something into her hands.

"Take it," she said. "It's iron. They can't take you if you carry iron."

Julia looked down at the amulet in Serena Locke's hand. It was a simple circle quartered by crossbars. She regarded it dully. Why did she want to take it? She couldn't remember. Her thoughts were hazy, ever changing.

*Come,* said the Faeries. *Claim your reward.*

Julia looked away from Serena Locke. The Faeries were reaching out their hands to her. They were shining, their wings glinting like sparks. She lifted her hand toward them and felt her body move forward effortlessly, as if she was being pulled by a current. Behind the Faeries, an opening appeared in the air, a rip in the fabric of the world. Through it, Julia caught a glimpse of a night sky twinkling with stars.

"Leave her alone!" Serena Locke shouted. "Take me instead. If you won't give me back my daughter, let me join her."

*We have the one we want,* said the voice of the blue Faerie. It was cold as ice. *We have no need of you, witch.*

Julia looked through the opening before her. As she drew closer, the stars disappeared and great black clouds covered the moon. Lightning splintered the dark, and a wind like the howls of starving wolves swept across the sky.

In the second before she was pulled through, she realized the truth. Turning, she reached a hand out to Serena Locke. "Help me!" she screamed.

She felt Serena Locke's fingertips brush hers, and for one heart-stopping moment she felt she might be saved. Then the Faeries surrounded her, and with the pinching of a hundred tiny fingers and the buzzing of wings, they carried her away.

# HAUNTED

**Ellen Schreiber**

My parents and I arrived at the Bleakmore Inn, a rumored-to-be-haunted hotel built in the late 1800s—the last place on earth I wanted to spend an autumn weekend. First of all, I didn't want to waste any time with my overly protective parents, and second, the decaying inn was more than a hundred miles from anything that resembled the living.

The Bleakmore Inn was an eight-bedroom Victorian estate, a skinny mansion with skeletal windows and two opposing chimney stacks. As we lingered on the front path of the ghostly and ghastly haunt, a cold chill ran through me. The inn might have been painted yellow, but through the dark and fog-permeated night air it appeared as gray and foreboding as an aging dinosaur. I half expected to see a toothless Igor slither out the oak front door and down the ancient steps to grab our suitcases, but no one came to help us with our belongings.

A few uncarved pumpkins were perched on the wrap-around porch, and fallen leaves crunched under our footsteps.

A swing, empty of swingers, eerily creaked as it slowly swung in the wind.

I guess the inn was beautiful—in its own way. I would have preferred something modern, the W with its minimalist design and unique overhead waterfall or the Venetian Hotel in Vegas with its handsome crooning gondoliers. At the very least, I'd have settled for a Holiday Inn with a heated pool and a game room.

My parents thought coming to a haunted inn would be a perfect getaway. But didn't they know that I, like most other girls, would have preferred a contemporary hotel with some life?

As soon as I entered the Bleakmore the hairs on the back of my neck lifted, like a vaulting cheerleader. I felt as if my parents and I weren't alone. I was right.

"I believe we have guests," a grandfatherly innkeeper mumbled into a phone from behind a centuries-old reception desk.

At first I didn't notice that he was blind, but when he hung up the receiver I spotted an aluminum walking stick leaning against his chair.

"May I help you?" he asked, now staring straight at us. He couldn't see, but he could feel our presence. I closed my eyes for what seemed like decades to see if my senses were as sharp as his. However, I felt nothing.

My parents set down their bags alongside a mauve velvet settee, and I wheeled mine in front of one of its two matching chairs. I unzipped my patterned heart hoodie and flipped my dark bangs out of my face.

My dad hadn't made reservations, so he checked for availability.

This was my opportunity to remove my iron shackles and explore the inn on my own.

"Don't go too far," my mother warned as she headed for a rack of local tourism brochures.

I passed an orange Tiffany floor lamp and small wooden table with an open guest book. No names were scrawled in it. I flipped through at least a dozen empty pages. The latest entry was left by a Mr. Curtis from Shelbyville and was dated a month ago.

Why should I believe this hotel was haunted? The *living* didn't even want to spend the night here!

If we were indeed going to stay, I wanted to make the best of it. Since the inn wasn't going to be inhabited by other teens, I'd have to make my own adventure. I explored the creepy hallway, with its white-flowered pale pink wallpaper, ornate-framed black-and-white pictures of the turn-of-the-century inn, and another photo, circa 1950, of a handsome teenage boy standing in front of a horse stable.

At the end of the hallway, an open door led to a small rustic kitchen. There was an adjoining dining room that included a cabinet full of white china and a window covered with white lace curtains.

I retraced my steps to find my parents still at the reception desk and the innkeeper gone. The elderly man must have needed help, but there didn't seem to be anyone around. Not a cook, maid, bellhop, or guest in sight.

I ascended the narrow circular staircase, with its muted beige carpet, and found a hallway lined with skinny wooden doors with black iron knobs.

Above each guest room door hung a gold nameplate. THE SHEFFIELD. THE MONROE. THE PEABODY.

I felt mysteriously drawn to the room at the far end of the hall. Its nameplate read THE BRADFORD. I wondered who had been here before me and what adventures those travelers were setting out on or returning from. Had those hotel guests been tourists, lovers embarking on a stolen night together, or honeymooners?

Light shining through a tiny window next to me caught my attention. A floodlight perched on the roof of the porch made it difficult to see out into the night. With the back of my hand, I wiped dirt off the window and pressed my face against the glass. I barely made out what appeared in the distance to be a stable.

I'd always been fascinated by horses. As a young girl, my room had been decorated with mares and ponies — everything from the wallpaper border and bedspread to the porcelain figures that lined my shelves. My favorite summers were the ones spent at River's Edge Horse Camp, and I'd even managed to bring home several blue ribbons. However, it had been ages since I'd seen a horse up close.

Ever so faintly, I heard what sounded to be a horse's whinny. I paused and listened, but all I heard was an eerie wind. Just then, the floodlight switched off. I stared into total darkness.

"Boo!" a woman's voice said.

I nearly jumped through all three floors! I spun around to find my parents standing behind me.

"This is your room," my mom said proudly, gesturing to The Bradford. "We have the one next door."

I got my own room! I could leave the lights, TV, and radio on all night or watch whatever I wanted to, uninterrupted, from the CW to MTV, without CNN, HSN, or ESPN invading my weekend.

"We have the whole inn to ourselves," my dad said, "but that doesn't mean you can blast your TV or clock radio." He gave me an affectionate kiss on the head and opened The Peabody door.

"Get some rest," my mother instructed. "Tomorrow we're going to explore the area."

Explore the area? I assumed that didn't include checking out the stable and going horseback riding, searching for a mall, or finding a hotel with an indoor pool. Instead, I was destined to spend a full day shadowing my parents in and out of old churches and browsing through dust-laden antiques.

Rain began to ping hard against the sides of the inn.

I entered the room called The Bradford and slid my hand along the wall until my fingers hit a light switch.

The overhead multicolored light fixture surged. It seemed to take all its strength to remain lit. I felt a chill in the air. Was there someone else in the room with me? Someone or something I couldn't see? As the light struggled, I left my suitcase by the door and turned on a bedside table lamp. Just as I switched it on, the bulb blew out.

Moonlight leaked into the bathroom through a crack in the window above the tub. Without much effort, I managed to find a light switch. The bathroom was as dinky as it was cold. It would have been fabulous to have a Jacuzzi with a plasma-screen TV, but it seemed I'd be lucky to get hot water. I checked myself out in the mirror—hazel eyes, shoulder-length, nonhighlighted flat brown hair. I would have loved to get a new do, but it had been a while since I'd been to a salon.

Just then the bathroom light flickered and failed.

I stood in total darkness.

I felt more frustrated than frightened. Candles, though sexy and romantic, are so nineteenth century. I wasn't prepared to spend two nights changing clothes, bathing, and entertaining myself as if I were Laura Ingalls Wilder.

I felt my way through the small room. I accidentally kneed my suitcase and let out a bloodcurdling scream. My parents must have been asleep, as my outburst remained unnoticed.

Safely in the lit hallway, I knocked on my parents' door. No one answered.

It was then that I saw him. Standing outside the room I'd just left and in front of the floodlighted window, glowing like a ghost. He was a gorgeous guy not much older than myself, slender with alabaster skin, sexy dirty-blond hair, and haunting blue eyes.

I was startled and I didn't know what to do. I was even more surprised when he saw me and smiled.

I turned around—I knew his gorgeous smile was meant for someone else. Perhaps a pretty blond who had just arrived with her family. Or his mother who was checking in. The smile had to have been directed toward anyone but me.

However, there wasn't anyone in the hallway but us.

"This place gives me the creeps," the handsome stranger said. "Until I saw you standing there. I'm Austin." He spoke his words softly, like an angel.

"I'm Amber," I managed to whisper.

He stepped forward.

My first reaction was to retreat, but instead I froze.

Not only did he look familiar, but this unknown handsome boy *felt* familiar. Strangely, I sensed a gentle loneliness emanating from him that I, too, had carried with me all of my life.

"Amy?" he asked.

"No—Amber," I corrected timidly.

"Amber—really?"

"Have we met? You look so—"

"I know I've never seen you before. I would have remembered," he said sweetly. "It's just your name. Are you here by yourself?" Goose bumps ran down my spine, and the hair on my arms and the back of my neck rose with every whisper from his perfectly formed mouth.

"Uh,no. Are you?"

"I'm on the fourth floor—the one allegedly filled with ghosts," he said proudly.

"I'm staying here."

"Really? There is supposed to be an electrical problem . . . in the Bradford. That's what they say, anyway. It might just be that the third floor is the haunted one," he said mysteriously.

I bit my lip nervously.

"I shouldn't try to scare you," he said, almost apologetically. "I didn't think there was anyone here this weekend," he hinted curiously.

"I was told there wasn't anyone staying here, either."

"Well, it will be good to have company. Someone my age for a change. And pretty."

Pretty. His words melted my soul.

We both paused awkwardly.

"It was great meeting you, Amber." He extended his pale hand. I didn't know what to do. This heavenly boy was so alluring. However, if my ultraprotective parents knew I was about to shake a stranger's hand, they'd surely end our vacation immediately.

Austin sensed my hesitation. "I know it's kind of weird to bump into a guy lurking in a haunted hotel," he said, pulling his hand back. "Maybe we'll meet again tomorrow night."

Just then, I heard my father's voice from inside his hotel room.

"Amber, is that you?" I could hear the sound of locks being unlocked.

What would my dad say if he saw me talking to Austin? I closed my eyes and waited. At any moment my dad was going to make a scene.

Dad opened the door. "What are you doing in the hallway?" he asked. "I thought I heard you talking to someone."

I glanced back. Austin had vanished.

"Uh, I was just singing. My lightbulb blew out and I need a new one. I'd prefer not to go downstairs alone."

"Wait here," my dad said, closing the door. When he opened it, he was draped in a robe. "Keep it down, honey," he directed with a whisper. "Remember, we are guests here." He quietly headed for the stairs.

I peered into the Peabody. My mother was fast asleep.

I couldn't relax. My body tingled all over. I was ready to jump out of my skin. The Bleakmore had way more nightlife than I'd ever imagined!

"Here," my dad said, quickly returning. He handed me several brand-new lightbulbs. "Don't stay up too long. We've had a long day and it's time to sleep."

But who could sleep?

Even as I closed my eyes in the lumpy Bradford bed, I couldn't get Austin out of my mind. His tousled blond hair, dreamy blue eyes, and perfectly sexy lips burned such an image on my brain. I could still see him standing before me. At school, I had friends and crushes, but a real boyfriend had always eluded me. I'd never met anyone as handsome as Austin. If only I had gotten the chance to feel our fingers entwined.

But why did this stranger look so familiar to me? I thought my dad said the inn was empty this weekend. Why would a teenage boy check in alone and stay in an old remote inn all by himself? How did he know so much about the hotel and about the Bradford's electrical problem? His evasiveness only added to his charm. Was this out-of-this-world dream guy real or just a figment of my overactive imagination?

No matter what, Austin was better than anything real or imagined. I held the extra pillow tightly in my arms and pretended it was him.

Just then I heard footsteps above me, pacing back and forth. Could they be Austin's?

I was dying to sneak up to the fourth floor. I wasn't about to sleep anyway, so a little exploring couldn't hurt. I crept out of the Bradford and tiptoed down the hallway. The stairs squeaked with every footstep. *Creak. Crack. Crunch.*

At any moment I could be caught.

The fourth floor was spookier than the third. It wasn't as well lit and the hallway smelled musty. I pressed my ear to Austin's door. The nameplate above his room was odd. It, too, read THE BRADFORD. I didn't dare enter his room without his permission. Just then the door opened.

I jumped back. Did Austin see me standing there?

"I thought I heard someone creaking on the stairway," he said. "I'm glad you came. I couldn't sleep, either."

I tried to peer past him. I wanted to know everything about

this dreamy creature. Was he here alone? And if so, why?

Austin stepped into the hallway and closed his door behind him.

"I have a place we can go," he said.

I followed him down the staircase and through the rustic kitchen. When he opened the back door, I stopped in my tracks.

"I shouldn't," I said.

"It's just over there." Austin pointed through the gentle rain toward the stable in the distance.

I paused. Then I realized I had to go.

Austin headed down a path, and I found myself following his every footstep. I knew this would be my last vacation if my parents found me leaving the inn with a strange boy, but I no longer cared.

The porch floodlight illuminated the way. A horse began to whinny, and her calls became louder with every footstep. I trailed close behind Austin, between the raindrops, exhilarated by my nocturnal adventure. When we reached the stable, Austin lit a gas lantern that was resting next to the open gate.

The bittersweet scent of the stable reminded me of River's Edge. As soon as we entered, a horse began to whinny as if she were frightened. I became concerned she'd wake my parents.

"Maybe this isn't a good idea," I stated.

"You've come this far."

I could hear the horse neigh and buck in her stall. She clearly didn't want any late-night visitors. We walked past four empty stalls. The horse at the end of the row continued to grow more anxious as we approached.

Austin walked right up to the stall's door. "I want to show

you this." He pointed to a wooden nameplate above the stall that I couldn't see from my vantage point. I inched forward. The nameplate was oddly familiar. It read AMBER.

I was floored!

"Funny, huh?" Austin chuckled. "I think it was meant to be . . . us meeting here at the inn. And this proves it."

I felt as happy as I did mystified. If Austin was a guest at the Bleakmore, how did he know about this particular horse?

"You've been out here before?" I asked.

Austin didn't answer. Instead he tried to calm down the horse. "It's okay, girl."

The horse was gorgeous. Her mane was as dark and thick as mine. However, on her it looked much better.

Austin unlocked the gate and stepped into the stall. He grabbed a bit that was hanging on the wall and cautiously fastened it on the anxious horse. "There, there," he said. The mare was almost hypnotized by Austin. I was amazed by Austin's confident yet gentle nature. Guys I'd known at school had only been interested in three things: sports, girls, and partying.

With one hand on the reins and the other stroking her mane, Austin held her steady.

"Go ahead."

But Amber started to snort. "It's okay, girl," Austin said in a gentle whisper. "This is my friend. Her name is Amber, too."

"It's okay. I really shouldn't . . ."

"Why not?"

Austin was right. I was dying to stroke her. She was as magnificent as Austin was, and I didn't know when I'd get a moment like this again. I reached out my hand and in an instant I felt warm fur against my cold, wet skin. All at once, Amber was peaceful and accepted me as if I were her handler.

I sensed Austin's gaze as I continued to stroke Amber's nose. Austin made me feel beautiful and, though we'd only met a short time ago, I felt I could be more myself with him than I had ever been with anyone.

"Here," Austin said, holding the reins toward me. I grabbed the leather as I'd done many times at summer camp.

Austin picked up a saddle from a bale of hay and placed it on the mare.

"What are you doing?" I asked nervously. "We can't just take her."

"It's all right. It's just for a moment."

I would have argued, but I trusted Austin.

"How come you are so good with her?" I asked.

"I have a sixth sense," he teased. I smiled back at him.

"We have only a short time." Austin cupped his palms, and before I knew it I was sitting on the most beautiful mare I'd ever seen. Austin led us out of the stall, through the stable, and toward a small fenced-in area. I felt like a princess on a stallion, being led by her handsome prince.

A light from the stable illuminated our way. The rain had stopped, and the ground was only mildly damp.

"Take her around," he said.

"But I've never ridden her before."

"It's like riding a bike, without the pedals."

I laughed. Austin had a great sense of humor and an even better smile.

"You've ridden before, haven't you?" he asked, as if he already knew the answer.

I nodded proudly.

"Then go!" Austin tapped Amber on the rear and she began to trot.

Time stood still as I began to ride Amber around the ring. One lap turned into two laps, then three, and all the while the most gorgeous guy I'd ever seen was standing at the fence's gate smiling back at me.

Eventually, Amber and I stopped in front of Austin. "I can't thank you enough," I said, exhausted and exhilarated. By Austin's glowing grin, I knew he was as pleased as I was.

The rain began to pick up again. We returned Amber to her stall, then quickly sought shelter from the impending downpour back at the Bleakmore.

Once inside the inn, Austin opened a door off the kitchen. He lit a candle that illuminated the room. In it was a small bar with a few bar stools.

Austin switched on a portable CD player so quietly I could barely hear the slow love song being played. He stood and held out his hand to me.

"I don't dance," I said apprehensively.

"It's okay, no one's watching."

"Not even a ghost?" I teased.

But Austin didn't respond. Instead, he took my hand. I knew my parents would be angry if they saw me here. However, I'd never felt so safe in my whole life as I did now with Austin. His hand was so much warmer and stronger than I'd imagined. He pulled me into him, and I felt as if I were melting into his chest.

We swayed for what seemed to be an eternity but was only a moment when we heard a creaking coming from the hallway.

"We're not supposed to be in here," he said, panicking. The footsteps grew louder. "Come, I know a back way."

We raced through a side door and up a set of servants' stairs until we were standing in front of the Bradford.

"Is this mine or yours?" I asked playfully.

"Yours," he said. "We have so much in common. Horses, staying in the Bradfords, being here at the Bleakmore. I've never met anyone like you before."

"Neither have I."

He stared at me longingly and flashed a sexy smile.

He leaned in to kiss me. I gently closed my eyes and waited for his lips, which I imagined to be tasty and sweet, pressed against mine. But they never came. I heard the staircase begin to creak and quickly opened my eyes. I began to fumble with the doorknob as the footsteps grew louder.

I turned around. Austin was gone.

When I awoke, I realized I must have slept the day away. I almost cried, thinking I'd wasted precious hours sleeping when I could have been spending them with Austin.

"I met the man of my dreams," I told my parents in the Peabody when they returned from exploring the area.

"But I thought you were sleeping all day," my dad questioned.

"No, I met him last night. Here."

"Honey, no one is staying in the hotel," my mom corrected. "It's just us."

"Just us," my dad confirmed.

"So are you saying I made him up?"

"We're not saying anything," my mom reassured. "Please, honey, keep your voice down."

"You're probably just tired from our travels," my dad assumed. "Now that you've slept all day you should be feeling fine."

"This time, you are *wrong,*" I exclaimed. "All I've ever wanted to do is fall in love. And now I have."

I raced up to the fourth floor. I banged on Austin's door. He was gone.

Frantically, I ran down to the stable. I searched everywhere, but Austin wasn't there. And more surprisingly, neither was the mare.

Frustrated and confused, I returned to the inn. Were my parents right? Had Austin and our magical night together been a fantasy? Was I so starved for companionship that the boy of my dreams had in fact been one?

I began heading back to my room to rethink my nocturnal adventure. It was then that I noticed the picture — the one I saw when I first explored the Bleakmore. A black-and-white vintage photograph of a handsome boy sitting on a black mare in front of the Bleakmore's stable. It had obviously been taken in the 1950s. The boy looked exactly like Austin!

I overheard the innkeeper talking into the phone. "I heard footsteps all night long," he complained. "Music coming from the bar. Voices in the hallway. And I swear someone has been staying in the Bradford."

Just then, Austin was standing behind me. I gasped.

I pointed to the vintage photograph. I could barely speak. "That's you."

He smiled, a beautiful smile. Just like the one in the picture hanging before me.

"That's why you know so much about the Bleakmore and the stable," I began, "and why you're staying here alone . . . why the innkeeper hears sounds coming from the Bradford. Why they say the inn is haunted."

Before Austin could respond, the innkeeper appeared behind the reception desk.

"Austin, who are you talking to?" he snapped. "Where have you been all day?"

"I rode into town to buy flowers for someone special." A bright bouquet of roses was sitting atop the reception desk. "I've been waiting for aeons for the girl of my dreams. I've finally met her. And now I'd like you to meet her, too."

The innkeeper eagerly stepped forward.

"Amber, this is my grandfather, Martin Bradford," Austin said. The innkeeper smiled, a smile similar to Austin's. "And the man in the picture is my great-grandfather, Louis Bradford. He bought the Bleakmore. People say I am the spitting image of him."

The reality of the situation hit me.

"This isn't you?" I asked, my eyes locked on the photo. "This is your great-grandfather?"

Austin nodded proudly. "What did you think, I was an apparition?"

I was horribly embarrassed. I wanted to hide, but that was out of the question.

"I live upstairs in the Bradford room," Austin revealed. "I help my grandfather run the inn and take care of the stables. I wanted to tell you, but I was afraid you wouldn't think it was cool."

I didn't know what to say or, for that matter, what to do.

"Austin," the innkeeper asked with concern, "what girl are you talking to?"

"The one standing right here," he said emphatically.

Austin's grandfather looked directly at me. I felt his gaze burn through my soul.

I wanted to run to my parents, to the Bradford, to anywhere but where I was. But I knew it was too late.

"You don't have to tell me *where* she is," his grandfather finally said. "Even a blind man can see a ghost."

Silence penetrated the room. I could only wait for Austin's reaction.

"Grandpa—" Austin admonished.

"I told you this place was haunted," the senior Bradford continued. "Has been for years. No one believes an old man. But *you* know the truth, Miss Amber," he said, still staring straight at me.

Austin didn't say anything. My handsome beau didn't know how to respond.

But when he turned to me and my eyes welled up with tears, then it hit him that his grandfather was right and he'd been gravely mistaken.

For the first time Austin looked at me as if he'd just seen a ghost.

Tears streamed down my face. I could hear the creaking footsteps of my parents coming down the staircase. As soon as they spotted Austin and me together, my parents and I would have to leave and never return.

I stormed out the front door and raced into the darkness

to the only place I knew to seek refuge—the stable. Amber's whinnies increased with every footstep I took, as if she were crying along with me.

When I reached the mare, she calmed down and nuzzled up to me. I held her around her neck and my falling tears dotted her coat.

My parents came here for a vacation. They chose the Bleakmore because of its remote location. Since it was rumored to be haunted, perhaps we would go unnoticed. Maybe our movements throughout the building would be chalked up to a legendary ghost from historical times, adding to the stories to be told to future guests.

I felt a presence behind me. I half expected it to be my parents, bags packed and ready to go.

I glanced back. Instead it was Austin, standing before me. I was sure Austin would be frightened of me. He looked just like he did when we first met in the hallway. But I was the one afraid. I barely made eye contact.

"I didn't expect to see you again," I said, choked up.

"I didn't, either. I'm so confused," he began. "I had to see you again . . . to know for sure."

"I'm sorry for everything."

"You look and sound as real as any girl I've ever seen before. But you are far more beautiful," he rambled as he tried to make sense of the situation. "I just can't believe . . . I mean, my grandfather has said for years . . . but I've never seen anyone, until you."

"I was just as surprised when you did see me."

"I guess I saw you because I wanted to see you."

His words sent chills through me. "I really thought . . .

the picture in the hallway . . . the Bradford room. Your pale skin and your knowledge of the inn and the stable. I thought you were . . ."

"A ghost?" he dared to ask.

"Yes. I thought you were . . . like me."

Austin paused. "I don't like to see you so sad."

"I just didn't want to disappoint or frighten you."

"Now it makes sense. Someone staying in the Bradford, the footsteps, and the voices. My grandfather was talking about . . . you."

I was overcome with sorrow. "I didn't mean to . . ."

But Austin smiled a reassuring smile. "I never thought I'd actually see a ghost, much less fall in love with one."

Any sadness I had suffered quickly vanished.

Austin stared into my eyes. He reached out his hand. He took my hand in his. His hand felt warm in my cold one. My whole body felt more alive than it ever had when I was alive.

"I want to do something I didn't have the chance to do before," Austin began. "Before I don't have the chance to do it again."

Austin leaned in to me and did the unthinkable but imaginable. In fact, I'd imagined it all my life.

He kissed me. He pressed his lips tenderly against mine, and I felt what I'd never felt on earth before. Love.

When I opened my eyes, I saw him smiling his gorgeous smile at me, his tousled, sexy, dirty-blond hair flopping over his dreamy blue eyes.

"I know we will see each other again," Austin reassured me. "It's just a matter of when."

I finally felt at peace, knowing Austin was right.

I was no longer haunted.

# WOLFSBANE

**Sarah Hines Stephens**

Sleep just was not happening. So I rolled over and pulled a spiral-bound notebook from under my mattress, grabbed my favorite black roller-ball pen, and began making a new list.

I love to make lists. I make lists of my lists sometimes. It helps me sort out my thoughts and feel like I am getting things done. If I am making a to-do list I always put a couple of things on there I have already done, just so I can check them off. Lists usually make me feel like I have things under control. Not tonight, though. Tonight's list was: Things That Make Me Want to Stick Hot Pins Under My Fingernails. And it went like this:

Football players<br>
Cheerleaders<br>
Belly shirts<br>
Pep squads<br>
Anything with the word "pep" in it<br>
Bubble gum<br>
Thongs

Press-on nails

MY SISTER'S INCESSANT WHINING!

I grabbed my bedraggled teddy bear and hurled him in the general direction of my sister's racket. The noise coming from her room was like metal scraping a smooth surface—that horrible squealing whine that makes the hair on your neck stand up. Awful? Yes. Keeping me from thinking? Yes. But compared to the bawling and howling that *had* been coming from behind her door, it was practically a lullaby. Not that I was getting any sleep.

"Shut up!" I yelled at my ceiling. If Lupe didn't shut it soon I was going to have to hole up in the garage. Or kill her. She was too deep in her pity party to care about eating or sleeping or anyone else in the house. She had been wallowing—and bellowing—for days. And nights. And my mood had finally gotten so bad I had to do something about it.

Yanking open my door, I stomped across the hall cursing her, and Chuck Richter. This was all pretty much his fault, which made it that much more annoying. Just thinking about Chuck brought the taste of barf to the back of my throat. He was hideous. Not exactly ugly, if you go in for the blond boy-band type, but hideous on the inside, and completely lacking in personality. He, and everyone else at Grover Cleveland, used his star athlete status to excuse his rank-ass behavior. Unfortunately, Lupe didn't see through his bullshit act until she was knee-deep in it. She had a weakness for the popular tribe. I didn't play that particular game. I approached high school life in more of a stealth mode and steered way clear of the plastic popular types.

I knocked once on Lupe's door and then let myself in. We have house rules about knocking and privacy and all that, but this was an emergency. Lupe's room was dark and had a weird closed-in smell, like unwashed hair. "Can you shut up?" I begged the lump on her bed. "Please?"

There was no response. She was almost completely hidden in her covers, with one hand reaching up to claw at her headboard.

"And maybe take a shower?" I asked, catching an unwashed whiff.

"Get out," Lupe yelled. Her voice was muffled under the blankets.

Okay, so my approach was a little harsh. But it's not like I'd been getting much sleep lately. I sat down on the edge of the bed and put my hand on the bump I figured was her foot. She pulled away. "He's not worth it," I said a little more gently. Amazingly, her moans started to subside.

"You were too good for him," I added. It was true. They were a couple destined to fail. He had a football for a brain and Lupe was the head of the International Club, the leader of the Academic Decathlon, and the prettiest junior on campus—maybe even the prettiest girl in school. The combo of looks and brains threw people. She would have gotten totally bored with Chuck and tossed him aside given another week, but she didn't get the chance. Chuck started dating someone else, somebody easier, without bothering to break up with Lupe first. I hoped it was her pride and not her heart that was suffering the most.

Underneath the blankets Lupe's crying became more of a whimper. "Did you see them at lunch?" she asked. "Devorah said he was all over her."

"Like stink on pig," I confirmed, cursing D for giving Lupe the scoop. Suddenly, the bile taste was back, along with a flash of the scene at lunch—Chuck and his new wench, Trina, on the grass island by the senior picnic tables, rubbing up against each other like they were trying to start a fire. How could I miss them? How could anyone? "Look, Trina is trash and Chuck is an idiot. In five years they will have a kid in kindergarten and you will be working on your Ph.D.. I don't know what you see in the sporting breeds. Now, can I get some sleep?" Talking about Chuck was making me irritable again.

"Oh, am I bothering you, Hazel?" Lupe snapped, sensing my annoyance. Her sadness was suddenly gone, replaced by fury, and it was all directed at me. She tossed back her blankets and I stood up quickly, trying not to flinch. Even in the dim light Lupe looked crazed. Her long hair, curly like mine, was matted into a huge snarl. Her face was twisted, her eyes were bloodshot, and she could have used an industrial eyebrow wax. The hairy caterpillars on her forehead were about to meet in the middle and shake hands. What would the Pep Squad think of her now?

"Pull yourself together," I said, backing toward the door. "And forget about him. You're just on the rag."

"Pull myself together?" Lupe growled. She lunged at me, and I grabbed for the doorknob. "Forget him? You could never understand." Lupe poked a long fingernail at my face, punctuating each word. She was really starting to freak me out. "You have no idea what it's like to be tortured month after month. Just get out and leave me alone."

Glad to. I slammed the door behind me. Lupe was right about one thing. I did not know what it was like to have my period. I was probably the only freshman at Cleveland who hadn't started bleeding yet. And secretly I was glad. It didn't sound like a picnic—especially for Lupe. She spent one week a month in total agony, and even though she locked herself in her room most of the time she made sure the rest of the house was fully aware of her misery.

But this was beyond her usual bleeding and bitching and moaning—way beyond. The combo of getting dumped and getting her period had sent Lupe over the edge. I mean, she'd given up basic hygiene! And nobody cried for three days straight.

Make that four. Lupe did not make it to breakfast or school or even out of the house the next day, either. "Don't you think it's time she rejoined the living?" I asked Mom before unloading my backpack on the table in the breakfast nook. That was Mom's favorite place to drink tea in the afternoon. She did it without fail. She was tea obsessed. She even grew her own twigs and leaves in the backyard. Which was cool, if you're into boiled bark.

The steam from her cup curled up around Mom's big dark eyes. She looked just like Lupe—same dark hair, thick brows, and long lashes. I had all of that, too, along with a deep desire for a package of laser hair removal treatments to get rid of the fine mustache that started showing up on my lip last year.

"Give her time," Mom said patiently before taking a sip. "She could really use some tea," she added, thoughtfully shaking her head.

*Right. The miracle cure.* I had to fight back a laugh. I was pretty sure a cup of tea was not going to cure what ailed my sister, but it was useless to tell Mom that. She was like a pusher when it came to her favorite drink. Later, I heard her outside Lupe's room peddling her addiction.

"Just try," she coaxed, standing awkwardly in the hall, holding a tray.

"No!" Lupe screamed.

"It might make you feel better. I grow it myself. It does me a world of good. Truly, sweetheart, it soothes the savage beast, especially in the moon times."

*Hippie,* I groaned inwardly. How many times had I heard her tell Lupe this same crunchy thing? Didn't she get it? It was as useless as her tea to try to talk Lupe out of the red cave or out of her precious diet sodas.

Lupe opened the door a crack and squinted out. "There's only one thing that will make me feel better," she said in a voice so low I could barely hear her. "Chuck's funeral." The way she said it sent chills up my spine. In the next instant, Lupe slammed the door, indicating the conversation was over, and we were in for another sleepless night.

Luckily (or unluckily), I was so tired that I fell asleep that night at my desk doing homework right after dinner. I woke with a start and a page of algebra pressed into my cheek. I felt instantly that something was wrong, something more than the fact I was asleep in a chair wearing all my clothes. The glowing numbers on the clock by my bed read 1:16. But that was not what was bothering me. What was weird was the silence. There was not a peep coming from Lupe's room.

*Maybe she's asleep. Finally,* I thought. I staggered down the hall to the bathroom to take off my makeup and brush my teeth. I flipped on the light switch and breathed in steam. The mirror over the sink was fogged. Somebody had showered recently. Somebody hairy. I practically gagged when I spotted the hair-clogged disposable razor on the side of the tub. It looked like it had been used to shave a gorilla . . . or a full head of hair.

"Lupe," I whispered as I turned back toward her room.

Already the "crazy" rumors about Lupe were swirling at school. If she'd done something as stupid as shaving her head she would never live it down! I could not let her do this. I could not stand to listen to her cry for the next two years. I opened Lupe's door, this time without knocking at all.

"Tell me you didn't—" The room was empty and the window was wide open. "Please tell me you didn't!" I said again to the billowing curtain. I looked out the window and down the street. Nothing moved. She was gone.

As quickly as I could, I scrambled over the sill and jumped, landing with a soft thump on the lawn, the same way I imagined Lupe had gotten out. Then I started to run. There was only one place Lupe would be going in the middle of the night. There was only one thing, she'd said, that would make her feel better. She was on her way to Chuck's house.

I started out at a dead run. I hadn't stopped for a flashlight or even to put on my shoes. There was no time. After four blocks there was still no sign of Lupe. The streets were silent, the sidewalks empty. Cutting through the woods was the fastest way.

The woods weren't exactly woods. That is, they were not a real forest, not by a long shot. They were the only patch of unpaved land left between the subdivisions that made up Glenwood. It was the place where neighbors walked dogs, kids played, and toys were lost—and the shortest route to the Richters'.

My pace slowed when the sidewalk ended. Without the glow of the streetlights I needed to step carefully to avoid sharp sticks and dog poop. It might not have been a forest, but it was big enough to lose your way and big enough to house a mess of squirrels, raccoons, and possums with their hairless ratty tails.

I shivered in the dark and hoped the rustling leaves were only the ones I was kicking through.

The farther into the woods I got, the darker it got and the slower I moved. "This is so lame," I whispered to myself. Damp seeped into my socks from the muddy path, and I wished I had stopped for shoes. . . . The dark shapes around me came into clearer focus. The moon was full, and bright enough to cast shadows, but the leaves were still thick on the trees even though it was almost November. I could smell the wet earth, the rotting leaves, and something else — metallic, like blood. A breeze rustled the bushes. It was a breeze, wasn't it? And then a noise like a siren, or a howl. I crouched instinctively, frozen, holding my breath and waiting for the sound again. Nothing. Only my breathing and the pounding of my own blood coursing in my ears. Suddenly, I felt stupid and really freaking cold. *What the hell am I doing?* I wondered.

I was answered by a raspy scream. *Lupe?*

I ran again, willing myself to go toward the noise while every fiber of my being wanted to run away.

Another scream. *Lupe?* It was a desperate noise, more animal than human.

I stumbled and fell to my knees in front of the bloody carcass of a cat. A calico. Daisy, the Richters' cat. *Lupe? Lupe, what have you done?*

The smell of wet hair and cooling blood was so strong it was overwhelming. I stood again, my mouth filled with hot spit. I swallowed back vomit, hoping this was the worst. Praying nobody else had heard or seen anything.

Shaving your head after a bad breakup would be weird, but killing your ex's family pet? Now I had more than Lupe's reputation to protect, I had my own school career to worry about, too. Try flying under the radar with this hanging off your family tree! I had to hide the cat. Looking around, I saw a fallen log. That could be good. I started toward it, but a dark figure filled the path ahead of me. I stopped so fast I stumbled, and in an instant the figure was on top of me. Lupe! I struggled to knock her off. Her face hovered just inches above mine, and I could feel hot breath on my cheek and hear her teeth snapping.

"What are you doing here?" she demanded in a rough voice.

"Get off." I could barely breathe, let alone speak. Lupe's knee was in my chest, and her fingernails dug into my wrists, piercing the skin. Her hair hung down into my face, curtaining hers.

"Why did you follow me?" Lupe's voice came from deep in her throat. She eased off the pressure on my chest a little bit but kept my arms pinned.

"I—I didn't want you to do anything stupid," I gasped. Much as I hated Chuck, I loved my sister. "I was worried."

"Worry about yourself," Lupe growled. She shook her hair back and I almost screamed. The hair in the razor was definitely not from Lupe's head or her face. Her thick brows were bushier than ever, meeting in the middle, and in the moonlight shadows I could see that even her cheeks were covered with soft dark fur. Lupe's narrowed eyes glinted mineral green and her long nose wrinkled up in an angry snarl, showing teeth. Sharp and yellowed.

I acted without thinking, without knowing what I was doing. I saw the soft flesh of her neck, covered as it was in fine hair, and in an instant I was tearing it with my own teeth, grown sharp. I saw my hand reaching. Claws and fur.

Oblivious to the pain, we rolled together. The snarling was fierce. Was it her? Was it me?

Then, in an instant, she was off of me and sprinting down the path toward home . . . on all fours.

I lay there on the path, my heart pounding. I breathed through my open mouth, tongue lolling, wondering if what I had seen, what I had done, was real. "This is a dream," I told myself. "I'm having a nightmare." But the blood was real, and so was the dead cat at my feet.

I clawed a hole in the dirt for Daisy, ignoring the tears running down my face and my own wailing. I covered the cat's body with soil, leaves, and rocks. Then I lifted my head to gaze at the moon and howled, for myself, for Daisy, and for my crazy sister.

Sunlight streamed in the crack in my curtains and I forced my eyes open. Oh, God. Was it only Thursday? Closing my eyes again, I tried to force the twisted images of my dreams out of my head. A deep pain over my pelvic bone made me open my eyes again. I sat up, pushing a fist into my lower stomach. My hand was covered in dirt, my nails were torn, and I was still wearing my clothes. Worse, my jeans were covered in blood. Mine. And more.

But it had been a dream. . . .

I wrapped my robe over my soiled clothes and staggered downstairs. So tired.

My mom was sitting on the couch, cradling my sister's head in her lap. Lupe's neck was scratched deeply—angry red lines in her otherwise perfect olive skin—but the wounds were cleaned.

Her eyes were closed, and her chest fell up and down with her breathing.

Mom stopped stroking Lupe's hair and looked at me for a long time. She made a sympathetic noise, like a whimper, and beckoned me closer with an extended hand. "The moon times are harder on some than others," she said, pulling me down next to her on the couch and nuzzling my cheek. "I see your time has come." My mom leaned forward and licked the scratches on my wrist. I could only nod.

"Drink," she said as she handed me her cup from the low table. "Drink this. It helps stave off the lunacy."

Too freaked out to argue, I took a sip of the warm liquid. It was bitter but tasted strangely good. I lapped up more, feeling it quench my thirst. "What is it?" I asked when I felt a tiny bit normal.

"Wolfsbane," she answered.

# 666

## THE NUMBER OF THE BEAST

# ABOUT THE AUTHORS

**Peter Abrahams** is the author of *Down the Rabbit Hole* and *Behind the Curtain*, the first two volumes in the award-winning Echo Falls mystery series for middle-school and young adult readers. He has also written sixteen crime fiction novels for adults, including *Nerve Damage* and *End of Story*. For more information about Peter, please visit www.peterabrahams.com.

**Laurie Faria Stolarz** is the author of the hugely popular young adult novels *Blue Is for Nightmares, White Is for Magic, Silver Is for Secrets,* and *Red Is for Remembrance.* Her latest young adult novel, *Bleed*, was published in the fall of 2006 with Hyperion. *Project 17*, a companion book, is slated for release in 2007. Born and raised in Salem, Massachusetts, Laurie attended Merrimack College and received an MFA in Creative Writing from Emerson College in Boston. To learn more about Laurie, please visit her Web site at www.lauriestolarz.com.

**Christopher Pike** is the well-known master of teen horror. From the mid-eighties to the mid-nineties, he virtually dominated the Young Adult market with his thrillers. He has returned to the book world with the publication of the Alosha trilogy, which is soon to be a major motion picture, and his adult novel, *Falling*, which will be published this spring. Presently Christopher Pike is preparing to shoot a film version of his most frightening teen novel, *Whisper of Death*.

**Joyce Carol Oates** is the renowned author of many novels, including *Big Mouth & Ugly Girl*, her first young adult novel, and *Freaky Green Eyes*. Her novel *Blonde* was a National Book

Award nominee and *New York Times* best seller. A recipient of the National Book Award and the Pen/Malamud Lifetime Achievement Award for Excellence in Short Fiction, Ms. Oates is the Roger S. Berlind Distinguished Professor of the Humanities at Princeton University. She lives in Princeton, New Jersey.

*New York Times* and *USA Today* bestselling author **Heather Graham** has written more than one hundred novels and novellas in a variety of genres, including *The Vision, Kiss of Darkness, The Dead Room*, and *Blood Red.* Under the name Shannon Drake, she has written numerous novels including *The Queen's Lady, The Island, When We Touch, Wicked, Reckless*, and *Beguiled,* a novel set in the Victorian period. An award-winning author who has been featured on *Entertainment Tonight,* Heather was a founding member of the Florida Romance Writers chapter of Romance Writers of America, and for several years running has hosted the Romantic Times Vampire Party, with all revenues going directly to children's charity. Heather was also awarded the RWA Lifetime Achievement Award. She lives in Florida with her husband and their five children.

**Bentley Little** is the Bram Stoker Award–winning author of hundreds of short stories and numerous novels, including *The Revelation, University, The Store,* and *The Resort.* Rejected by society and hated by all who know him, he lives in a hovel and has no pets, no friends, no family.

**Chet Williamson** has written many novels in the field of horror and suspense. Among them are *Second Chance, Ash Wednesday, Dreamthorp* and The Searchers series. Over a hundred of his short stories have appeared in such magazines as *The New Yorker, Playboy, Esquire, Twilight Zone, The Magazine of Fantasy and Science Fiction*, and many other magazines and anthologies. *Figures in Rain,* a collection of his short stories, won the 2002 International Horror Guild Award. He has been a final nominee for the World Fantasy Award, the Horror Writers Association's Stoker Award, and the Mystery Writers of America's Edgar Award.

**Jane Mason** grew up on the shores of Lake Superior and has taken many icy swims in its depths. Fortunately she never had a virtual run-in with a ferry or experienced a freaky hallucination from nearly drowning. Now she lives in Oakland, California, with her husband, three children, and an assortment of animals, and writes books for kids and teens with her friend Sarah Hines Stephens. She swims in a pool and the Pacific.

**Amelia Atwater-Rhodes** grew up in Concord, Massachusetts. Born in 1984, she wrote her first novel, *In the Forests of the Night*, praised as "remarkable" (*Voice of Youth Advocates*) and "mature and polished" (*Booklist*) when she was thirteen. She has since published *Demon in My View*, *Shattered Mirror*, and *Midnight Predator*, all ALA Quick Picks for Young Adults, as well as *Hawksong*, a *School Library Journal* Best Book of the Year and a *Voice of Youth Advocates* Best Science Fiction, Fantasy, and Horror selection.

**Joshua Gee** first learned about tetrodotoxin while investigating Haitian "zombi" poisons for *Encyclopedia Horrifica*, a nonfiction compendium of all things gory, ghoulish, and ghastly. At this time, Investigator Gee does not wish to disclose why he also knows so much about involuntary hospitalization. According to eyewitnesses, he is frequently sighted in New York City and at www.joshuagee.com

**Robin Wasserman** is the author of *Hacking Harvard,* the Chasing Yesterday trilogy, and the Seven Deadly Sins series. Things she is afraid of: Cockroaches. Fire. Failure. Tuna fish. A devoted horror fan, she first read Stephen King's *It* when she was thirteen, and has reread it at least once a year ever since. It scares her every time.

**T.E.D. Klein** attended Brown University, in the same neighborhood where horror writer H. P. Lovecraft once lived. He fulfilled a childhood dream when he became the editor of a fiction magazine, *Twilight Zone*; later he edited a police magazine, *CrimeBeat.* His horror novel *The Ceremonies* inched briefly onto the bestseller list, and a story in his collection *Dark Gods* won a World Fantasy Award. He wrote a movie for Italian thriller director Dario Argento, but the result was so embarrassing that he's never told his parents about it. He lives in New York City and upstate New York, just across the dirt road from a cabin popularly believed to have been visited by extraterrestrials.

**David Moody** is a British author of horror and science fiction novels. He often writes about the end of the world and he doesn't believe a story always has to have a happy ending. His biggest influences are *Night of the Living Dead* and *Day of the Triffids.*

David has written many novels, including the popular Autumn series of zombie books. A movie version of the first book is currently in production.

He lives just outside Birmingham, UK, with his wife, daughters, and a houseful of pets.

**Melissa de la Cruz** is the author of many books for teens and adults, including the popular Au Pairs series and the novel *Fresh Off the Boat.* Her latest works include the Angels on Sunset Boulevard trilogy, stories in *Mistletoe* and *21 Proms,* and the anthology *Girls Who Like Boys Who Like Boys: True Tales of Love, Lust and Friendship between Gay Men and Straight Women,* which she coedited. To find out more about Dylan's story, check out her vampire series, Blue Bloods. She has also written for many magazines, including *Teen Vogue, Seventeen,* and *CosmoGirl.* Melissa divides her time between Los Angeles and New York and has spent many summers (but so far only one winter weekend) on Shelter Island, where she is always on the lookout for a vampire in danger. Check out her Web site at melissa-delacruz.com.

The winner of both a Bram Stoker and a World Fantasy Award, **P. D. Cacek** has penned over one hundred short stories, appearing in such anthologies as *999, Joe Lansdale's Lords of the Razor,* and *Night Visions 12* and, to date, four novels. Currently working on her fifth (and possibly sixth) novel, Cacek lives in Fort Washington, PA . . . in a haunted house across from a haunted mill. When not writing, she can often be found with a group of costumed storytellers called The Patient Creatures (www.creatureseast.com). You can visit her Web site at www.pdcacek.com.

**Isobel Bird** is a practicing Wiccan whose teen series, Circle of Three, developed a cult following among otherwise well-behaved, bookish readers. Isobel lives and celebrates the moon in northern California.

**Ellen Schreiber** is the author of the popular vampire love story series Vampire Kisses, *Teenage Mermaid*, *Comedy Girl*, and the upcoming Vampire Kisses 5—*The Coffin Club* and Vampire Kisses Manga—*Blood Relatives*. Ellen grew up being creeped out watching reruns of the black-and-white TV show *The Twilight Zone* and suspenseful Alfred Hitchcock movies. Though she wasn't allowed to watch scary movies as a young girl, she is making up for it now.

**Sarah Hines Stephens** writes books for all ages and hides her face when forced to watch horror movies. She occasionally howls at the moon and likes tea, but really prefers coffee. Sarah loves to work in collaboration (especially with her friend Jane Mason) and has written about cats, monkeys, aliens, and princesses but never before werewolves. She relished the chance to write about girls with real teeth and claws. Sarah lives in Oakland, California, with her husband (the horror buff) and two young children.